T0182707

The
Watchful
Wife

Suzanne Leal is the author of novels *The Teacher's Secret*, *Border Street*, *Running with Ivan* and *The Deceptions*, for which she won the Nib People's Choice Prize and was shortlisted for the Davitt Awards and the Mark and Evette Moran Nib Literary Award. A senior member of the NSW Civil and Administrative Tribunal and facilitator at community, corporate and literary events, Suzanne is the host of Thursday Book Club, a relaxed, friendly book club connecting readers online.

www.suzanneleal.com

The Watchful Wife

SUZANNE LEAL

ALLEN&UNWIN
SYDNEY · MELBOURNE · AUCKLAND · LONDON

First published in 2023

  This project has been assisted by the Australian Government through the Australia Council, its arts funding and advisory board.

 This project is supported by the Copyright Agency's Cultural Fund.

Allen & Unwin
Cammeraygal Country
83 Alexander Street
Crows Nest NSW 2065
Australia
Phone: (61 2) 8425 0100
Email: info@allenandunwin.com
Web: www.allenandunwin.com

Allen & Unwin acknowledges the Traditional Owners of the Country on which we live and work. We pay our respects to all Aboriginal and Torres Strait Islander Elders, past and present.

 A catalogue record for this book is available from the National Library of Australia

ISBN 978 1 76106 777 8

Set in 12.75/18 pt Adobe Garamond Pro by Bookhouse, Sydney
Printed and bound in Australia by the Opus Group

10 9 8 7 6 5 4 3 2 1

For David

Prologue

THE KNOCK CAME EARLY THAT morning. Was it six or seven?
I hardly remember.

My first thought was a ridiculous one: my mother had come
to admonish my slumber.

The idle will not prosper. I knew that. And what greater
idleness could there be than staying in bed, in that half-
awake, half-asleep idyll, when there was work to be done?
I was thirty-two years old, yet still the child inside me cowered
at the thought of my mother's displeasure.

But I did not open the door to my mother that morning.
I found, instead, two strangers—women—in trousers and dark
woollen jumpers.

'Can I help you?' I asked, trying to keep my voice from
wavering.

'Police,' said the one on the right, who was tall and thin.
'Can we come in?'

No, you cannot.

'Yes, of course,' I replied.

That, I would later discover, was my first mistake. If a police officer—or two—come knocking and ask, as they will, *Can we come in?* your answer is this: *Do you have a warrant?* If they say no, then you say no, too. I know that now. I did not know it then.

So instead of sending them away, I led them through the front door and into the lounge room. 'Would you like a seat?' I asked, my trembling voice polite.

I saw them exchange a glance that said, *Who is this ludicrous woman?* I knew that look well. Once, it might have made me crumble. But now I straightened my back and lifted my chin instead.

The police officers failed to take the seat I offered. They stayed standing. So, I stayed standing, too. And there we all were, the three of us standing in a room meant for sitting; all just looking at one another.

The tall, thin officer broke the silence. 'We wish to speak to Gordon O'Hanlon,' she said.

'He's not awake,' I replied. This, as far as I knew, was true.

Another glance from them, another lift of the chin from me.

'Can you wake him?' Once again that tall officer spoke while the other one—short and stout—stayed silent.

I nodded. Of course, I *could* wake him. I didn't want to, but certainly I had the capacity. And for a moment, irritation at the inaccuracy trumped my fear of those women. For that brief moment, I was not the wife of a man in trouble but simply an English teacher.

When I returned to the bedroom, I saw my husband was not asleep, after all. Instead, he was getting himself dressed:

in trousers, a collared shirt and woollen jumper. His feet were bare, but as I watched on, he reached across for his black leather shoes and a rolled-up pair of socks. With a tie and a jacket, he'd be fit to show his face in my Free Church. Well, the Free Church that had once been mine.

'There are people here,' I said to him. 'They are women.' I couldn't bring myself to say the word *police*. I was already breathing quickly and if I uttered that word, I feared I might hyperventilate. So I did not say it.

'I'll go out to them,' he told me, socks on now, as he wriggled into his shoes.

I nodded and watched him leave the room. Should I follow or stay?

Stay, I decided, and to busy myself I began putting the room in order. I made the bed, I straightened the clothes in the wardrobe, I repositioned the hairbrushes that lay on our chest of drawers, then I waited.

But not for long, because I just couldn't stay still.

So I ventured back to the lounge room. I expected those police officers to still be standing and was surprised to find them seated instead: the two of them on the sofa; my Gordon in an armchair, our coffee table between them. Stopping in the doorway, I watched and listened.

'N-n-no,' my husband was saying, 'that is not true. That cannot be t-t-true.' He was stammering now as he did, at times, when he was nervous.

'Why are you stuttering, Mr O'Hanlon?' asked that short, stout officer I hadn't heard speak before. 'Do you have something to hide?'

He shook his head; he shook it hard, like a dog with a toy in its mouth. But my husband had nothing in his, and once he'd stilled, his empty mouth hung open. This made him look odd. *Close your mouth*, I had to force myself not to call out.

'Is there anything more you'd like to tell us, Mr O'Hanlon?' asked the tall, thin officer. Her voice had changed now. Crisp and professional at the front door, her tone was almost a growl as it ricocheted through our lounge room.

'I didn't do anything,' my husband insisted.

'So why, then,' she snarled, 'do you think you were suspended?'

I waited, heart quickening, breath catching, to hear Gordon's answer.

None came.

Not a word.

What now? Were they going to take him from me? Were they going to lead him out of our house and lock him away? These were the questions I asked myself as I kept out of sight, my arms by my side, my hands clenched tight.

Save him, save him, save him, I prayed. Since I could talk, I'd prayed to a God who frowned from the heavens, appalled at the sinners before him. *He is not one of them*, I reassured my Lord. *He has done nothing wrong. Please, please*, I begged, my hands intertwined now, *please, don't let them take him away.*

They didn't. They didn't take him away. The tall officer slid a card across the table before she stood up. As soon as she did, the short one rose, too. And without thanking my husband for his time or shaking his hand, they headed for the door.

Once they were gone, neither of us touched the card that tall, thin officer had left us. But face up on the table, it was easy enough to read. *DSC Johnston*, it said. *Sexual Offences and Child Abuse Unit.*

I stood there aghast as those sickening words seared into me. *Stop!* I wanted to scream after those women. *You have made a mistake. A dreadful, dreadful mistake.*

Part one

1

THAT DAY—THE DAY THE POLICE first came to our door—
was the day Miss Habler died. At the time I knew nothing of
this. At the time, I knew only one thing: my husband was in
trouble. I could hardly have managed much more.

Miss Habler had been my Sabbath School teacher. And so
committed had she been to this task that, in all the years she
taught me, not once did she miss a lesson.

Neither did I.

Like Miss Habler, my parents were godly people. Very
godly. Indeed, had my father's position in the public service not
been quite so secure, he might even have entered the ministry.
He became an elder instead; an elder of the Free Church of
Kirkton—the church we attended, my parents and me. On the
Sabbath, we'd leave the house at 7.30 am, when the ungodly
of Kirkton were still asleep and would not witness the sight of
us setting out down the footpath: my father in his polyester
suit—no matter the weather—my mother and me in one of
our long-sleeved, ankle-length frocks.

To cover my head—in winter as well as in summer—I wore a wide-brimmed hat secured with elastic looped under my chin, which pulled too tight and made my skin itchy. On my feet were the laced school shoes my mother insisted I wear because they were sturdy and good for walking. Loudly they'd slap on the footpath—more loudly, it seemed, the closer we came to Tracy Cameron's house—as I prayed she wouldn't yet be out of bed. I always disliked my loud clumping shoes—purchased two sizes too big so they might last—but on those Sabbath walks I despised them the most.

Just before I turned ten, however, something miraculous happened: my feet grew so fast that, within a month, my new school shoes no longer fit me. So together my mother and I went to the shoe shop to buy me some more.

'Can I help you?' the manager enquired.

My mother pointed to a heavy black shoe. 'A pair like that.'

Turning to me, the manager gave me a wink and smile. Her hair, cut shockingly short, was soft and honey-coloured. 'Mum's getting you sorted for school, is she, love?'

'And for church,' I added, unable to hide my dismay.

'Oh love,' said the woman, her smile disappearing, 'they're not really the sort of shoes you'd want to be wearing for good, are they?'

'One pair of good walking shoes, that's all she needs,' my mother replied, voice clipped, lips tight. An imposing figure, in my head she was twice the size of my father even though there was less than a head between them. Broad-faced, her long brown hair kept back in a very tight bun, hers was a moist, fair complexion that quickly turned red whenever she felt displeased:

a timely warning to keep myself quiet. And, in the shoe shop that day, I watched in alarm as her face began to darken.

To my surprise, the manager did not fall silent, but simply pressed on. 'How about something with a buckle then? We've got buckled school shoes for girls, which would be dressy enough for good.'

My mother's eyes, narrowing now, flashed with irritation. Would she erupt? Right here in the shop? Her hands white and clenched, I honestly feared she might. *Stop talking*, I silently warned the manager.

But although her voice dipped, the manager would not stay quiet. 'They're going on sale next week,' she said. 'The girls' school shoes, I mean, and only the ones with a buckle. Fifty per cent off.' She gave my mother a wink. 'Look, I shouldn't be doing it, but I'll bring the sale forward. Just for you, mind,' she added, her voice becoming a whisper, 'so please don't tell anyone else.'

My mother's large head gave a tilt to the right as she sucked in her bottom lip. 'Half price?' she murmured.

Smile widening, the manager tapped the side of her nose with a finger. 'But just for you. Why don't we go slightly larger, so they'll last a bit longer?'

And keeping her lips pressed tightly together, finally my mother had nodded.

2

I TURNED TEN ON THE day of the Sabbath. *It's the eighteenth*, I wanted to exclaim to my parents, *the eighteenth of August and I am ten.* Ten years old! And what an effort it was to say nothing at all; the only way to avoid a scolding. For in my family and in the Free Church, birthdays were not to be mentioned and never to be celebrated.

So as we walked to church on that cool winter's morning, I did not speak of my birthday. Nor did my parents. Wistfulness might well have swelled in me then—at the thought of my schoolmates, showered in presents and laden with cake for us all to share—yet it did not. For when my head dipped down, I glimpsed my new shoes. And the sight of them, so shiny and new and dressy, restored the smile to my face.

It was a long walk to church—well over an hour—and the sight of the spire filled me, as always, with something close to relief. Built on what had been a peaceful street—before Woolworths moved in—our church was on a corner block, covered in well-mown grass. Scraggly limbs of unruly eucalypts hung over the fence that divided the church from our neighbours. Other than that, our church and its grounds presented a picture of perfect order. More than that, really, for made as it was of sandstone and boasting a very tall spire, our church was impressive. From the outside, I mean. Inside it was much more subdued.

A wide sandstone arch framed our church doors: so thick they seemed made for a fortress. The doors were both kept locked, except on the Sabbath when the one on the right was propped open.

Directly inside was a foyer so dark that, even with lighting, it stayed dim. *So why didn't someone open both doors to let the day in?*

This, I'd decided, was a question for Reverend Burnett, by then our minister for over twenty-five years, and for whom, that day, I had some personal news. Because Sabbath School began before the morning service, our church would be empty upon our arrival; apart from Reverend Burnett, who would already be there. On that day, the day of my tenth birthday, he was in the front pew, his eyes on the notes on his lap, the Bible open beside him.

To get to my Sabbath School class—in a room annexed to the church—my mother and I walked straight down the aisle towards Reverend Burnett. To get his attention, I spoke very loudly. 'When I grow up, I'm going to be an elder.'

My mother had caught my hand in hers, and as my words spilled out, her hold on me tightened, squashing and tangling my fingers together.

When Reverend Burnett glanced up, he was frowning. 'Ellen Wells,' he admonished, 'remember the words of the scriptures. Let your women keep silence in the churches: for it is not permitted unto them to speak. And if they will learn anything, let them ask their husbands at home.'

'But—' I began to protest, until, rendered mute by the force of mother's painful grip, I lowered my head instead. *But I have no husband*, was what I'd wanted to say.

My teacher, Miss Habler, had no husband either. She did have a cousin, and that—believe it or not—was Reverend Burnett himself. This so confused me, I'd often catch myself staring from one to the other in search of the family resemblance. But if it was there, I never quite managed to find it. They were both old, of course, but this, it seemed, was all they had in common. While Reverend Burnett's light skin had a yellowish hue that made him look ill, Miss Habler's complexion was rosy. And where his eyes were navy and stern, her eyes were lighter and sparkling. He had a burr from a childhood in Scotland while Miss Habler had been raised right here in Kirkton. In our manse, no less, for she was the child of our previous minister, now long departed.

If Miss Habler felt the shame of being unmarried, she never let anyone know. Alone and unapologetic, she'd enter the church, head held high, steps quick and firm on the carpetless floor.

In this, our Free Church—with its bare walls and hard wooden pews—mirth was never encouraged. But in its separate space, our Sabbath School room was slightly more festive. For although our classes never rang with laughter, Miss Habler could always bring the Bible to life and did, on occasion, make me smile. Under Miss Habler's direction, the Bible became a world not only of men but also of women. Like Mary Magdalene, so loved by the Lord that, even in death, he came to her. Or the widowed Ruth who, ever devoted, refused to leave her dead husband's mother. Or Martha who cooked and cleaned to distraction.

Unlike the empty walls of our church, those in our Sabbath School room were adorned with the prophets: Moses stuck in the wilderness; Abraham, holding a knife to the throat of his son; and David fighting the monstrous Goliath. But of all the prophets stuck to the wall, John the Baptist was my favourite. And when he had to come down because Hester Boyce screamed at the sight of his head on a platter, I missed him. I really did.

The passing of John the Baptist was, of course, a sober reminder of the problem with birthdays. After all, hadn't Pharaoh marked his by killing his baker, and King Herod by beheading my favourite prophet? Tangible proof of how much God disapproves of birthdays. Perhaps even more than He hates Christmas and Easter.

So on the day I turned ten, having slipped through the door to my Sabbath School class, I was more than surprised—I was shocked—when Miss Habler wished me a happy tenth birthday and gave me a package wrapped up in brown paper. Holding it in my hands, I felt my heart race. With excitement, oh yes, but mostly with fear. For what if my parents walked in? What if they witnessed Miss Habler's transgression? Or worse, what if God had been silently watching us all along?

If Miss Habler shared my disquiet, she didn't reveal it, even though she glanced at the door more than once. But when

I turned over the package, my fingers pressing into its thick paper wrapping, she nodded. *Go ahead*, said her nod. *Open it.* So I did. I opened my illicit birthday package. It had the weight of a pocket-sized book and that's what it was: a hardback book called *Anne of Green Gables*, with a girl on its cover. A girl who might be ten, just like me.

'I think it's time you met Anne Shirley,' said Miss Habler, quite softly, her eyes, round and grey, looking straight at me. Under her navy felt hat, her hair—also grey—was pulled tightly back, although one wisp had made an escape. Like all the women at our Free Church, Miss Habler wore long-sleeved, high-necked dresses, which fell below the knee. In contrast to my mother, however, who wore more shapeless frocks, Miss Habler favoured those with a belt.

Clasping my new book, I was speechless. I liked to read— no, I loved to read—but in my house there was only the Bible.

'But my parents—' I began, my heart battering hard.

Cutting across me, Miss Habler's voice was soothing. 'I will speak to them,' she said, her eyes on the door once more. 'I will assure them that Anne Shirley is a God-fearing girl, whose story I've asked you to read.'

I nodded, my throat so tight with gratitude I was unable to say a word.

'A book of religious instruction,' Miss Habler continued, 'unrelated to this particular day.'

There was a noise at the door as the others began to arrive, so quickly I slipped the book into my pocket before taking my place at the desk.

That day we were four: Gerard and Stewart Campbell, Hester Boyce and me. Gerard and Stewart were brothers who looked so similar they might have been twins, but weren't. Rather, Gerard was one year my senior and Stewart almost two years my junior. Hester Boyce was, like me, an only child and also in Year 4. She was a thin, sallow girl with a high, scratchy voice that made my own sound like honey. At her school, she once confided, they called her Fester Voice.

Change your school and change your name, I'd urged but she hadn't. Instead, she'd sought comfort from Job, whose trials were greater than hers. And while I loved to hear about Job's shockingly difficult life, his camels—his three thousand camels—most intrigued me.

On the day of my tenth birthday, however, it was time to learn about somebody else: a woman whose name was Jael.

'The Canaanites were a wicked people,' Miss Habler told us that morning, 'living on land meant by God for the Israelites. Now, King Jabin, the Canaanite king, had a general, Sisera, who fled to the home of a man called Heber, an ally of the king. There he was welcomed by Heber's wife, Jael. Unbeknownst to Sisera, however, Jael was not his ally at all. "Come in, my lord," she falsely encouraged, leading him into her tent to drink, eat and rest. But the moment he slept, she crept towards him, carrying a tent peg and mallet.'

Captivated, I drew in my breath as a spike of excitement ran through me.

Miss Habler's eyes twinkled as, one by one, she surveyed us. 'Do you know what happened next?' she asked with a smile, pausing as we all shook our heads.

'Well,' she said, her voice rising a little, 'she placed the point of the tent peg on Sisera's temple and hit the peg with the mallet.'

When I felt myself flinch, Miss Habler laughed, raising her voice until she was almost shouting. 'Then Jael, she drove that peg through Sisera's temple. And so hard did she drive that peg, it stuck right through him and into the ground below. This,' she announced, her voice triumphant, 'was how the great General Sisera died: at the hands of a woman.'

And, then with the most enormous smile, Miss Habler opened her Bible. '*Most blessed of women be Jael,*' she read, her voice lilting and cheerful. '*She put her hand to the nail, and her right hand to the workmen's hammer; and with the hammer she smote Sisera, she smote off his head, when she had pierced and stricken through his temples. At her feet he bowed, he fell, he lay down: where he bowed, there he fell down—dead.* And that,' she said with a chuckle, 'is the story of Jael.' Closing the Bible with a bit of a bang, her expression turned serious. 'What then,' she asked the class, 'is the lesson Jael teaches us?'

Frowning, I set myself to thinking, while Stewart and Hester also stayed silent. Only Gerard raised his hand. 'If you want to hammer a peg into someone's head,' he said, the words coming out in a rush, 'make sure you hammer it hard. Because if you don't and that person wakes up, he'll be very angry with you.'

Miss Habler nodded. 'Thank you, Gerard,' she said before her head turned towards me. 'And you, Ellen,' she said, 'what do you think about it?'

'Well,' I began, trying hard to gather my thoughts, 'I think Jael was clever for making Sisera trust her so much that he fell asleep in her tent. For that was the only way she could kill him.'

'Exactly!' said Miss Habler, smacking her lips together. 'And in this way, God reveals how the gifts of ordinary people can be used to show his glory. For Jael was an ordinary woman, with ordinary skills. It was, for example, her job to set up the tents that sheltered her community. She was good at hammering tent pegs into the ground, so when it came to pounding the skull of General Sisera, she had all the skills she needed, didn't she?'

'Yes,' we all murmured, 'she did.'

⟶

After the Sabbath School hour was over, Miss Habler led us back to church in time for the ten o'clock service. I joined my parents in our usual pew, five rows from the front: my mother on my right, my father beside her, an empty space to my left. Silently, we waited for Reverend Burnett to rise to the pulpit and begin the morning prayers. Eyes to the front and keeping very still, I slipped my hand in my pocket and let it rest on the book I'd been gifted. Curiosity burned inside me, my fingers itching to draw it out, fold back the opening page and learn what I could about that girl called Anne Shirley.

But I did not draw out the book, I did not fold back the opening page and I did not begin to read it. Instead, my back very straight, I waited for Reverend Burnett to tell us to pray and, once he had, I rose to my feet.

In the Free Church of Kirkton we stood to pray but stayed seated to sing. The music of our church was that of the Psalter—the Book of Psalms set to music—the only accompaniment the sound of our voices, tuned to the fork struck by our Cantor—Gerard and Stewart's father—who gave us the opening note.

Beside me my mother would sing very loudly, certain of her own range. Turning her shoulders towards me while her head still somehow faced forward, she'd sing in admonishment whenever my notes fell flat.

Reverend Burnett walked with a stoop but when he mounted the pulpit to pray and to preach, he stood tall, his yellow skin reddening as he looked down from the lectern.

'Once the heathen nations of Canaan had been subdued,' he began on that day I turned ten, 'Israel had no real leader, and her people began to follow false gods, disobeying the laws of the Lord. At this time, Israel was oppressed by Jabin the King of the Canaanites and his ruthless captain, Sisera who fled to save himself. Sisera ran and ran until he came to the tent of Heber the Kenite, where, instead of Heber, he found his wife, Jael.'

At the sound of her name I straightened, my heart beating faster, for I knew full well what awaited that ruthless captain. As Reverend Burnett's voice rose, I caught the hint of a smile on his face. I, too, felt my lips twitch, as my body buzzed with excitement.

'Now Heber was an ally of Jabin and his general Sisera,' said Reverend Burnett. 'So Sisera would have been relieved to be welcomed by Heber's wife, Jael, who gave him milk and invited him in to rest.

'But when General Sisera was sleeping,' continued Reverend Burnett, a curl in his voice as once more it softened, 'did Jael simply leave him to repose?' Pausing, his eyes drilled into mine, I was sure of it. 'Well,' he asked, 'did he?'

Transfixed by his stare, slowly I shook my head.

Blinking once—a satisfied blink—his face became more animated. 'No, no,' he said, his voice booming now, 'she did not leave him alone now, did she? Instead, she found herself a tent spike, a large one. She took that spike—that great heavy spike—and with a hammer, she pound it right through his temple. Yes, she did. She pound so hard she smashed that general's head.'

My skin was tingling now, my eyes squeezing tight—both horrified and thrilled by our minister's words.

'A gruesome act,' he conceded, 'but a righteous one, too: an act to protect God's chosen people.' Leaning into the lectern, he tapped a finger into the wood. 'Now some might decry Jael's deceptive behaviour in luring Sisera to his death. To those people,' he said, his eyes moving from pew to pew, 'I say you are wrong. Yes, she was deceptive, but there was a battle to be fought. There was a war to be won. And on the battleground, Jael's deception was needed to secure a victory and, with it, the freedom of God's people.'

Fired by my minister's words, I was nodding now. I was not the only one: beside me my mother was bobbing her head, and beside her, my father was, too.

'For in Jael,' said Reverend Burnett, 'we see true faith and courage.'

That's right, I thought. And so, on that day—the day I turned ten—I learned two important lessons, one from Miss Habler and one from our Reverend Burnett: that God might be found in those who deceive; in ordinary people whose ordinary skills might be put to good use.

Later, much later, these were lessons I would well remember.

3

OURS WAS NOT A CHURCH for loitering after the service was over. Instead, we'd join the queue to shake hands with Reverend Burnett to thank him for his sermon.

Once my parents had finished their greetings, Miss Habler made her approach. 'Mrs Wells,' she said, her eyes not quite meeting my mother's, 'I wanted to let you know about the homework I've set for Ellen. It's a book—she has it with her— and I'd like her to read it this week.'

Was it my imagination or did I catch a slight waver in Miss Habler's usually steady voice?

My mother's face reddened, her eyes flashed and, waiting for her reply, I felt myself flinch. Then, to my surprise, she nodded.

That evening, I took to my room straight after tea and settling down in my bed, opened Miss Habler's gift to read about Anne Shirley, who, I smiled to discover, wore her clothes long and her hair in plaits, just like me.

—

Of course, Anne Shirley and I were still quite different. I was no orphan nor did I live on a farm. My hair was not red and my skin didn't freckle. Yet, so much did I enjoy the tales of her life that, whenever I could, I'd slip into the pages to join her. And as I devoured the words in front of me, there were times—many times—when I swear I became Anne Shirley herself, with Diana as my best friend.

Beyond the pages of *Anne of Green Gables*, however, the truth was this: I did not have such a friend. But if I could have chosen one, it would have been Yvette Sanderson. Not because we were kindred spirits—we weren't—but because if Yvette was your friend, everyone else would be, too.

Yvette was, it was generally agreed, the prettiest girl in our class. Her skin, unlike mine, tanned easily and she wore earrings to school every day. She had long blonde hair she mostly left loose, which, I knew, was an act of vanity. This was why my hair—which reached past my shoulders and right down my back—had to stay plaited.

In Year 5, Yvette was again our class captain. To captain our class—even just for one term—was something I yearned to do. But to be in the running, you needed a nomination. And no-one nominated me.

So year after year, I continued to cast my vote for Yvette.

We were twenty-four in my Year 5 class: fourteen boys and ten girls. In the classroom, we sat where our teacher told us to sit—in tables of six—but at lunch and recess we could sit where we liked. Outside, the boys and girls kept their distance. The girls sat mostly together in a group controlled by Yvette. To be part of the group, you had to be asked, and I'd never once been invited. At school, Yvette rarely talked to me at all. Elsewhere, though, she might strike up a conversation. Provided we were alone. On one such occasion, I managed to gather my courage and ask if we could be friends.

At first she was quiet, as though thinking it through, until with a look of regret she declined. 'It's not that I wouldn't like to,' she said, 'but friends need to hang out together at home, not only at school.'

I bit my lip and said nothing: I wasn't allowed to go to other girls' places and had never had anyone home to mine. Instead, I spent my time learning to sew and knit with my mother. These were, she would tell me over and over, vital skills for a woman. Cooking and cleaning, too. And woe betide the woman who lacked them: for how on earth would she find a husband?

I had no real interest in finding a husband, but I did learn to sew well enough to make all my clothes, including school tunics. This was a fortunate thing, as my parents would not allow me to wear a ready-made tunic. Instead, my mother copied the pattern then made it much longer.

I sewed my out-of-school dresses from fabric chosen by my mother. Like Marilla—who adopted Anne Shirley— my mother also chose scratchy material. And like Marilla, my mother required my frocks to be simple, with sleeves fitted right to the wrist. I, by contrast, longed for a dress with puffed sleeves, like the one Anne herself had finally been given. But because I had no-one to surprise me with such a gift, I needed to think of some other way to get it.

So I sat myself down at our sewing machine and, once again, slightly changed my mother's dress pattern. I couldn't replace those straight full-length sleeves with ones that ballooned and stopped at the elbow, but perhaps I might manage a modest-sized puff that began at the top, then narrowed all the way to the wrist.

This is how I came to own a dress with slightly puffed sleeves; the dress I wore to my Year 5 end of term dinner.

When the note went out suggesting the dinner, I handed it to my mother reluctantly, for I knew what her answer would be.

That night, nothing was mentioned, but in the morning, there it was on the kitchen table, signed to return to the school, confirming we'd all be attending. I read it again, sure I must be mistaken. Three times I checked before it sank in: I would be there. I would be there at the end of year dinner, together with all of my classmates.

—

On the night of the dinner, my stomach was filled with a fluttering. And when, alone in my bedroom, I put on my dress and buttoned it up, my fingers were shaking. In my room I had no mirror—that would be vanity—but we did have one in the bathroom for my father to shave. And when I slipped in to look at myself and caught sight of my beautiful sleeves, I couldn't remember when I'd ever felt happier.

With trepidation, I made my way out to the lounge room where my parents were waiting.

'What's wrong with your sleeves?' my mother exclaimed, extending a hand to pull at the fabric that puffed out at the top.

I lowered my head and tried to adopt a shame-faced expression. 'I made a mistake with the cutting and wasn't sure how to fix it.'

'You should have asked me,' my mother harrumphed and, when I meekly agreed, nothing more was said of it.

To the dinner I wore my buckled school shoes. The other girls wore sandals and the boys all had sneakers. Yvette Sanderson's sandals were silver and sparkling to match her blouse, which sometimes flipped up to reveal her belly.

Yvette's mother, whose name was Sandra and whose hair was yellow, had a very smooth face somewhat darker than her neck. Her lips were painted bright red—harlot red—while her eye shadow matched her blue eyes.

'Call me Sandy,' she said to my mother, but my mother did not. For the occasion, my mother had dressed in her grey serge skirt and a white poplin shirt with a removable grey serge collar. Her hair was parted and clipped, as usual, into a very low bun.

Yvette's mother did not wear her hair tied back. Instead, she let it fall over her naked shoulders. I must have been staring for she gave me a quizzical smile as she pulled at the front of her blouse. 'It's a peasant top,' she said. 'Do you like it?'

I'd been sipping my juice and it was all I could do not to spit it right out when she asked me the question. Had I not been with my parents, the answer would have been clear. *Yes, Mrs Sanderson*, I would have replied, *I do like it*. And this would have been the truth, for the fabric had an attractive sheen, and the sleeves, gathering as they did at Mrs Sanderson's elbows, gently billowed.

But how could I compliment a woman whose shoulders were bare? To buy some time, I cleared my throat which, to my surprise, made a sound so unexpectedly loud, it caused heads to jerk up and some of my classmates to titter. And although my body was hot with shame, I refused to look down. Instead, I smiled at Mrs Sanderson and told her the colour was lovely.

Still fingering the cloth, she looked slightly bemused. 'Well, yes,' she said, after a moment, 'white is a colour, I suppose.'

—

Mrs Sanderson had organised the dinner, with help from Tracy Cameron's mother, who called herself Bim, even though her name was Karen. 'It's a great deal,' she said. 'Ten dollars for the kids, twenty-five for the adults, and that includes alcohol.'

Joshua's father, who was sitting a few seats down, popped up his head. 'What, even for the kids?'

Well, that made all the parents laugh. Except for mine, of course.

It was not until the end of the night, however, that my mother raised her objection. 'I don't think my husband and I should have to pay for alcohol,' she said, her voice loud, 'given we are both teetotallers.'

The table fell silent—completely silent—except for Joshua's father who suddenly leaned so far to the left, I thought he might topple right over. Clutching on to the back of the seat where Joshua's mother was seated, his whisper emerged as a tongue-tied bellow. 'Tee what?' he asked.

'Teetotallers,' Tracy's father repeated, eyebrow raised. 'No alcohol. Nothing. Not even a beer.'

Tracy's mother looked disbelieving. 'Not even a champers at Chrissy?'

'Bugger the champers at Christmas,' added Joshua's father, straightening up once more. 'What about New Year's Eve? What about a glass to welcome in the New Year?'

My face reddening, I glanced across at my parents, waiting for their answer. But they said nothing at all.

Turning to face them, Yvette's mother was looking perplexed. 'What, you don't want to pay?'

'Not for the alcohol,' my mother confirmed. 'Of course, we're happy to pay for the food.'

'So how much do you want to pay for the food?'

Although my parents exchanged a look, not a word passed between them. 'Fifteen dollars,' said my mother, her voice resolute. 'We'll pay fifteen dollars each.'

Yvette's mother blinked, a strange half-smile settling on her lips. 'Oh,' she said, 'I see.'

'We'll be short then. We'll be short twenty bucks.' The voice, loud and flat, came from the far end of the table. When I craned forward, I saw it was Kevin's father, who had a large, red face. 'Short twenty bucks,' he repeated, lifting up his right index finger. 'But tell ya what, I've got an idea, a real good idea. How about I shout the lot of youse? How about I just go over to the, to the—' His voice faltered, eyes glassy as he looked around the table. 'To the bar,' he said, his voice raised in triumph. 'How about I just go over to the bar, get another round for youse all—' Then he paused, hesitating. 'Except for them ones there, because they're—' he stopped, his face blank before suddenly lighting up '—because they're totalled.'

'Totalled,' hooted Gavin Thompson's father. 'Ha, ha, totalled.'

Slipping through the tight smile on her face, Kevin's mum's voice was insistent. 'Mick,' she said, 'let's go!'

Kevin's dad was finally on his feet, rocking as he tried to slip a hand into his back pocket. 'What?' he demanded, although no-one had asked him a question. 'You think I'm not good for it?' he continued, eyes darting around the table. 'Is that what you think?'

Yvette's father was up now, too. Walking over to Kevin's father, he swung an arm over his shoulders. 'Sure, you're good for it, but if you do that, you'll be ruining the girls' organisation. This is what we're going to do: everyone's going to sling in a fiver to make up for the shortfall.' Narrowing his gaze in on my parents, he gave a bit of a nod. 'Not you two,' he said. Mostly, Yvette's father had a cheerful face, but tonight he wasn't smiling.

As we drove home, my mother hissed at my father, her voice low so I wouldn't hear what she was saying. I did though. I heard everything. I always do.

'What a hide, asking us to subsidise their drinking. Lucky they didn't try to charge us for their cigarettes as well,' she spluttered.

—

At school on Monday, Tracy headed straight for me. 'Your parents are real cheapskates,' she said. 'Everyone thinks it's outrageous, and my mum simply couldn't believe it.'

When, at Sabbath School that week, I repeated what Tracy had said, Miss Habler cocked her head to the side. 'Cheapskate is nothing more than a vulgar word for a person who is frugal,' she told me. 'And frugality is a virtue, never a source of shame. It is—in part, at least—the way to lead a godly life. So honour the Lord and take care of what money you have.'

I followed Miss Habler's advice, as I always did, and was frugal with my spending. This is how I was able to save my money, bit by bit, for when I might need it. Which, of course, later I did.

4

OUR CHURCH CELEBRATED TWO THINGS, and two things only:
Baptism and the Lord's Supper. Anything else was abhorrent,
especially Christmas and Easter.

I'd learned not to envy my classmates when they spoke of
Santa Claus and the presents they'd get, the brightly lit trees,
and the bonbons they pulled for the treats that were hidden
inside them. Easter I found more difficult: first because of the
Easter raffle then because of the egg hunt.

Each year, my school held a raffle with baskets of chocolate
eggs as prizes, all wrapped up in cellophane. And when I was in
Year 6, an Easter egg hunt was offered to the class that raised
the most money. Part of the playground would be roped off
and chocolate eggs hidden throughout it. Each student in the
winning class would be given a basket and fifteen minutes to
gather up all the eggs they could find.

I already knew about Easter egg hunts; I knew, for example,
that every year so many eggs would be hidden in Tracy
Cameron's backyard that no-one could possibly find every single

one of them. Months and months later and there she would be, cartwheeling on the lawn, when she'd see it: yet another Easter egg she'd missed.

Now I had the chance to be part of an egg hunt, too.

On the whiteboard in our classroom was a list of all twenty-eight students in our class, 6C. Beside our names were points added for good work or good behaviour, or deducted for poor work or poor behaviour. I was hardworking and well behaved so my points were always rising. To prepare for the Easter raffle, however, an extra column was added to show the money each student had raised by selling their Easter raffle tickets. At the end of the very first week, Yvette's number was five, Tracy's four, Kevin's seven, Joshua's six, while mine was a zero.

But what could I do to change it? How could I possibly ask my parents for money to support such a pagan event?

Two weeks were left to raise the money, only two weeks to ensure that we, the students of 6C, would win the competition. As the days passed, the points kept rising and rising. Only mine did not change.

'You know your problem? You're not a team player.' It was Friday morning, the recess bell had rung, and I'd just stepped out of the classroom when Tracy Cameron appeared in front of me, hands on her hips, head cocked to the side, lips pursed.

She was right. I wasn't a team player. I didn't play netball or softball or basketball. In fact, I didn't play sport at all. Because of my respiratory problems. That, at least, was what my mother had told Mr Floyd, who was our principal.

As far as I knew, I had no respiratory problems. I didn't even own a puffer. In truth, my mother's objection had nothing to do with my health. The girls' sports uniform was the problem: the pleated skirt so short it shocked my mother only slightly less than the scungies worn under it.

'This is where loose morals begin,' she warned me. 'And how young girls lose their modesty.'

It was her job to protect me from such a fate and to keep me pure. For this reason, I was never to wear the school sports skirt, and certainly never to be found in scungies.

So on that Friday morning, when Tracy confirmed what I already knew—I was not a team player—all I could do was nod.

'You're right,' I agreed. 'I'm not.'

Confusion passed across Tracy's green eyes, before her top lip lifted up in a sneer. 'And because of you,' she continued, 'we'll probably lose the Easter hunt competition.'

Her voice rose to a pitch. 'I mean, not even a dollar to help out the school? My mother couldn't believe it. My mum and Yvette's mother wrapped up all those Easter baskets and you can't even con—' for a moment she stumbled '—contribute to the school climbing bar.'

This, I remembered, was how the Easter raffle money was to be spent: on a new climbing bar for all the boys, and the girls, too, if they were wearing scungies.

⁓

I never intended to do what I did. Everything just happened so quickly. I'd just arrived home after school when it caught my eye, laying there on the hallway floor. Peering closer, I felt my jaw drop. Orange-red and twice folded, it was a twenty-dollar note that must have fallen from my mother's purse or even my father's pocket. In short, a note that wasn't mine.

Or was it? For in that moment, these were the words that came to me: *Ask and it shall be given you; seek, and ye shall find; knock, and it shall be opened unto you.*

Had I not asked? Had I not sought an answer to my problem? Had I not prayed to be saved from the shame of my class's failure? I had knocked at the door of my Lord and He had opened it to me. In my own hallway I'd been given the answer, in the form of a twice-folded banknote.

I picked it up and, to keep it safe, slept with it under my pillow. And when I arrived at school the next morning, I handed it to my teacher.

In return, she showered me with raffle tickets, so many I could scarcely fit them into my pocket; so many I didn't have time to count them. To be honest, I didn't care about the tickets themselves. I cared for only one thing: the number 20 Mrs Carris was writing beside my name, the number to propel me straight to the top of the class and all of us to victory.

And we were victorious.

So delighted was I by our success, I forgot all about the tickets my twenty-dollar note had earned me. Until Mr Floyd, our principal, drew the raffle at Monday's assembly.

When he called out my name, I stayed quiet. I didn't move, not even a muscle. And when he called my name a second time, still I said nothing.

Sitting on the floor behind me, Yvette gave me a push. 'That's you,' she said. 'You've won. You've won the biggest basket.' She sounded baffled. I was, too.

Stumbling to my feet, I made my way to the stage where Mr Floyd was beaming. 'Lucky day, Ellen,' he said. 'Easter hunt class winner and Easter basket winner.'

That's when the fear took hold of me. As my arms reached around that enormous basket of chocolate eggs, my mind screamed out to drop it and run. For how could I return home with such a prize? And how could I possibly explain my win without first confessing my theft?

The answer came in class with my teacher's congratulations. 'Gosh,' she said, peering through the cellophane and into the basket, 'there's enough for a second Easter hunt.'

During lunch, I repeated her words to myself. Over and over I said them.

A second Easter hunt.

That was it.

That would be my salvation.

I stayed back after school that day and, once the classroom had emptied, finally gathered the courage to speak to my teacher.

'Ellen,' she said, 'what are you still doing here?'

I swallowed, unsure how to raise it. 'My Easter basket,' I began.

She smiled. 'That was a lovely surprise, wasn't it?'

I gave a quick, jerky nod. 'I'd like to give it back,' I said, my voice rushing, 'to the school, for another Easter hunt.'

Mrs Carris had very dark eyebrows, thick at the start before they narrowed. Now both of them lifted.

'Oh Ellen,' she said, her voice rising, 'you don't have to do that. Really, you don't.'

Clearing my throat, I did what I could to try to sound more convincing. 'I want to,' I said. 'Perhaps for the class that came second.'

Mrs Carris leaned forward a little. 'That's very generous,' she said, 'very generous indeed. But are you sure that's what you'd like to do?'

Relief softened my body and I nodded. And once I'd begun, I just couldn't stop. I simply kept nodding and nodding and nodding.

'Okay, Ellen,' said Mrs Carris, her voice turning gentle. 'You can leave it with me.'

'Thank you, Mrs Carris,' I said, hot with gratitude. 'Thank you so much.'

I returned to my desk, scooped up the basket and, as bits of cellophane stabbed at my cheeks and my nose, carried it to my teacher. I picked up my school case, but before I could leave Mrs Carris was calling me back, an Easter egg in her hand.

'Here,' she said.

Biting my lip, I stayed put.

My teacher stretched her arm forward. 'Come on, just one.'

'Just one,' I echoed, tentatively reaching for it.

The egg was wrapped in a glittering gold foil, the words Crunchie stamped all over it. And when I saw that, oh, how the smile spread over my face. Until I remembered.

'I can't take it home,' I told her, my voice very flat, hoping she wouldn't make me explain. For how could I tell her that I was a thief who had dishonoured her parents by stealing their money?

'You could eat it on the way home,' she suggested. 'It's a bit of a walk, isn't it?'

She was right. It was a good way to my house; twenty-five minutes, even if I walked very quickly.

'It'll be energy for the walk,' she encouraged me.

Weighing her words, I cradled the egg in my hand, imagining how it might feel to undo the wrapping and press my finger into it. If only I dared.

'Tell you what,' said Mrs Carris, 'I'll open it and we can share.'

So I passed it back to my teacher and watched her peel back the foil, then press at each side until that Crunchie egg caved right in. Breaking off a piece, she popped it in her mouth then broke off a bit for me.

'You should eat it now,' she counselled me, 'before it starts to melt.'

So I did: right there and then, I popped it into my month. As the chocolate dissolved, my eyes closed over and soon only pebbles of honey-sweet Crunchie were left in my mouth. And when I opened my eyes, Mrs Carris was smiling straight at me.

'Off you go, then,' she said, as she gave me the rest of that egg.

That afternoon, I walked very slowly, stopping to snap off more and more of my Easter egg. But when I was just about home with still more to finish, I started to panic. Our street was leafy, with tall, large-trunked trees lining the road and a small reserve on the corner. In the reserve I hid myself, crouched behind a gum tree. Once safely hidden, I crammed the rest of the egg into my mouth: too much, really, as brown liquid began to ooze from my lips. Wiping it off, I lifted my hand well away from my tunic and cleaned it on a tree trunk. Next, I screwed the gold foil wrap into a very tight ball and hid it in the fork of that tree. Then I hurried home, passing houses with rose trees and daisies until I reached our own front yard, and its carpet of sharpened grass blades.

—

The two Easter hunts took place the next day: our winning class before recess and the runners up, 5W, straight after lunch.

Everyone in our class was given a basket and once the eggs had been hidden, we started our hunt. Mrs Carris made us all line up and wouldn't say *on your mark, get set* until everybody stood still. Then we were off. Half of us ran and half of us didn't, but we all kept our eyes to the ground—until Yvette found an egg in the tree and Kevin two more on the windowsill of the school hall. I myself found four eggs in all—two in the grass, one in the bowl of a bubbler and the fourth behind the rubbish bin. I'd hoped for another Crunchie egg, but that didn't happen.

Not that it mattered. What mattered was this: after that day, if I heard my name in the playground, it wasn't always followed by laughter. And when I'd turn to see who it was, I'd find a girl or boy from 5W calling out to say thank you.

Throughout that last year of primary school, high school became the main conversation. Half my Year 6 class had enrolled in Kirkton High. It was a co-ed school, which was why I wouldn't be joining them. In early years, girls and boys learning together was more or less acceptable, but in high school, my parents warned me, it was completely out of the question.

There was, a short distance away, a girls' school—Mary MacKillop College—I thought my parents might like to consider. But when I suggested this to my mother, her face turned purple. 'A Catholic school?' she exploded. 'A place filled with Papists? Have you gone mad?'

I knew about Catholics and their worship of idols, but had no idea this school would be full of them.

'They're not like us,' Miss Habler reminded me when I next saw her. 'They pray to Mary instead of to God; they even kneel down to her statue. Worse still, they worship the Pope, a mere mortal.'

Which, of course, made them all heathens.

———

And so, instead of attending that heathen college, I travelled for more than an hour to Brightvale Girls High where, once again, mine was the longest tunic. And although my cheeks burned hot as I walked through the playground, the staring and gaping was nothing new to me. Keeping my head held high, I walked through the grounds of Brightvale Girls High, pretending to know exactly where I was going.

I walked and I walked until I stumbled across the library, its double glass doors thrown wide open, as if in welcome.

So I walked inside.

It was big—four times the size of my primary school library—and bright, so bright; its full-length windows encircling the mezzanine level so light poured in from all angles. The floor was a carpet of vivid lime green, the back wall a fire-engine red, and the ends of each book shelf were deep yellow.

And the books! So many books!

'Well, hello,' came a voice as I stood transfixed.

I must have started for the next thing I heard was a laugh. 'Sorry love. I didn't mean to scare you.'

To the right of the entrance was a long white counter and behind it stood a woman. Her hair was grey and cut very short, with a fringe at all angles and wisps of hair around a face that would have been gaunt were it not for her luminous smile.

'You're new, aren't you? Year 7, I'm guessing.'

I nodded.

'Welcome,' she said, in an accent I couldn't quite place: not Australian like mine or Scottish like Reverend Burnett, but somewhere in between. 'I'm Miss Bell and I'm the school librarian.'

'Ellen,' I offered. 'I'm Ellen.'

'Delighted to meet you, Ellen,' she said. 'Now, you're clearly a reader, to have sought out the library so quickly. What is it you like to read most particularly?'

I felt my brow furrow as I tried to decide what to say. For in truth, the answer was this: the books I most liked were those I could only read in secret. Books of imaginary lands and imaginary people: Alice who fell down a rabbit hole, Dorothy who woke up in Oz and Peter Pan from Neverland. Cocking my head to the side, I surveyed Miss Bell, still trying to determine what answer to give her.

'Come on,' she said, 'there must be something you love?' Her eyes, wide and curious, settled on mine and something in them made me trust her.

So I took a deep breath and I made my confession. 'Adventure,' I breathed, my voice low and nervous. 'I like to read adventure and magic.'

Miss Bell clapped her hands like a child, instead of the grey-haired woman she was. 'Well,' she said, in that accent of hers, 'have I got something for you!' Bending down, she disappeared behind the library counter. When she stood up again, she was holding a hardcover book. 'Here you go,' she said, handing it to me. 'Tell me if you've read it.'

The cover showed a wintry scene of a boy with a bear, a lion and something not quite human.

'What's it about?' I asked, as I ran my hand over the jacket.

'A magic land,' she replied. 'The magic land of Narnia.'

My interest piqued, I held onto the book more tightly.

'Let's sort you out with a library card,' she said, 'and you can read it at home.'

My heart sank as I watched Miss Bell fill in a wallet-sized card and slip it into a plastic cover. 'All yours,' she said, handing it to me. 'You can borrow up to four books at a time.'

'You want this one?' she queried, her eyes on that lion-witch book I was holding.

I can't, I wanted to tell her. *I can't take home a book about magic and demons and the other strange beasts that fill it.* Instead, I just nodded, and once it was scanned, the book was mine for two weeks. Longer if I cared to renew it.

Finding a seat in a quiet corner, I opened the book and started to read. Once I'd begun, I just couldn't stop and on I went, page after page, so completely engrossed that I jumped sky-high when the bell rang.

'Do you know where you're going?' Miss Bell asked when I passed her on my way out.

'The quadrangle,' I ventured and she nodded and gave me directions.

I'd imagined the quadrangle as something quite lovely, with trees and soft, thick grass, surrounded by rows of white-painted classrooms. The quadrangle at Brightvale Girls High was nothing like that. It was simply a large asphalt square sloping down from the street to a two-storey building with a wide front balcony.

There must have been two hundred girls gathered there, a sea of green-and-white tunics.

A noise then, a blowing, whistling noise, that came from a microphone held by an old-looking man. Standing with his legs apart, he tapped then blew into the microphone. 'Welcome,' he said, 'to Brightvale Girls High. I'm your principal, Mr Harris, and I'm delighted to see so many of you joining us in Year 7 this year.'

He had a nasally, gravelly voice that, over the microphone's whistling, made it hard to follow. Leaning forward, I tried to catch what I could.

'Brightvale Girls High,' he was saying, 'I am proud to say, is a most excellent school, known both for its academic success as well as its sporting prowess.'

Netball, softball, tennis and volleyball: these were the sports in which the school excelled.

'And to ensure the standard stays high,' he continued, 'here at Brightvale Girls High, we have sport twice a week.'

No, I thought. *Oh no.*

For my mother had made it very clear: under no circum-stances would I be wearing the sleeveless shirt, tiny wrap-around skirt and stretchy shorts that comprised the Brightvale Girls High sports uniform. Once a week I could manage, I thought. Once a week I could grit my teeth, ignore the comments and try to play sport in my tunic. But twice a week? I wasn't so sure.

—

When I first clapped eyes on my English teacher, I had to stifle a cry of surprise. For he was a man with hair almost as long as mine. Here in my school; here in my very own classroom.

'Welcome,' he said, once we'd all settled. 'I'm Mr Tobin and I'll be teaching you English.' His was a pleasant voice, so pleasant I began to relax to the sound of it. Windows lined the wall to his right filtering shafts of sunlight that lit up his face and his hair, making him look like Jesus. And when his eyes met mine, they had a softness that seemed otherworldly. And from that very moment, despite his appearance, I was transfixed by our long-haired teacher.

On that very first day, Mr Tobin gave us a list of books he required us to read. Some we would study while others, he said, were for our general interest.

The Count of Monte Cristo was first up. A classic, our teacher assured us, as he handed a copy to everyone.

'Two weeks,' he said. 'You have exactly two weeks to finish it.'

But I'd only needed a week. Night after night, I stayed up in bed, absorbed by the story of Edmond Dantès and how cruelly he'd been betrayed. *Punish them*, I hissed into the pages. And when, finally, that punishment came, a thrill of delight had surged through me.

5

AT BRIGHTVALE GIRLS HIGH, OUR class was taught sewing and knitting by Mrs Serasinghe, whose accent betrayed a schooling elsewhere, so soft and clipped and clear was her English.

There were those in my class who found this amusing. 'Girls, girls, settle down,' they mimicked our teacher, over and over again, refusing to quieten.

'Girls,' Mrs Serasinghe repeated, 'please be quiet.'

But those girls would not stop talking. And as their noise grew louder—and our lesson kept being delayed—an indignation rose up inside me so strong it lifted me to my feet. 'Silence!' I said to the girls behind me, my voice low and deep and loud. 'Be still!'

And they were.

But although I'd brought the classroom to order, I'd done myself no favours. For when I went outside to have my lunch that day, I heard a hissing behind me.

'Think you're smart, do you?' It was Erica Garcia. 'No-one likes a suck-up,' she told me, 'especially a suck-up in a ridiculous uniform.'

I glanced down at my very long tunic then over to hers, which only just covered her thighs. And as I tried to decide which of us was wearing the more ridiculous garment, I found myself starting to smile.

With that, Erica flew into a frenzy. 'Why don't you just fuck off?' she said. 'I mean, you know you look like a freak, don't you?'

And as she walked past me, she clipped my shoulder and pushed me so hard I almost lost my balance. Shocked, I took a moment to catch myself. Erica, meanwhile, had joined a circle of girls from our class, all sprawled on a shady grass patch. Pointing her finger my way, they stared at me with disdain.

Perhaps, I reflected, I should have stayed quiet in Mrs Serasinghe's classroom.

—

Our sport days were Thursday and Friday, and on both days, I wore my tunic to school as usual.

Mr Marlon, our sports teacher, took us for ball skills on Thursdays and gymnastics on Fridays. He was a tall man with dark blonde hair and a long, floppy fringe that mostly covered his eyes.

When, on one of those very first Thursdays, I again missed every ball I was thrown, he gave me a look of despair. 'Why aren't you in your sports uniform?' he added.

Erica answered for me. 'Most probably forgot,' she said, and I didn't correct her.

Mr Marlon stepped towards me. 'You're not one of those students who finds sport a waste of time are you?' His voice had risen now, his face suddenly so close I could feel his breath on my skin.

I dared not move for fear of upsetting him more, so I cricked back my neck as far as I could to try to put some space between us. I knew what I needed to say. *Not at all, Mr Marlon, I think sport is very important.* But to call throwing a ball *very important* was such a stretch, I wasn't sure I could make it. So I just shook my head which, to my relief, seemed to appease him.

'Don't forget to wear your sports uniform tomorrow,' he warned me.

And when, once again, I turned up in my tunic, I was hardly surprised by his threat of detention.

That morning, we had to run up a soft spongy mat before dropping straight into a somersault. Erica went first. Before her run-up, she pointed one foot and lifted her hands up and out to the side. Then, in short, high steps, she ran down the mat, dropped to the floor and, curling into a ball, effected a perfect roll.

Peta Stevenson was next and, unlike Erica, neither pointed her toes nor lifted her hands before running. Instead, she jogged down the mat then, stopping halfway, bent in a squat and rolled over.

Just before me was Angela Lim, who was slight and quiet with long dark hair that fell to her shoulders. Her run down the mat was more a fast walk and she rolled, not like a ball, but more like an unfurling streamer.

'Tuck your head in,' Mr Marlon warned her, 'so you don't break your neck.'

Break your neck?

I'd been nervous already but now my hands shook as I stared down the length of that mat.

'Let's go, Ellie,' Mr Marlon called out.

Ellie?

'Now,' he said, becoming impatient, 'unless you want that detention.'

I did not want that detention. But the threat did nothing to loosen my body and still I stayed there, stiff and unmoving. *What now?* An intervention, that's what I needed, something completely miraculous. Closing my eyes, I silently fashioned a prayer. *Lord,* my voice rang inside me, *help me run down that mat and roll over. Incline thine ear unto me*, I beseeched him, *and in the day when I call answer me quickly.*

And he did. Remarkably, miraculously, my left leg shot out, then my right and, had my stride not been clipped by the length of my tunic, surely I would have been running. On reaching the middle of the mat, I fell to the floor, and wrapping my hands around my knees, bent forward, tucking my head to stop my neck from breaking. Then I rolled onto my back and, repeating my prayer, pushed myself over.

But as I stood up, instead of applause, I heard laughter. And when I took a step forward—one that was wider than usual—I knew exactly what had happened: my school tunic had split right open.

Mr Marlon gave me an unpleasant smile. 'And that's why we have a sports uniform.'

———

To stop my tunic from splitting further, I took tiny steps all the way to Mrs Serasinghe's classroom. Slowed by my stepping, I arrived late, trying my best to smile as I took my seat at the front.

As soon as I saw my teacher, my smile wavered. And when she looked straight at me, a questioning note in her eyes, I felt myself sag and, to my horror, started to cry.

Stop, I willed myself. *Don't look at me*, I silently begged her.

But her eyes didn't leave mine, creased with such concern I could hardly bear it. 'What's wrong, Ellen?' she asked, her voice gentle.

'She split her tunic,' Peta Stevenson called out before I could answer. 'Right up the back. At gymnastics.'

'Even though Mr Marlon told her to wear her sports uniform or she'd get a detention,' Erica yelled over her.

Mrs Serasinghe lifted a hand. 'Thank you Peta and Erica,' she said, 'but I was asking Ellen.'

Despite my efforts, my tears hadn't stopped and, because they were coming so fast, I struggled to wipe them.

'Does your tunic need mending?' Mrs Serasinghe asked me. I nodded.

'Then stay after class and let's see what we can do.'

So when the lunch bell rang, I stayed put in my seat.

'Okay,' said Mrs Serasinghe once everyone had left, 'why don't we get started.'

In her classroom was a door to a storeroom with shelves of fabric, cottons and patterns and, right in the middle, a head-less, armless dressmaker's dummy in a sleeveless sky-blue dress.

'Why don't you pop that dress on,' Mrs Serasinghe suggested, 'while I take a look at your tunic? I'll just need to undress Bertha.'

'Bertha?' I echoed.

'My model,' she said with a laugh, her hand on the neck of that headless dummy, as she lifted off the blue dress.

Without a frock to cover her, I saw that Bertha the dummy was not only missing her head and her arms, but also her legs. The rest of her—little more than a torso—was made of a stiff material that, had it been two shades lighter, would have matched my own skin. Idly, absently, I let my gaze follow the curves of that dummy—from the bulge of her chest to where her thighs met—until, suddenly mindful of what I was doing, my face burned with the shame of it.

Turn away, I counselled myself, yet I could not, gripped as I was by the urge—such an urge—to run my finger up and down that naked torso. A moment later and to my amazement, Mrs Serasinghe did exactly that.

'Bertha's a size 10,' she said, pressing into the model, 'which means I can use her for larger sizes, too.'

I nodded, appalled, unsettled, entranced by her wandering fingers.

'Now pop off your tunic,' she told me, her voice becoming brusque, 'so I can mend it.'

With a click, the door closed behind her, and there I was, alone in the storeroom. I took a deep breath, slipped off my tunic and put on that slip of a sky-blue dress. It was odd to be wearing so little; to have the air dance over and under my arms, my shoulders, my armpits. And, alone in that room, this time I did not stop myself: up and down I ran my fingers along that dummy's bareness, up and down, up and down.

'Let me know when I can come in,' Mrs Serasinghe called out, making me jump.

'Doesn't that colour suit you?' she mused when, hands once again by my side, I said I was ready. 'It really brings out the blue in your eyes.'

I shook my head, embarrassed. 'My eyes aren't blue.'

More muck-coloured, my mother would chastise me, having hoped for a child with her brown eyes instead of my own murky mixture.

Mrs Serasinghe seemed surprised to hear it. 'I'm not sure about that. It might depend on what you're wearing.'

When she motioned for me to turn a half-circle, I saw a mirror stuck to the back of the storeroom door. And in the mirror, I caught sight of a girl whose eyes did indeed seem to match the blue of that sleeveless dress she was wearing.

Holding my tunic in front of her, Mrs Serasinghe examined the tear. 'It shouldn't take much to repair,' she murmured.

I followed her back into the classroom and to the row of sewing machines along the back wall. Sitting down at the closest machine, Mrs Serasinghe threaded it with green cotton then quickly mended my tunic. 'That should be fine now,' she said, holding it out in front of her, 'but don't forget to wear your sports uniform next time.'

I nodded, as though to pretend if only I might curb my forgetful nature, all would be well. But perhaps my nod was too half-hearted or somehow uncertain. Whatever it was, Mrs Serasinghe kept asking me questions until I could no longer hold the truth inside me.

'I don't have a sports uniform,' I confessed.

'Is the uniform shop out of stock?' she asked me.

I shook my head. 'It's just, well, it just that my parents won't let me wear it.'

She looked surprised. 'They object to you playing sport?'

I shrugged. 'It's more the uniform itself, because it's immodest.'

'Immodest?' she echoed, her voice so low she could have been speaking just to herself. 'So that's why your tunic's so long?'

I nodded. 'And the rest of my clothes.'

Now she was thoughtful. 'Would it help if I wrote to your parents? If I reminded them that you're actually required to wear it?'

I wanted to laugh. 'No,' I managed to tell her, 'I really don't think that would help.'

———

The very next Tuesday, Mrs Serasinghe again asked me to stay after class. 'I've got something for you,' she said, once the classroom had emptied.

This puzzled me: I had no idea what that something might be.

And when she gave me a soft brown-paper parcel held together with string, still I felt confused.

'Aren't you going to look inside?' she asked.

I nodded and blushed and, savouring the wonder of such an unexpected gift, opened it slowly. Inside were two garments: the first, a white T-shirt with a bottle-green collar, the same as our school's sports top, only with long sleeves. Holding the top against me, I flattened the sleeves along my arms, and fondled the cuff at the wrist. 'Thank you,' I whispered.

My teacher smiled. 'Keep going,' she said.

From the parcel, I took out the second item: a skirt, as it happened, the colour of our school sports uniform, only triple the length. 'Oh Mrs Serasinghe, a skirt!'

She shook her head. 'Not a skirt,' she corrected, 'a skort.'

I thought I'd misheard her. 'A what?'

'A skort: a pair of shorts that looks like a skirt.'

I narrowed my eyes, certain she was making it up.

'Look,' she said, taking it from me, 'I'll show you.' And holding the skirt before me, she pulled up the front to reveal long wide-legged shorts underneath it. 'It's practical for sport.'

Surprised, grateful and so, so thankful I wouldn't be facing Mr Marlon's detention, I found myself without the words to express any of this to my teacher. All I could manage was a very soft, 'Thank you.'

Mrs Serasinghe gave me her gentle smile. 'My pleasure,' she said. 'I hope it makes things a bit easier.'

I nodded then blinked and blinked again so that I wouldn't start crying.

All week I kept my clothes hidden and, when Thursday came, I woke early to put them on.

When, dressed and ready for school, I walked into the kitchen, my mother was stirring the porridge, consumed by the task. This gave me the chance to slip into my chair and wait for my father to join us. Once he had, my mother carried the porridge across to the table and served us each a bowl. Then, leaving the food untouched, we closed our eyes.

'Gracious God, our guest,' rumbled my father, his voice a low monotone, 'we have sinned against Thee, and are unworthy of Thy mercy; pardon our sins, and bless these mercies for our use, and help us to eat and drink to Thy glory, for Christ's sake. Amen.'

When I opened my eyes, my mother was glaring at me. 'What are you wearing?' she snapped.

My heart hammered hard as I swallowed. 'My sports uniform,' I said. 'One of the teachers gave it to me, so I wouldn't get a detention. It's not immodest,' I continued, my voice quickening as I stood up to show her. 'Look.'

My mother's eyes travelled down from my neck to my ankles before they swivelled across to my father, who didn't look up. And when, ten minutes later, I headed to school, I was grateful my mother did nothing to stop me.

Under Mrs Serasinghe's instruction, we'd advanced from sewing to knitting, first a scarf then socks. 'Great for birthday presents,' she told us. 'And you could use cotton instead of wool to make something lighter for Christmas.'

A buzz rippled through the classroom, but not through me; not until I came up with my own idea. *What*, I mused, *was to stop me from also giving out presents, if not for birthdays or Christmas, then simply for a surprise?*

And so, once I'd finished my socks and my scarf I wrapped them up in separate parcels and took them home.

But when I handed my father his gift at dinner that night, he left it unopened.

My mother, by contrast, unwrapped hers at once. 'What's this?' she asked, pulling out the blue scarf I'd made her.

I felt my neck stiffen. 'A scarf,' I replied, my voice uncertain. 'I made it myself.'

'Oh,' she said. 'Why?'

Why did I make it for her, was that what she meant, or why did I make it at all?

'For class,' I ventured, 'with Mrs Serasinghe.'

'Mrs who?' asked my mother, her face scrunching up.

'My teacher.'

'Well, I hope she's taught you more than this. Any half-wit can knit a scarf.'

And when, spreading it out on the table, she examined my work, I immediately saw the flaws I'd missed in the classroom: the tension uneven, the width not always regular. And had I been a more daring person, I'd have scooped up my scarf and quickly snatched it back from her.

My father's parcel had still not been touched and for some strange reason, this was worse than my mother's critical eye.

'Are you going to open it?' I asked him.

'Can't say I need a new scarf,' he replied.

'It's not a scarf,' I murmured, becoming impatient as he half-heartedly squeezed the package.

'Do you want me to open it for you?' I started to ask, but before I could finish, my mother was doing it for him.

'They're very thick,' she said, holding up the dark green socks I'd knitted. 'How on earth will he manage to squeeze into his shoes when he's wearing them?'

Later that night, as I lay in bed, I thought that perhaps avoiding birthdays and Christmas was not such a bad thing after all.

—

Midway through my very first term, Miss Bell lent me a book that belonged to her and not to the library.

'What is it?' I asked.

She raised her hands to the sky, feigning surprise. '*Harry Potter and the Philosopher's Stone*, of course. It won't be published here until June, so my sister sent it to me from the UK.'

I screwed up my face. 'Harry Potter?'

'Boy wizard. Everyone's raving about it.'

'Really?' From the cover—a boy in glasses standing next to a train—I found this surprising.

'Just try it,' she pushed me. 'Give it a few pages before you make up your mind.'

Well, from the first page, I was spellbound.

'Take it home with you,' she insisted.

I shook my head. 'I'd rather just read it here,' I said, as I searched for a reason. 'So . . . well, so I don't lose it.'

Not since *Anne of Green Gables* had I been so entranced by a book. The awful Dursleys, the magical train platform, the Hogwarts School of Witchcraft and Wizardry and, more than anything else Harry, Ron and Hermione, who quickly became my own friends.

Day after day, I sat in the library at lunchtime, immersed in the story. And once I'd finished the very last page, I did as I had with *Anne of Green Gables*: I returned to the start and I read it all over again.

Not until I'd read it twice more did I finally hand it back to Miss Bell. In return, she gave me more and more books from the library and for the rest of the term, I read my way through her selections.

As the holidays loomed, I started to panic: how on earth would I manage the break without books?

But Miss Bell was a step ahead and, in the last week of term, suggested some I might like for the break. 'You can borrow the lot,' she said, with a grin. 'They should just about get you through both weeks.'

I tried to mirror her smile, but couldn't.

'Everything okay?' she asked.

I made to speak but no sound came out. Clearing my throat I tried again. 'My parents don't like me to read,' I began, finding myself with nothing left but the truth.

Her face creased in confusion. 'What, not at all?'

'Not really. Well, except for the Bible, of course.'

'But what about English, and History? What about all the books you need to read for your classes?'

'If they're on the class list, I'm allowed to read them,' I said, 'but I've already finished them all.'

A silence, then, as Miss Bell surveyed me.

'And if I were to give you a list of compulsory reading myself?' she suggested, her words slow and thoughtful. 'How would that be?'

Before I could answer, she had another idea. 'After the break, we could discuss all the books on the list. Like a tutorial. I could write to your parents to explain what I'd asked you to do.'

A tutorial! Yes, a tutorial at Miss Bell's direction. It was a good idea, a great idea, and, like a layer of ice in the sun, it made something crack inside me; something that pushed the air into my lungs, letting the breath rush freely through me.

And so, on the last day of term, I filled my bag—a large Globite schoolcase for serious students—with the books Miss Bell had picked out for me. And although they weighed so much my Globite was even harder to carry, I didn't care. Not at all.

6

AS THE YEARS WENT BY at Brightvale Girls High, my classmates began to transform. Tunics that had sagged now strained while skirt hems grew shorter and shorter. My tunics, however, stayed loose, disguising my body completely.

Only in the shower could I properly consider the shape my body was taking, the surprise of my fast sprouting hair and the spreading pink of my nipples. I had to be quick, though—the cost of hot water and, in all things, the need for restraint—for within seconds, it seemed, a rap would sound at the door.

'Hurry up,' my mother would call, her voice seeping in through the keyhole.

And yet, on occasion, transfixed by my body, I'd still take my time; soaping crevices and hollows more slowly than needed and running a finger along my new curves, daring to loiter, daring to encircle my thickening pink nipple until it grew hard with the growing heat in my body.

At school, faces were changing as well. Some became clownish—eyelashes thick and black and clumped together; lips stained red or purple or pink; over-flushed cheeks and black-rimmed eyes—while others were spotted with red, angry pimples over the nose and the cheeks and sometimes the chin and the forehead. Only my face, it seemed—neither spotted nor painted—stayed unchanged.

On the school bus—noisy, even where I sat at the front —were students not only from Brightvale Girls but also from Brightvale Boys.

'Show us your tits,' the boys would call out, mostly, it seemed, to nobody in particular.

That would prompt a guffaw from the girls who sat at the back of the bus, including Peta Stevenson and Erica Garcia, who, now in Year 10—like me—had earned this privilege.

'Piss off,' they'd call out, louder and louder until finally the driver would stop the bus, and threaten to throw them all off.

One afternoon, however, Peta's answer was different. 'All right, I will.'

And then, there she was; right there in the aisle, her sports shirt lifting higher and higher until it covered her head instead of her chest, revealing a lace brassiere.

At first I was shocked but then I was laughing. Was this what my mother had feared when I came to this school? That I too would be lifting my sports shirt in public? Was that why I'd not been allowed a sports uniform? At first my laughter was soft, but the more I considered Peta's missing head and half-exposed breasts, the louder it grew.

And grew and grew until Peta's head reappeared. 'Stop laughing, Ellen, you fucking weirdo!' she yelled out, sticking her finger up at me.

Most of the time, I'd just read in the bus, and immersed in my book, would take little notice of anything happening around me.

I was not the only one on the bus who read. One of the students from Brightvale Boys did, too. He caught the bus only sometimes and, when he did, sat by himself at the front, just as I did. One Friday morning, however—when the bus was more crowded than usual—he took the seat next to me.

To make sure his legs didn't touch mine, I leaned closer and closer towards the window until the side of my face was pressing into the glass.

That's how I stayed until, hearing a rustling, I turned to find him taking a book from his schoolbag. Curious now, I craned my head in an effort to read the title.

Without a word, he tilted the book to show me: *To Kill a Mockingbird*.

'Do you know it?' he asked. His voice was low and quiet and he had an odd accent.

I nodded. I did know it. Well, knew of it at least.

'And,' he continued, 'what did you think?'

I baulked, not wanting to admit that I hadn't yet read it at all.

I made a murmuring sound as though considering his question, before returning it to him. 'What about you? What do you think?'

He nodded, angling his head in my direction still without making eye contact. 'I still have some way to go, but for now, yes, I like it.'

'I'm Konrad,' he added. 'Konrad Baran.'

'Ellen,' I countered, lowering my head. 'I'm Ellen Wells.'

Then we both returned to our reading.

⸺

At school that morning, my thoughts kept drifting to Konrad Baran and the book he'd been reading.

'Good choice,' said Miss Bell when I asked her about it. 'I'll grab you a copy.'

She did, and I started to read it immediately. Such a terrific story, so wonderfully told. Well, that's what I thought until I came to the end.

'What?' I hissed into that very last page, completely dumbfounded. *What?*

It wasn't right. No, Miss Harper Lee, it was not. For how dare she shovel such misery into its pages; how dare she drag that man along with her, without pulling him out at the end?

Mr Atticus Finch, I wanted to call into those pages, fix up that mess, return to your story and, this time, try to do better.

⸺

Two weeks passed before Konrad Baran and I next spoke. It was a Tuesday morning, rainy and humid, and when he got on, the bus was already quite full.

About to pass by, he stopped, then softly asked if he might sit beside me.

'Yes,' I whispered, dipping my head, shy now, too.

Instead of trousers, he was wearing school shorts and when he sat down, I stared at his legs. Then when the driver took corners too quickly—making Konrad and his bare legs lurch into mine—oh, the surge that sparked through me.

'Is that good?' he asked, keeping his voice very quiet.

I felt my breath catch. What could I say? How could I possibly answer that question? Was it good? Was it good to feel the warmth of his leg beside mine? Well, yes, it was. But I'd never have dared to admit it.

When I stayed silent, he repeated his question, now resting his eyes on my book.

Only then did I realise. 'Oh, you mean this?' I replied, mortified now, as I brushed my hand over Charlotte Brontë's bestseller.

'We're reading *Wuthering Heights* for English,' he said. 'There were three of them, you know. The Brontë sisters, I mean. All writers.'

'Oh,' I said, trying my best to regain some composure. 'Imagine that.'

——

For the rest of the week, I prayed the bus would be full and Konrad would once again ask to sit next to me. But on the days the bus was crowded, he wasn't there, and when there were enough free seats, he sat alone as usual.

On Friday morning, however, something strange happened: as I got off the bus and headed to school, I heard my name being called. Turning around, I found Peta Stevenson in front of me.

'One of the guys wanted to give you this,' she said, handing over a folded note with my name on it.

I looked at the note then looked back at Peta, uncertain what to do next.

'Well, aren't you going to read it?' she grumbled, becoming impatient, 'just read it.'

So I did.

Ellen, it said, *do you want to come to the formal with me next Friday? Konrad.*

Konrad? Konrad Baran?

How astonishing!

But why would he give such a note to Peta when he could have asked me directly?

'He was too nervous to ask you himself,' Peta murmured, as though reading my thoughts.

Dumbstruck, I could only stare at her.

'So,' she said, a mischievous smile lighting her face—*were we now friends?* 'Will you go?'

Would I go? Well, would I?

Yes.

Yes, I would go.

Of course, I would go.

These were the words that leaped into my head, overtaking anything else. With these thoughts came images, too, that danced and fluttered around me. Pictures of the dress I would make myself for the formal. Blue, deep blue; in a soft, soft fabric—perhaps even silk. I had money—not a lot but some—earned sewing clothes for the children from our church. Surely,

I thought with a jolt of delight, I could use it to buy the fabric to sew a most wonderful frock.

'Well?' prompted Peta. 'Will you go?'

I nodded, eyes wide, heart pounding as finally I found my voice. 'Yes,' I told her, 'I will.'

Peta's eyes gleamed. 'I'll tell him,' she promised.

At school that day, I tingled and tingled, my excitement so strong, I struggled to keep it inside me. And that afternoon when the students from Brightvale Boys clambered onto the bus, my breathing grew quick as I searched—without success—for Konrad Baran.

—

With less than a week to the formal, there was no time to waste. So when, on Saturday morning, my mother announced her shoes needed collecting from the bootmaker, I jumped at the chance to do it. For only two doors down was a fabric shop with heavily discounted stock.

When I entered the shop, the manager looked surprised. 'Just you today?'

I gave what I hoped was a nonchalant smile. 'Yes, just me.'

She returned my smile. 'Well, how can I help you?'

I took a deep breath. 'I'd like some silk. For a dress.'

'Silk?' she echoed, sounding impressed. 'For you?'

Yes, for me, I wanted to reply, *for a formal, to make myself the most beautiful dress.*

But I couldn't risk spilling my secret, not yet.

'For a friend,' I said instead.

The rolls of silk were at the back of the shop. So many colours and so many shades of blue: from the palest azure to a navy so deep it seemed black.

'How much is this?' I asked, my hand lightly touching a thin roll of mid-blue.

'Thirty dollars,' she answered.

My heart leaped a little. 'Thirty dollars for the roll?'

She laughed. 'Afraid not. It's thirty dollars a metre.'

Perhaps she saw my face fall for her tone quickly softened. 'Tell me,' she said, 'is your friend set on silk?'

I considered the question. 'No,' I replied, 'not really.'

'So how about I show you something cheaper but just as lovely to look at?'

'Your friend,' she continued, 'is her colouring a little like yours?'

For a moment, I just looked at her, scared I would trip myself up. 'Yes,' I said in the end, 'her colouring is a little like mine.'

She nodded. 'Something in French navy might be nice.'

French navy?

'It's lighter than standard navy and looks good with fair skin and dark hair.' She paused. 'And do you need a pattern or have you already got one?'

'I'll need one,' I said, before catching myself. 'For my friend, I mean.'

The manager nodded. 'And what sort of style is she looking for? A high neckline, or perhaps something lower?'

While she'd been speaking, my hand had begun to make its way up my own neckline: a Peter Pan collar buttoned up to my throat. 'High,' I whispered.

'And what about sleeves? No sleeves, short sleeves or long sleeves?'

I swallowed. 'Long.'

'And the dress itself, below the knee?'

I nodded.

She smiled. 'I think I may have just the thing.'

Once I'd agreed with her choices, she took everything down to the register: zipper, pattern and the French navy roll of soft polished cotton.

'That'll be thirty-four dollars,' she said with a smile.

I swallowed. Thirty-four dollars. Out of my range. But only just.

I did a quick calculation. 'Do you think I could make do with three metres instead?' I asked her.

She folded her arms, considering. 'Of course, there's a ten per cent discount for regular customers,' she said slowly. 'So why don't we just round it down to thirty?'

I smiled. I almost laughed. 'Thank you,' I said to her softly.

—

There were, in our house, three bedrooms: one for my mother and father; one for me and one for the only indulgence in our otherwise frugal household: not one but two sewing machines.

I started on my dress that very same day, while pretending to work on the trousers I'd been asked to make for the son of one of our elders.

Over the next few days, I worked hard; so hard that by Thursday morning my beautiful dress was finished. Only then as we sat down to breakfast, did I tell my parents about the formal.

'A formal?' my mother exclaimed, her face turning red. 'And who on earth is Konrad?'

'The b-bus,' I stuttered, 'he sometimes catches the school bus.' I swallowed, waited a moment. 'Can I go?' I asked, my voice beginning to waver.

'You most certainly cannot!' she thundered.

'I wouldn't join in the dancing,' I whispered. 'I'd just stay seated all night.'

'Dancing?' My mother was sounding frenzied now. 'Do you mean to say there'll be dancing?' She turned to my father, who, until now, had been silent. 'John,' she screeched, 'what do you have to say about this?'

My father's head reared up as his hair—grown long on one side and swept over to cover his baldness—fell in front of his face. 'I say no,' he replied, pushing it back into place.

＿

My heart beat hard that morning: harder and harder the closer we came to Konrad's bus stop. What would I say when I saw him? Or worse, what would I do if he didn't turn up at all?

But he was there that morning. And as the bus was full he asked to sit beside me.

Nodding, I tried to decide how best to bring up the formal. Slide into it gently, I cautioned myself: chat for a bit before telling him what had happened.

'I can't come,' I blurted out instead.

When he looked confused, I tried to make myself clearer. 'I'm really sorry, but I can't come with you tomorrow night.'

Still he looked perplexed.

'To your formal,' I said. 'It's because of my parents. Because they won't let me go.' I stopped. I swallowed. I took a deep breath. 'But thanks very much for inviting me.'

'Inviting you?'

I nodded. 'To the formal.'

He frowned. 'I'm sorry?'

'To the formal. Your school formal.' We were facing the front of the bus instead of each other, but now he swivelled his head towards me.

'But I didn't,' he said.

'Didn't what?'

'Didn't invite you to my formal.'

Now I was confused. 'Yes, you did: Peta gave me your note.'

He'd swivelled so far we were almost face to face. 'What note? I didn't write any note.'

And that's where I should have left it. Just as that creeping, squirming sense of unease was rising inside me, I should have simply gone quiet. Stupidly I insisted. 'Yes, you did. I can show you.' And I could. For ever since Peta Stevenson had passed me that note, it had stayed in my wallet, tucked behind my bus pass. And now, I handed it back to Konrad.

He took a quick look then returned it. 'I didn't write that.'

I shook my head, thinking I must have misheard. 'What do you mean?'

'It's not my writing,' he said, speaking more slowly now, as though I had trouble with English. 'I didn't write that note.'

'Oh,' I replied, 'I see.' And I did. Finally, I did. For it was all beginning to dawn on me. Lowering my head, I clasped my hands together, willing the bus to go faster, willing the bus to speed to Brightvale Boys High so Konrad Baran would no longer be there beside me.

For the rest of the trip, we were silent. And when the bus finally reached his school, Konrad quickly stood up, mumbling something I couldn't make out, before he was gone.

Alone in my seat, I tried to piece it together. And when, on alighting the bus, I saw Peta Stevenson just ahead of me, on impulse I ran over to her.

'That note, from Konrad Baran,' I shot out as fast as I could before I lost my nerve, 'he said he didn't write it.'

Peta stopped walking. When she turned to me, her lips were twitching and then she started to laugh. 'That was a joke,' she chortled. 'I wrote it myself.' A hand on her hip, she ran her eyes down me—from the top of my head to my ankles. 'I don't know why you even believed it. You didn't really think he'd ask *you* to the formal, did you? I mean, really?'

—

Three days later when I woke to the Sabbath, the sadness still hadn't lifted. And as I began to get ready for church, it only increased. For when I opened my wardrobe, there at the back was my lovely new dress; my French navy frock, with its boatneck bodice, its long narrow sleeves and full, ankle-length skirt.

Taking it out, I held it to me, inhaling its newness. Returning it to the wardrobe, I put on the dress I'd made from a dark brown poplin my mother had bought on sale several years earlier.

I was now seventeen and I had been helping Miss Habler with her Sabbath School classes for more than a year. And although I loved the work and the children I taught, nothing could lift my spirits that morning.

I did try to smile as we prepared for our classes together but Miss Habler would not be fooled.

'Oh Ellen,' she asked, 'what's wrong?'

Her voice was so gentle, so filled with concern, I looked at her in dismay, unsure I'd be able to keep it together.

'Take your time,' she said.

So I sat down beside her, I gathered myself and told her what had happened. I started with Konrad sitting beside me then moved on to Peta and the note I'd been given. And as I approached the end of the story and the shame engulfed me, I had to clench my teeth to keep myself going.

All this time, Miss Habler had stayed quietly beside me, hands in her lap, wisps of hair peeping out of her burgundy hat.

'I should like to see this dress,' she said once I'd finished. 'Perhaps you could wear it to church next week?'

Wear it to church?

I blanched. The very thought of it made me startle.

'How can I, Miss Habler? My parents know nothing about it.'

She nodded: this was something I'd revealed already. 'But the design itself is modest?'

'Yes,' I assured her. 'It is.'

'As it happens,' she began, 'I've been wanting to acknowledge your work with me here. With a length of fabric, I was thinking—' Here she paused. 'Perhaps that might explain your new dress.'

I stared at Miss Habler, astonished. *What on earth was she suggesting?*

With a click of her tongue, she gently chastised me. 'It's very straightforward,' she said. 'I'll pay for the cost of the dress: fabric, cottons, pattern, whatever you had to buy. Then there'll be nothing to hide. I'll simply tell your parents I'd like you to have a new dress for church, to thank you for all your help.'

⸺

And so, on the morning of the following Sabbath I woke not to sadness but instead with a spark of excitement. Quickly I rose to put on my new dress, smoothing it down more than was needed, just to feel its soft silken fabric.

'What's that?' my mother asked over breakfast, jabbing her finger towards me.

'A dress from Miss Habler,' I said, trying to keep my voice steady. 'Remember, she told you about it. She paid for the fabric but I sewed it myself.'

'That was quick,' my mother retorted, and on detecting a hint of praise in her voice, surprise and relief travelled through me.

When I joined Miss Habler that morning—clad in my lovely new frock and my old beige hat—she was in the Sabbath School room, her long thin body folded into a child-sized chair.

'Oh my,' she exclaimed as soon as she saw me, 'but isn't that the most beautiful garment?'

I did my best to temper the pride that might have engulfed me—so pleased did I feel to be wearing that dress—but nothing could quell the surge of affection that rose in my heart for Miss Habler.

7

'SO WHAT DO YOU THINK you'll do next year?'

I'd blinked at the question, not sure how to answer.

For if I were to have told Miss Bell the truth, this is what I'd have said: as soon as my final school year is over, my mother will find me a husband, to spare me the shame of spinsterhood.

'You should think about teaching,' she offered.

'Teaching?' I echoed.

'Why not? You'd be great: you're clever, you love to read, you listen, you're organised, and because you like to learn, you'll be able to lead by example.'

My face grew warm at her words, so warm I put up my hand to stop her, unused as I was to such flattery.

But her words kept coming back to me.

A teacher. *A school teacher.* A teacher like Miss Bell and Mrs Serasinghe. Me? Unthinkable. Unimaginable.

And yet.

For hadn't Miss Habler herself been a school teacher?

Yes, and look what happened to her, my mother's voice bounced inside my head, *she ended up a spinster.*

'A teacher?' my mother repeated when I gathered the courage to raise it. 'Why on earth would you want to do that? And besides, what would be the point? You'd be giving it up as soon as you're married.'

I nodded, swallowed, then took a moment to answer. 'I know,' I said, keeping my voice very measured, 'but could I apply in the meantime?'

My mother sighed and harrumphed, but stopped short of saying I couldn't.

Miss Habler beamed when I told her the news.

I returned her smile with a grimace. 'So long as she doesn't find me a husband too quickly.'

He'd have to be part of our church community, that went without saying. But only two of our members were wifeless: Mr Stevens who was as old as my father and James Johnson whose bad breath made dialogue difficult. I didn't want to marry either one of them.

When I confessed this to Miss Habler—the words rushing out of me, high and filled with alarm—I feared she would chastise me.

She did not. 'I felt exactly the same way,' she said, her voice a murmur.

My head yanked up. 'You did?'

She nodded. 'My parents wished me to marry but I didn't agree with the choices they gave me. Besides, I wanted to finish my studies. And of all the suitors my parents put forward, I couldn't be sure any would stand for a wife who wanted to study.' She gave me a smile. 'So I refused to consider even one of them.'

'And after you finished your studies?'

The smile disappeared. 'By then, my circumstances had changed. First the Lord called for my mother. Two months later—days after my graduation—He came for my father. And as I was their only child, the family home became mine. So there I was, no longer under anyone's power.' Her lips lifted. 'And I wasn't sure that I wanted to change that.'

I lowered my head to better consider her words. 'But my parents are in very good health,' I murmured softly.

8

SO I WENT TO UNIVERSITY—the country's oldest—with its gracious stone buildings, moss-covered grouting and enormous lecture theatres.

In one such theatre, we had our English literature classes. The building itself was not level. It plummeted, instead, at a very steep angle to a space that, except for a lectern, was empty. Scuffed wooden steps divided the room, a continuous desk on either side of the steps and one long bench to sit on.

On my first university day, I'd taken a seat at the front. I was still arranging my folder, my pens and my paper when a woman sat down beside me.

'Good God,' she exclaimed. 'I've been racing around the whole bloody campus like a chook with its fucking head chopped off.'

Appalled and curious, I stole a look at her. To my surprise, she was dressed in a tablecloth—a white, lace tablecloth—with a hole for her head so that, like a poncho, it covered her shoulders and back. Under this, she wore nothing but black: a black skirt with a sleeveless turtleneck top. Her hair was blonde—so blonde it seemed white—and her lips were painted bright red.

But before I could study her closely, a sound came from the front of the room and, when I turned to check what it was, a red-haired man was heading towards the lectern.

'My name is Dr Alex Romano,' he told us, 'and I'll be teaching you this year. More about that a bit later. For the next few moments, though, I want you to put down your pens and lean back in your seat with your eyes closed.'

What?

'"Let Me Not to the Marriage of True Minds" is a sonnet,' he continued, 'by that great master, William Shakespeare. It's also one of my favourite pieces of poetry. If you already know it, you might understand why. If you do not, your life is about to be enriched. So relax, sit back, keep your eyes closed and listen. Just listen.'

His voice became slower—deeper, too—as he started to read aloud.

'Let me not to the marriage of true minds
Admit impediments. Love is not love
Which alters when it alteration finds,
Or bends with the remover to remove.'

I was soothed by the lilt in his voice, so soothed I felt a bit sleepy. And the sleepier I grew, the more distant my lecturer's voice became.

'Love's not Time's fool, though rosy lips and cheeks
Within his bending sickle's compass come:
Love alters not with his brief hours and weeks,
But bears it out even to the edge of doom.

If this be error, and upon me proved,
I never writ, nor no man ever loved.

'And that,' said Dr Alex Romano, his voice suddenly louder, startling me out of my stupor, 'must be one of the greatest love poems ever written.' His eyes swept the hall. 'Over to you,' he said, addressing us all. 'Any thoughts before I tell you a little bit more?'

My neighbour's hand shot up. 'I'd like to suggest a change.'

Dr Romano cocked his head to the side. 'A change?'

'To the poem. I think it needs to be changed.'

His eyebrow lifted. 'Yes?'

'To get rid of the sexism. I mean, it's so blatant, isn't it?'

For a moment he paused. 'Can you explain what you mean?'

'That last bit,' she said, 'the bit about time being a bloke.'

'Time being a bloke?' he repeated.

'Well, yes,' she said. 'It keeps saying *his* whenever it talks about time. And, like, why should time be male at all? I'd be suggesting a change to get rid of the sexism.'

I watched my lecturer swallow. 'And how would you do that?'

Sucking the end of her pen, my neighbour turned thoughtful. 'Probably just make it *she* instead of *he*,' she said after a moment or two. 'You know, restore the balance a bit.'

Someone called out from the back. A woman. 'No, no,' she said, 'get rid of *his* altogether and replace it with *time* instead.'

Dr Romano looked concerned. 'Wouldn't that be a bit repetitious?' he ventured.

'It'd do the job though,' countered my neighbour.

That got her a laugh. 'An interesting point,' said Dr Romano.

An interesting point? No, it wasn't. It was a ridiculous point.

'You can't change a poem just because you don't like it,' my voice rang out.

The lecturer laughed. 'Clearly something to think about when we consider the purpose of art and what to do with the problems it raises.'

When the class was over, everyone rushed up the stairs as fast as they possibly could. Instead of joining the crowd, I took my time, waiting until the stampede was over and the room was almost empty. Only then did I pack up my bag—still the same Globite I'd used throughout high school. Built to last, the salesman had assured my parents and he had been right. Yet, despite their durability, Globites were surprisingly rare on campus. Most other students wore satchels or backpacks and—struggling now with my oversized model—I envied them for it.

'Can I help you?'

The voice came from behind, and I turned to find a man level with me, even though he stood on the lower step. His hair was messy, the front swept across his forehead and over his face, one eye peeking through it.

He gave my bag a quick tap. 'I can carry it for you,' he offered.

'It's not heavy,' I said. But the size alone made it awkward and I kept bumping my legs as I hauled it up the stairs.

'Give it to me,' he insisted.

'I'm Jamie,' he said, once we'd reached the top and stepped into the sunshine. 'Jamie Kellaway.' Then he stretched out a hand towards me. I'd never shaken a man's hand before and only after some hesitation did I finally take it. When our palms met, his fingers curled up and he gave my hand a squeeze.

'Ellen,' I said, my voice a bit phlegmy. 'Ellen Wells.'

'I agree with you,' he said, before he let go of my hand.

I didn't know what he was talking about.

'The poem,' he said. 'About it being wrong to try to change it.'

'Well, of course you'd think that: the patriarchy always protects itself.' I knew that voice, and when I looked around, I saw I was right: there was that tablecloth woman.

'I rather see it a different way,' Jamie replied, 'I'd like to be seen as a protector of art, rather than of the patriarchy.' He turned to me, eyes twinkling now. 'And what about you, what do you think about it?'

'Don't try to co-opt her,' she warned him, 'or bully her into an answer.'

But before Jamie could open his mouth to reply, there was shouting behind us.

'Steph!' someone was calling. 'Over here.' When we all turned to look, a woman was waving her hands towards us. My neighbour's face lit up and, turning around, she left without a word.

'Saved,' Jamie Kellaway whispered, making me smile. 'What about a drink to celebrate?'

Caught by surprise, I found myself nodding. 'Tea?'

He laughed. 'Sure. I know a really good cafe. It's a bit of a walk, but worth it.'

He still had my case but wouldn't let go when I held out my hand to take it. 'It's fine,' he said. 'I thought it'd be much heavier. I'd assumed you'd come straight from the airport.'

I shook my head. 'I came by bus,' I said, and for the second time he laughed.

We walked across the pedestrian bridge to the neighbouring suburb, and into a cafe called Holly's.

'I like your dress,' he said once we were seated. 'So retro. Where did you find it?'

Find it?

It was a dress I'd only just finished: white spots on navy, a Peter Pan collar and a row of white buttons down the front. 'I made it,' I told him.

'Wow,' he said, 'that's wild. I love the whole look: the clothes, the long hair. It's all great.'

I blushed, unaccustomed to praise for the way I looked.

Except by Mr de Rossi, of course.

Our geography teacher, Mr de Rossi also liked to take pictures. And in our final school year, he took our photographs for the school magazine. 'Swivel to the side, then look back,' he said when it came to my turn.

I did what he asked: I turned to the side and, frowning a little, looked back again.

'What about a smile?' he said with a wink. 'Just a small one will do.' And when I obliged, he snapped again, and once more.

Later that week, we passed in the hall. 'Your portrait shot,' he said, 'it's great.'

I tilted my head, sure he had to be joking.

'It is,' he insisted. 'Swing by the staffroom and I'll give you a copy.'

When I presented myself at his door—curiosity trumping my shyness—he gave me a A4-sized envelope.

Reaching inside, I pulled out a photograph, so large it only just fit inside. At first I didn't see it was me, for the girl in the portrait was smiling and glowing, her skin clear and bright, her large blue-grey eyes staring straight into the camera.

'I look—' I began, unsure what to say next.

'Stunning,' said Mr de Rossi, his voice slightly confused, as though he couldn't fathom it either.

—

'And what about you, darling?'

Startled, I found a woman standing beside me, pen in one hand, notepad in the other. She had one eyebrow raised, as though she'd been waiting some time for my answer.

'Oh,' I said, flustered. 'Um, a tea.'

Her eyebrow stayed raised. 'What sort?'

'Well . . .' I began. 'Lipton?'

She shook her head. 'Nup, sorry. Earl Grey, English Breakfast or peppermint?'

Peppermint in tea? I'd never heard of any such thing. 'Earl Grey,' I replied.

Jamie ordered a coffee that came in a very small cup, like something a child might drink from. I, by contrast, was delivered a large pot of tea with a small jug of milk and a matching cup and saucer.

'So you're enrolled in Arts?' Jamie asked me.

I'd lifted the teapot and was starting to pour when I turned to answer his question. A stream of liquid missed my cup and spilled on the saucer and over the table. Biting my lip, I berated myself for being so stupid.

Pulling serviettes from our table's dispenser, one by one Jamie handed them to me.

'Education,' I replied once I'd mopped up the mess I'd made. 'I'm doing a Bachelor of Education.'

'So you can become a teacher?'

'Yes,' I replied, a thrill surging through me. Still I could hardly believe it: both that I'd actually started the course and that my parents hadn't stopped me.

'An English teacher?'

I nodded. 'I've taken History, too, but it's English I most want to teach.'

He didn't want to teach. He wanted to be a psychologist, so he could work with prisoners.

That was a surprise. Of all the things to do, why choose to spend time with criminals?

'Prisoners,' he corrected me. 'I said prisoners, not criminals.'

Pedantic, I thought at the time. Only later—much later—did I completely change my opinion.

⸺

The following week, Jamie sat beside me in English and, after we'd finished, asked if I'd like to have lunch.

Yes, I thought, *I would*.

Once we'd left the lecture hall and were back outside, I looked around for a place to sit down.

'I often eat on the grass or a step or on one of the benches,' I told him.

His eyes crinkled. 'I was thinking of something more like a cafe or restaurant.'

'Oh,' I said, surprised for I'd brought my lunch with me, as I always did. But perhaps it would keep for a day.

So we went to a cafe that Jamie knew well, and on his advice I ordered something I'd never tried before: Greek salad.

When it arrived, I was caught out by two things: olives and cubes that were white, but otherwise unidentifiable. Warily bringing one to my lips, I didn't expect it to be so salty or to crumble so quickly. To be honest, it made me feel like gagging.

Jamie gave me another big smile. 'Good, isn't it?'

I nodded, swallowed, then gulped down another three olives and two salty squares. 'Wonderful,' I agreed.

—

When, a couple of weeks later, one of our lectures was cancelled, Jamie had another suggestion. 'Why don't we see a movie?'

'A movie?'

He nodded. 'There's a cinema nearby. It's half-price on Tuesday and they play classics all afternoon. What do you think?'

No. That's what I thought. For films were the work of the devil, Reverend Burnett had always warned us.

'Say yes,' said Jamie. 'You'll love it—it's a really great cinema.'

With his eyes on mine, I felt something crackle inside me; something that, with all its fizzing and sparkling, must have prompted my answer. My reckless, impulsive, wicked answer. *Yes.*

So we headed off together, Jamie once again taking my case while I walked beside him.

'You really could do with a new bag,' he suggested. 'Something less awkward.'

'Like that,' he said as we approached a shop window.

Hanging down from a hook, was a bag in burgundy leather. A satchel, really, big enough to fit whatever I needed for university.

'Do you want to take a look?' he suggested.

I hesitated. 'It'll be too expensive.'

He gave a click of his tongue. 'I doubt it. It's a second-hand shop, so nothing costs very much.'

The sales assistant was oddly attired, a scarf tied around her head that caught some of her long, grey hair but left the rest spilling out. And although her skirt was as long as the dress I was wearing, her top was more like a brassiere.

'This won't last long,' she said as she took down the bag to show us. 'I only just put it out.'

When she handed it to me, I felt my breath catch. It was perfect: the colour so rich, the strap so strong and the size exactly right. 'A real bargain,' the woman assured me.

Unconvinced, I was loathe to look at the price tag.

When, finally I did, I thought there must be a mistake. 'Four dollars?' I queried.

'Uh-huh,' she said. 'An absolute bargain.'

So I bought that bag, I ripped off the tag and I wore it out of the shop; so pleased I was almost skipping.

Only when we reached the crest of the road did my high spirits dampen. For there, lit up on the building before me was the word *CINEMA*. Despite my growing unease, I let Jamie lead me through the door and into a darkened foyer. At the far end, beside a flight of carpeted stairs and behind a counter, sat a man with no hair.

'If you're after the Retro Choice, it's already started,' he rebuked us.

Jamie laughed as he took out his wallet. 'That doesn't matter,' he said, 'we can't have missed very much.'

Two, even three, at a time, Jamie jumped the stairs as I did my best to keep up with him. Once we'd reached the top, Jamie pushed through the double doors, and I followed.

'Oh,' I cried out, shocked by the blackness engulfing me. Only once my eyes had begun to adjust did I notice a row of lights leading down a flight of wider, longer stairs. And when, then, finally I lifted my eyes, oh, the shock of that gigantic screen in front of me.

Jamie touched my arm gently. 'There's two seats here,' he told me. I could make out rows of people around us, their faces in shadow as they stared up into the screen. All except one who swivelled his head and hissed at us both to be quiet.

Once sitting down, I tilted my head to properly take in the enormous screen before me. And oh, oh, oh! How my mouth gaped in horror. For covering the screen was a desert of statues: huge human-bodied idols with strange animal heads. The light from the screen lit the faces of those seated around me and, risking a glance, I marvelled at their captivation.

Reverend Burnett was right, I thought to myself. This was, indeed, a place of darkness and idolatry. A cold place, too—so cold—and I regretted not dressing more warmly.

Cast down your eyes, I counselled myself at the sight of those half-human idols who were filling the screen.

So I lowered my eyes, daring only to look once more when I heard the cheerful tones of a woman. A mother, it soon became clear, to a girl of eleven or twelve with the unusual name of Regan.

But as fast as they had appeared, so too were they gone, replaced by the house of a Papist, filled with statues and crosses.

Things got worse after that. Much worse. First the girl Regan stopped smiling and her body began to writhe. And then, oh my, oh my, oh my, her sweet voice transformed, and out of her mouth came guttural sounds, and language so filthy I thought I must have misheard it.

My back ramrod straight, my jaw strangely locked, I watched on in horror as that child mutated: her head lurching then swivelling, not just to the side, but around. A full half-circle it turned, so the girl was looking straight out at me, while her back remained in full view.

'You know what she did?' that ghastly, head-swivelling child asked me, her voice no longer her own, but instead the voice of the devil.

That was it. That was all I could manage. Around me, the room turned blacker and, although I stayed as I was in my seat, that was the last I saw of the horror.

The next thing I knew, I was the one who was moving, my body bouncing and tossing around, just like that sinister child. *What?* I wanted to scream but nothing came out. I was being carried, I slowly realised—an arm under my knees and another around my back—by Jamie Kellaway.

'What—' I tried again, this time letting out a very small sound. 'What are you doing?'

'Getting you out of the cinema,' he said, his breath short and laboured.

He carried me down the stairs and back to the foyer where he laid me across a row of chairs pushed together. Too dazed to sit up, I stayed on my back, the strap of my new bag digging into my shoulder.

That was when I remembered. 'My bag,' I whispered, still unable to speak very loudly. 'My Globite.'

'Don't worry,' said Jamie. 'I'll get it.' And he did. Within a minute or two he was back, with both my bag and a glass of water.

Slowly, gingerly I tried to sit up.

'Drink this,' he said as he gave me the water, 'before I help you get home.'

I shook my head. 'I'll be fine. I'll just catch a bus.' But when I tried to stand up, my legs felt unsteady.

'I'll catch it with you,' he insisted. *No, please no*, I wanted to say, but my head was pounding and I didn't have the strength to protest.

So we sat on the bus together, me by the window, the breeze cooling my prickling face and, by the time we had to get off, I'd completely recovered.

But when I said as much to Jamie—*I'll be fine from here*—he ignored me.

'You shouldn't be walking alone,' he said, 'not after what happened.'

So I let him walk me as far as my street. 'I'm okay now,' I told him.

He shook his head and gave me a wink. 'Since I've come this far it would be rude not to say hello.'

I felt my heart sink. But what could I do? I couldn't just send him away, and besides, he was still carrying my Globite. So, despite my misgivings, he accompanied me home and, after I'd knocked, we stood by the door together.

First there was nothing, then there were footsteps and, after a while, a soft creak as the front door opened while the screen still stayed closed.

Through the mesh, my mother's voice was muffled as she fiddled with the key. 'I thought you said you'd be at the library all day,' she muttered, before finally unlocking the door. And then, oh my, to see her face when she saw not only me but Jamie there, too.

Taking a step forward, he put out his hand, a friendly smile on his face. 'I'm Jamie,' he said. 'Jamie Kellaway.'

My mother did not take his hand. She just stared at him as he, in turn, kept talking.

'I took Ellen to the cinema,' he began to explain. 'I didn't know what was on until we got there, then we were late so we had to rush in. I really should have warned her, I know. I'd forgotten how shocking *The Exorcist* can be if you haven't seen it before.' And then, to my horror, he started to chuckle. 'All that Satan stuff. Sometimes, it even gives me the jitters, I'll admit it.'

He stopped for a moment, his tone turning serious. 'I really didn't expect her to faint, though. To be honest, when I felt her slump onto me, it scared the daylights out of me. I thought, my God, what's going on? I've got to get her out of here, out into the fresh air. So I bundled her up and took her back into the foyer. She didn't want me to bring her home but I thought,

I can't leave her, can I? Say she faints on the bus or when she's walking home?'

I really thought he might never ever stop speaking at all; by the time he finally drew breath, I was beginning to completely despair of it. Had he observed nothing at all as he'd rambled on? Had he not seen the colour drain from my mother's stern face as her expression became more and more thunderous?

'How dare you!' she screamed, the moment he'd finished, her finger pointing to his face. 'How dare you take my daughter to that house of Satan. How dare you lure her into his lair!'

And that was just the beginning.

When I could bear it, I glanced at Jamie, his head now at a slightly odd angle and looking completely perplexed.

'Get out!' was how my mother ended her tirade. 'Just get out!'

So he did. His face bright scarlet, he made his way back down our front path, still carrying my Globite.

'My bag!' I exclaimed, my voice too loud, making him jump before he let go of the bag and, without glancing back, hurried away from our house.

After that, Jamie no longer sat beside me in class, and when our lectures were over, he never came to find me, although often I wished that he would.

9

AS THE END OF MY studies approached, I started to worry. What would happen, I asked myself over and over, if no school wanted me as their teacher? So when I was offered a job at Hopetoun Girls High, I jumped at it.

The school was built on the side of a hill and I frequently had the sensation that the buildings themselves—not only the land—sloped downwards. Single classrooms—built to be temporary but never pulled down—surrounded the brick, two-storey building that ran the width of the schoolyard. This is where I gave my first lesson, to a roomful of Year 9 girls.

When I entered the classroom that day, I clutched at my folder, trying to hold down the panic that threatened to rise up inside me.

Seated in rows, the students kept their eyes on me. Perhaps it was my newness—or their own curiosity—that kept them quiet that day. Whatever the reason, pandemonium only broke out two days later. That's when the shouting and laughing and calling began; the throwing of erasers and balls of paper all over the classroom.

I tried to stop them; I tried to speak but my voice was too high, too shrill to make any headway. What on earth could I do? I panicked, the urge to flee overwhelming.

That's when it happened. At the very moment I was about to run, I was filled with a God-like strength. And in place of my high, squeaky voice, what emerged from my throat was a tone so loud and so low the whole class stopped—mid-shout, mid-laugh, mid-jeer—and stared at me in astonishment.

'Quiet!' I roared. 'From now on you will all be quiet. Absolutely quiet, do you hear me?'

And for the rest of the lesson they were.

—

At Hopetoun Girls High, my long dresses and skirts quickly gained the students' attention.

Where does she get her clothes from?

I mean, where the fuck would you find that?

These were the whispers I'd hear, especially on playground duty.

If I felt like giving a bit of a scare, I'd sidle over to whoever had asked the question. 'Actually,' I'd say, 'I make all my clothes myself.'

After that, word of my sewing skills spread quickly.

The first to approach me was Julia Nguyen—a Year 8 girl in none of my classes—who knocked on my door one lunchtime.

'Miss,' she said, 'they said you can sew clothes and stuff.'

I nodded.

'I cut one of my skirts to make it shorter, but it's not straight.'

A brief glance sufficed to see just how awry her cutting had gone. So what could I do but give up my lunch to save that poor girl's butchered garment?

During lunch the following week, Julia brought her friend Bella, who was wanting to repair a dress. Soon after, Rosie Stratford joined us. That's when things stepped up a notch. For unlike Julia and Bella, who were happy to hem and repair, Rosie wanted more: Rosie wanted to start from scratch. She wanted to make her own clothes. And because Hopetoun Girls High had no sewing classes, she asked if I would teach her.

From then on in, each Wednesday lunch, I'd help the girls with their sewing and knitting, and by the end of Term 1, there were more than ten girls in the group we called the Wednesday Sewing and Knitting Circle. The school even gave us a room to use. It was only basic—worn and colourless really—but I didn't care. I'd never been one for adornment.

Others in our Circle were not so easily pleased. Instead of leaving the room as it was, they attacked it with energy, cleaning then painting those grimy walls, scrubbing the floor and rearranging the desks and the chairs to make the room more welcoming. Julia brought in a kettle, Rosie some tea bags and coffee and I supplied cups and the milk. And when a discarded sewing machine was found in the sports storeroom, I claimed it for the group.

To encourage beginners as well as students who knew how to sew and knit, I'd bring in fabric and wool from home, with a selection of knitting needles. Rosie Stratford pounced on a pair, as well as a ball of olive-green wool.

'Teach me how to knit,' she begged me, 'I want to make a jumper.'

I was amused. 'A jumper? Sure you don't want to start with a scarf and see how you go from there?'

Rosie's eyes shone as she shook her head. 'Not really,' she said, 'I'd prefer to jump in and see how I go. I can always start over again if I have to.'

I couldn't argue with that. 'Let's give it a try.' I agreed.

Rosie is someone who brings the sun with her and she made our Sewing and Knitting Circle sparkle.

One Wednesday lunch, her father popped in unexpectedly. Ian Stratford managed the bank down the road where he had the school as a client. An active parent, he came to all the school functions, including the monthly P & C meetings.

'Hope you don't mind me turning up like this,' he said. 'I've been meaning to get in touch to sort out a time for a chat but I keep forgetting to do it.'

'Do you want to join us?' I asked, puzzled to have him there at our Circle.

That made him laugh. 'No, thanks,' he said, 'but you've got a member for life in Rosie. Which is why I'm here. I've been thinking the group could do with a sponsor.'

I was perplexed. 'A sponsor?'

'To manage the stock.'

The stock?

His eyes were as bright as his daughter's. 'I'd like to sponsor the group to the tune of two hundred dollars a term. To put towards fabric and wool, and anything else you need.'

'Oh—' I began, so shocked I felt speechless.

'I'd like to,' he said. 'It's a great thing for Rosie and the other girls, and this is a way to say thank you.'

10

WHEN I STARTED WORK AT Hopetoun Girls High, I continued to live, as always I had, with my parents. Until suddenly—quite suddenly—I could no longer bear it.

It was the day of the Sabbath and I was almost twenty-seven when I made my decision.

In church that morning, Reverend Burnett had praised the long-suffering Ruth who, on the death of her husband, devoted herself to the care of his mother.

At home over lunch, my mother returned to our minister's sermon. 'Today, the will of God was made clear,' she told me. 'Today, I understood the path that has been ordained for you: that you will not marry but instead, with Ruth as your model and guide, you will devote your time to our care as your father and I grow older.'

Stabbing a piece of tomato, my fork had been hovering mid-air, when all of a sudden, my fingers sprang open and it clattered onto my plate.

'I might still marry,' I ventured although even I found this unlikely. In all the time I'd been teaching I'd had no suitors and at church James Johnson and old Mr Stevens were still my only prospects.

'No,' said my mother, becoming more and more resolute. 'I don't believe you will. Your path is that of a daughter, not of a wife or a mother.'

An ice-cold feeling of dread overcame me. Yes, I was a daughter and, yes, I had followed the scriptures by remaining at home while unmarried. But I could not spend the rest of my days caring and cleaning: I was a teacher; a teacher of English and a sewing and knitting instructor.

Surely my mother could not be suggesting that, at a time of her choosing, I should give up my work to devote myself entirely to her and my father?

I did not protest that day. I did not say to my mother, *No, no, I will not do that. I will not give up everything for you.* I simply lowered my head, picked up my fork and ate my tomato.

Then I planned my escape.

⸻

One thing I had was money, for I had been saving almost all of my salary. I also had a car. At Miss Habler's insistence, I'd learned to drive, and once I'd been given my licence, Mr McGregor—a fellow church member whose eyesight was failing—sold me the car he'd had since 1964.

'You can't go past the Hillman Imp,' he assured me. 'It rockets along on the racing track, too.'

And although I found this hard to believe, I did push hard on the pedal sometimes, thrilled by the rush that surged through my body as I watched the speedometer climb.

With cash and a car already, I just needed somewhere to live. One meeting with the local agent solved that, and within a few weeks I'd rented a flat not far from the school.

Now I just needed to move my belongings without attracting my parents' suspicion. So I purchased a suitcase large enough to fit what I needed but sufficiently small to secrete in my car. Now, the Hillman Imp has an unusual feature: the engine is at the back instead of the front while the boot is under the bonnet, which is where I hid my new suitcase. When I left for work in the mornings, I'd pack the back seat as usual, with the crate containing my books and my marking, before adding a little bit extra: a few of my clothes which I'd later transfer to my suitcase. After a week, the suitcase was full.

My sewing machine was the last thing I took, carrying it out to the car before I drove to school on the morning of my final departure. That evening, instead of going back to my parents, I went to my newly leased unit. My stomach turning, my heart leaping, I walked up the stairs, took a deep breath, and let myself in the front door.

Only then did I finally exhale.

And oh, the joy, the joy of being in a place that was mine. My very own place where the lights turned on, the stove ignited, the water was hot and I had all the clothes I needed.

But before I could let myself revel too much, I needed to tell my parents. I put off the task until later that evening. This, I'll admit, was deliberate. My parents would never take calls after eight; anyone ringing at such a late hour didn't deserve to be answered. So when I called at 8.37 pm, I was certain they wouldn't pick up. I was right. And when, instead, the answering machine clicked in, I cleared my throat and read from the notes I'd prepared. I'd found a unit, I told them, but didn't say where. I'd see them at church I added before, hands shaking, I ended the call.

On Thursday, a letter arrived at Hopetoun Girls High addressed in my mother's handwriting. With a quickening pulse, I went to the staffroom to open it.

Dear Ellen, it read. *You have shamed yourself, you have shamed us both and you have shamed the Lord himself. The place of a single woman is with her parents: well you know that. And in leaving, you have not only dishonoured your parents, you have also brought dishonour upon our church. And, as you well know, the dishonoured cannot be accepted let alone welcomed into the House of the Lord.*

I felt my eyes prickle. *Don't*, I warned myself. For I couldn't let myself cry. Especially not here. Straightening my back, I took a breath then another.

Well then, so be it.

I had sent myself out into the wilderness and there I would stay.

And for close to a year, I did. I didn't see my parents, I didn't go to my church and I stopped helping Miss Habler at Sabbath School.

I missed all this and yearned for a Free Church-filled Sabbath. A lifetime of prayer and singing and sermons, and now, shut out from it all, I had nothing. I could, I suppose, have found myself somewhere else to worship, but I never quite mustered the courage. Instead, I stayed alone in my flat, trying to keep the day holy. But this made me sad and when the sadness leaked into my school days, I finally sought Miss Habler's counsel.

At first she was quiet. 'There's a church family in some hardship,' she finally ventured, 'and Reverend Burnett has called for assistance, especially with clothing and food. Given your skills, perhaps you could help.'

'With sewing?' I asked.

'And knitting. You could do both on the Sabbath.'

I looked back at her, dubious. 'Really?'

She nodded. 'It's no breach of the Holy Law to work to attend to the needy. You could sew and knit for that family all day long if you were minded to do it.'

I felt my lips curl into a smile and, from then on in, this was how I spent each Sabbath.

Some months later, Miss Habler had another suggestion. 'Why don't you join me at church tomorrow?'

It was such a ridiculous proposition I almost laughed out loud. After my mother's furious letter, how could I even consider it?

'You never know,' said Miss Habler. 'Her anger may well have cooled by now. She might even surprise you.'

'Unlikely,' I said with an unhappy chuckle.

And yet, the suggestion stayed with me. Perhaps I could give it a try. I could always leave if I had to.

And so, despite my misgivings, I rose early the following morning to make sure I'd arrive in good time.

But if I'd hoped to slip into my Free Church unnoticed, I was to be disappointed. For the moment I stepped into the vestibule, there I was: face to face with my parents. Too surprised to avert my eyes, I stared straight at them, my feet turned leaden, my arms long and stiff by my side.

We did not engage in idle chit-chat, my parents and me. We did not catch up on the months that had passed. And neither asked me a question.

'How are you?' I ventured, instead.

Before they could answer, there came from behind a voice I knew well, one that filled the vestibule. 'Ellen, you have been missed.'

Spinning around, my head quickened with answers, excuses, apologies. But while I was still wondering what to say, our minister threw me a question. 'How's the rural placement going?'

I struggled to make sense of what he was asking. *The rural placement?* What rural placement? But before I could work it out, my mother was answering for me.

'Beneficial,' she said. 'Very beneficial. She's only just returned from her time there.'

Still completely confused, I found myself nodding.

'Welcome back,' said Reverend Burnett. 'It's good to have you here again.'

'It's good to be back,' I replied, and that was the absolute truth of it.

I sat with my parents in our usual pew, each of us silent. Reflecting on the grace of the Lord, that's how it might have appeared. But I was not considering grace; I was considering the lies my mother was telling. And whether I should be filled with horror or overcome with gratitude.

11

WHEN GORDON O'HANLON ARRIVED AT Hopetoun Girls High, he stood out: a very tall man who dragged his foot when he walked was an unusual sight. Because of a stroke, he told me later, that had threatened his whole left side, but in the end, had only affected his leg. Still, it set him apart; this tall, handsome man with a leg that didn't work properly. And he was very handsome, with his dark brown hair and his light brown eyes which, magnified by his glasses, made him seem constantly wonderstruck.

Eighteen months later, I'd marry him.

Was it love at first sight? I don't think so. Love at first sight did not happen to a woman like me. That was for women who walked very tall and tossed their hair when they laughed. These were the women who knew about love at first sight. Not me.

So when, in my thirtieth year, Gordon O'Hanlon, tall and limping, arrived at Hopetoun Girls High, I had no expectation.

I certainly did not plan a romantic attack—I wouldn't have known where to start.

There was something interesting about him, however, right from the very beginning: that combination of height, good looks and a foot that dragged. The incongruity of it confused me. And not only me. It seemed to puzzle the students, too, the older girls in particular. They would all stop to stare at the tall new teacher who'd smile and wave whenever he caught them looking.

Although I was never Gordon's superior, I did become his mentor. For this I can credit Tony Jackson, head of the English department, whose advice to Gordon was this: if you need to know anything about the school, anything at all, ask Ellen.

And Gordon had done exactly that. Not all the time, just now and again. About homework to set, texts to choose, school resources to locate. And I was pleased to help.

The classroom doors each had a square window: too high for the younger students to see through, but just right for those who were older. For me, too. And when I approached Gordon's classroom, I'd sometimes tilt my ear to the door to listen. And if I could do it without being caught, there were times I'd look in as well.

When I did peer in, I liked seeing Gordon in action. For his classes, he'd arrange the desks in a horseshoe shape with spaces between them, like a curve of dotted lines. A clever way, I thought, to have students both close and out of reach of each other.

Spying on his Year 10 class one day, I was impressed to see even the most languid of students sitting up instead of slouching. And if a few of them doodled a bit, they still seemed to be listening to Gordon's even, unhurried voice.

Leaning against his desk, he faced the class then, standing up, turned around to write on the whiteboard.

As he kept writing, Maxine Popchev—a girl for whom I'd never felt an affection—slipped through the gap beside her desk and began to move from one side of the room to the other. I thought she was doing a dance until I saw that her foot was trailing. When this got a laugh from some of her classmates, she shuffled back to repeat her performance.

Oblivious, Gordon continued writing as Maxine kept up her nasty performance: back hunched now, as her foot scraped the floor and her movements became more and more exaggerated.

Mid-scrape, and finally Gordon turned around to catch the impersonation. And when he registered what was happening— just what that girl was doing—his light skin started to redden.

At that moment, my hand flew to the handle as I readied myself to fling open the door and drag the girl out of the class-room. She needed rebuking; she needed some discipline. At the very least, she could do with a really good shaking.

In the end, I did none of these things. Taking my hand away from the handle, I caught back my anger and swallowed my outrage.

But only just.

—

The following Monday, Gordon split his trousers.

Little wonder, really, for the trousers were worn and a size too small. This I'd noticed some time earlier. Unfortunately for Gordon, he'd split his trousers at school. Fortunately for him, he wasn't in class at the time. He'd been on his way but hadn't arrived when *rip*, straight down the middle they'd torn.

So instead of turning right into his Year 9 class, he turned left into our staffroom. Perhaps he'd hoped to find it empty. He certainly seemed surprised to discover me there. Quickly enough, though, his surprise turned to relief then gratitude. And that was the start of everything.

When he saw me sitting alone at my desk, he hesitated, but only for a second. Then he blurted it out. 'I've split my pants.'

His words made my spine stiffen: I was instantly back in Mrs Serasinghe's classroom. 'Don't worry,' I soothed him as Mrs Serasinghe had soothed me. 'They shouldn't take much to repair. But first,' I said, as I felt my face flush, 'you'll need to take them off.'

And he did. He slipped off his shoes, then took off his trousers, a hand on the wall for balance. And there he was, wearing only a shirt and his underwear.

Modesty would have me avert my eyes while curiosity held my gaze on his torso and limbs; on all those parts that were covered and all those parts that were not.

'Give me five minutes,' I mumbled as my eyes swept across him, my face growing hotter and hotter.

His was a large split, but my sewing is quick and, as I'd promised, the repair did not take long.

When I was done, he turned to put his trousers back on. I should have turned, too, but I confess I did not. Instead, I watched the back of his body as again he balanced himself, slipping one foot into a leg of his trousers and his second foot into the other. And when he zipped up his fly, the fabric strained against his buttocks and I prayed my stitches would hold.

They did.

They held.

Turning back, he gave me a grateful smile. 'Thank you, Ellen,' he murmured, and I liked the sound of my name when he said it.

⸺

The sewing machine was in my living room corner and seeing it after school that day gave me the idea: I would sew Gordon O'Hanlon new trousers. And unlike his old trousers—the ones I'd repaired—mine would be strong and well made and they would not split.

The very next day, I purchased a length of lightweight wool in dark grey and, on a whim, one in a deep shade of green. Then I got started.

The first pair of trousers I sewed at night and the second over the weekend. Then I wrapped them both up in brown paper, and tied them with string, as Mrs Serasinghe had done for me.

Driving to school on Monday morning, my heart jumped at the sight of the parcel there on the seat beside me. *Shush*, I told myself. But my heart would not be quietened, not while I was in my car nor when I arrived at my school nor as I walked across to the staffroom.

At the doorway, I squeezed my eyes closed then, opening them up, shot a look in front of me. Desks surrounded three sides of the staffroom, most of them facing the wall. Only the luckiest among us—not me and not Gordon—had desks by the window. Ruby Chan had one: her back was the first thing I saw in the staffroom that morning.

When I called out hello, she mumbled back, then turned to continue her work. We were the only two in the staffroom, so I popped the parcel on Gordon's desk, praying she wouldn't notice.

I was back at my desk when a terrible thought occurred to me. Without a note, how could Gordon be sure the parcel was meant for him? It was not too late, I counselled myself. I still had time to write something down and placed it on top of the parcel. But what should I write and how should I start it? *Gordon*; *To Gordon*; *Dear Gordon*. Too brusque; too little; too much. Better without a salutation at all.

For the note itself, I remained stumped. What tone to use? Something light, something cheery. *Thought you might like these—enjoy!* No. They were not chocolates. Something amusing might work but I'd never been very witty.

I was still in a quandary—the note unwritten—when Gordon himself walked in. And, ill-prepared as I was, what a fright it gave me to see him.

Before I could think how to stop him, he was on his way to his desk. What would he say when he saw the parcel just sitting there on his desk? He would be confused. He might even hold it up to try to find out whose it was. Or he might not. He might unwrap it himself and, mystified, wonder who on earth could have left such a gift.

There was only one thing to do: gathering up what I'd need for my classes, I fled the staffroom. For the rest of the day, I stayed away, venturing back only when the school and the staffroom had emptied. And when I mustered the courage to check Gordon's desk, I saw that the parcel was gone.

12

AS I DROVE TO SCHOOL the next day, I tried to work out what to do. Simply walk into the staffroom as though nothing had happened? As though I had not sewn trousers for Gordon O'Hanlon and left them, without so much as a note? Or should I seek him out and get it all off my chest?

So completely did these thoughts consume me, I paid little heed to the footsteps behind me. Until a hand reached out to touch me.

'Oh,' I exclaimed, turning around, 'it's you.'

'The trousers,' he began, letting go of my arm, 'did you make them?'

Nodding a little, I felt my head prickle as my body grew warm with embarrassment.

'Thank you,' he said. 'They're great. Perfect, in fact.'

The next day, he wore the grey trousers, the green ones the day after that. From then on in, this was the pattern he seemed to adopt, wearing my trousers exclusively. Except on a

Friday when his attire would veer to the casual and he'd often arrive in jeans.

But whenever he wore a pair of my trousers, he'd give me a smile and I'd try not to blush or lower my eyes in reply.

—

Saturday afternoon, that's when I would shop. And because my unit was close to the shops, I'd walk and take my trolley. With its floral cover and bright white wheels, it was not a popular choice among shoppers. So it surprised me to find an almost identical one—only tartan not floral—in aisle three; right next to Gordon O'Hanlon.

'Ellen,' he said when he saw me, his face breaking into a smile, 'what a surprise!'

It was the end of winter but he was in shorts, his legs kept warm, perhaps, by a forest of curly black hair. And once again, the sight of his uncovered legs so took my attention that, for a moment or two, I lost track of what he'd been saying.

'Coffee,' I heard once I'd refocused. 'We could have a coffee once you've finished your shopping.'

'Or tea?' I asked.

'Or tea,' he agreed, with a smile.

There was a cafe—one of a chain—close to the grocery store, but this was not where Gordon took me. He knew a better one, he told me. So pulling our trolleys, we walked there together. Setting out on his right leg, which was strong and muscular, he'd bring his smaller, leaner left leg to join it, before stepping out again on his sturdier leg and bringing his left leg towards it. An awkward endeavour, but with its own rhythm; a rhythm that soon pleased me.

The cafe Gordon had chosen was long and narrow, with a scattering of people inside it. Along one wall was a row of windows where we were offered a table. The waitress who served us was young—little more than a teenager—with a wide, wide smile, and four or five earrings making their way up her ears.

'Which cake would you recommend?' Gordon asked her.

Pen to her cheek, she considered the shop's front display. 'To be honest, the sponge cake's fantastic.'

'Done,' said Gordon with a smile, before he turned back to me. 'Why don't you have one, too?'

Looking across at that cake display, I felt myself waver: with its layers of strawberries and cream, it did look delicious. Too delicious, I decided, hardening myself, and opting for toast.

Gordon and I sat on either side of a table so narrow our heads might have touched if I hadn't been careful. And this made me nervous, so nervous.

I fell into silence. Thinking hard, thinking quickly, I tried to fill it. 'So—' I began, but my voice came out squeaky. Clearing my throat, I tried again. 'How are you finding the teaching load?'

'I like teaching,' he said, 'and I like Hopetoun High.'

'There are stirrers, of course,' he conceded, 'but I don't mind a challenge.'

'*Really?*' I wanted to say, but before I could open my mouth to reply, the waitress was back with two small plates: one containing a large slice of cake, the other two pieces of toast, with butter and jam on the side.

'You should have ordered the sponge cake,' said Gordon, as he cut his in half and slid a piece onto my plate. 'Forget the toast,' he said. 'You'll love it.'

And I did. With its vanilla sponge, smooth sweetened cream and plump red berries, how could I not?

Time passed quickly that afternoon, too quickly, and only when the waitress began sweeping around us did I notice the sun had dipped.

'I'd rather you didn't walk home in the dark,' said Gordon when we stood up to leave, 'so why don't I come with you?'

I shook my head. 'I'll be fine. Really I will.'

He didn't insist. 'How about a walk on Saturday?' he asked instead, and this time I smiled and nodded.

—

On Saturday morning, I sprang out of bed eager to check on the weather.

'No, no,' I muttered, shaking my head at the blackening sky and willing the sun to shine. *Be gone*, I rebuked those threatening clouds, fist clenched, jaw tight. *Be gone, be gone, be gone.*

But they would not go. And then it started to pour.

At ten past nine, my mobile phone rang and Gordon's name flashed up on the screen. And although his words were no surprise, each of them stabbed right into me: 'The weather's so bad, I think we should cancel the walk.'

'Oh,' I said, as my throat constricted.

But then he continued: 'So why don't we do something else?'

Something else?

I tried to swallow, hoping to loosen my throat. 'Today?' I finally croaked. 'Do you mean something else today?'

'Yes, today,' he said, then he hesitated. 'Un-un—' he began, then tried again, until the words came rushing out. 'Unless you'd rather leave it?'

I shook my head. Twice, three times I shook it before I gave him a proper reply. 'No,' I said firmly, 'I don't want to leave it.'

'Good,' Gordon said, sounding relieved, his voice now slower and clearer. 'That's really good. In that case, I thought we could go to the movies. There's a festival on and they're showing *Willy Wonka and the Chocolate Factory*, the original one. Have you seen it? In the cinema, I mean?'

My body tensed. 'No,' I managed to murmur.

'You'll love it. It really comes to life on the big screen.'

'Does it?' I asked, trying to keep my voice neutral. Ever since that one time with Jamie Kellaway, I'd never returned to the cinema.

'How about I pick you up in an hour?' Gordon suggested.

'Fine,' I spluttered. 'That's fine.'

After the call, my thoughts quickened, torn as I was between joy and disquiet, until a memory came back to me. *Cold*. The cinema had been very cold.

So I put on the sky-blue jumper I'd knitted myself. And instead of tying my hair back, as usually I did, I left it out to keep my neck warm.

When the doorbell rang and I opened the door, Gordon simply stared at me.

What? I wanted to ask. *What is it?*

For a moment or two, he stayed quiet. 'You have the most beautiful hair,' he said, his voice little more than a murmur.

—

The cinema was newer and lighter than the one I'd been to with Jamie. From the foyer, glass doors looked out to the street which gave me some comfort. Inside the theatre, however, it was still just as black.

We sat quite close to the front and when the film began, Gordon leaned closer, his breath lightly tickling my ear. 'It's a great film,' he promised. 'You'll love it.'

The opening music was light and tinkling as the screen filled with chocolate: light brown powder and folds of thick dark liquid; wafers lined up on a factory belt bare and crisp before they received their coating.

Then the chocolate was gone, replaced by a small corner store, overrun with children and bursting with lollies. One child only was standing outside, face pressed to the glass as he peered inside. He was Charlie Bucket and his family were poor. How especially wonderful then that he should beat the odds to win a trip to Willy Wonka's chocolate factory! For wasn't Willy Wonka's the most marvellous place; and didn't I laugh to see Charlie float up in the air, higher and higher, until he had to burp his way down again?

Gordon laughed, too. Then he gave my hand a squeeze.

Shock, surprise, delight coursed through my body. Clenching my teeth to gather my courage, I squeezed back, and for the rest of the film, we held hands.

Afterwards, Gordon drove me to dinner in a car much newer than mine: silver with black banding, and a spare tyre strapped to the back of it. And while we were driving, Gordon kept hold of my hand.

The joy this gave me rose and rose, all the way to the restaurant. Until we were seated, when it dissolved. For instead of a knife or a fork or even a spoon, only chopsticks were set at my place.

'The food's terrific—Cantonese style,' Gordon told me. 'Don't worry,' he added, 'you'll love it.'

But it wasn't the food that was making me nervous. Chinese I'd eaten before, just not with chopsticks.

Gordon's eyes were on the menu. 'What do you feel like?'

A fork.

'I can choose,' he offered and, my focus still on the chopstick dilemma, I simply nodded.

The wine came first, a bottle between us, and I tried not to flinch when Gordon filled up my glass. Don't think about Reverend Burnett I counselled myself, as cautiously, gingerly, I took a sip of that evil drink. Moistening my lips, I had one more sip, then another.

'Cheers,' said Gordon, knocking my glass with his.

'Cheers,' I replied, very softly.

'Help yourself,' he urged me, when our entrees arrived, tilting a plate of dumplings towards me. But with no fork to help me and not wanting to use my fingers, I suggested he go first.

Hovering his chopsticks over the dumplings, quickly he trapped and popped one into his mouth.

A triumph, I marvelled, and with a surge of bravado, reached for the chopsticks beside me. Then I baulked. For try as I might, I just couldn't copy his deft pincer movement.

As I floundered, a flash came before me: toasting marshmallows at camp, just before my parents took me home instead of letting me stay for the weekend.

'Find a stick,' our teacher had told us. 'Stab it into your marshmallow and then you'll be able to cook it.'

That's what I'd done then; so that's what I did now. I pushed my chopstick into one of those dumplings and when I lifted my hand, there it was, successfully skewered.

Perhaps I exuded some of the triumph I felt, for Gordon rewarded me with a smile. Then he asked me a curious question. 'Do you have an elastic band?'

'An elastic band?'

'Or a hair tie, something like that.'

From habit, I felt for a plait but that night, of course, I'd worn my hair out. So I searched in my satchel until I found my brush, a hair tie wrapped around its handle.

'Pass me your chopsticks,' he said once I'd given it to him. Bemused, I watched as he took the paper sleeve from his chopsticks, folded it lengthways then rolled it up tightly. Placing it between my chopsticks, he secured it with the hair tie. Only then did I understand what he was doing. He was making my chopsticks into tweezers so I'd be able to use them.

And when I managed to secure my next dumpling not with a stab but by trapping it between my chopsticks, Gordon raised his glass to me.

'So,' he asked, once the dumplings were gone, 'what made you become a teacher?'

Miss Bell, I thought, and Miss Habler as well. 'Because I love reading,' I said, which wasn't a lie. 'And you?'

He gave me a smile. 'To be honest, I think it's my jeans.'

It was not the answer I might have expected. 'Your jeans?'

He nodded. 'My parents were both school teachers, so I suppose you could say I take after them.'

Only then did it all make sense. 'Oh,' I said, 'science genes not trouser jeans.'

For a moment he looked at me, puzzled, then he started to laugh, a low deep rumble that became louder. 'Science genes not trouser jeans,' he repeated, spluttering now, a hiccup between his laughter.

That's when I caught it. His laughter, I mean. As though it had jumped over the table to lodge in my throat. Then I was laughing as hard as ever I had, laughing until my stomach was aching.

We're causing a scene, I admonished myself when finally I found some control. 'They'll throw us out if we're not careful.'

But Gordon just shook his head. 'I don't think they will,' he assured me.

13

WHEN I ARRIVED AT SCHOOL on Monday, I forced myself not to run to the staffroom, so great was my urge to see Gordon. And although I walked instead, still I found myself perspiring, beads of sweat dotting the edge of my hairline. Once at the door, I stopped to gather myself. Only then did I step inside.

He was not at his desk. Nor was he at the sink or by one of the soft chairs in the corner. He was not in the staffroom at all. Only Ruby was there.

Hiding my disappointment, I greeted her.

'Good weekend?' she asked, with what seemed like a note of sarcasm.

I tried not to sound too excited. 'Yes, thanks,' I replied. 'It was.' That was usually enough to finish things off but to my surprise she now seemed keen to continue.

Swinging around on her chair, she turned to face me. 'Oh really? Did you do something special?'

Feeling a smile at the back of my throat, I tried to push it back down again. 'Not really,' I said, trying to keep my face steady. 'You?'

The spark of interest had faded now. 'A couple of parties,' she said, swivelling back to her desk and from then we worked in silence. I am normally a diligent worker, well focused on my work. But whenever I heard the door open that morning, my eyes immediately darted towards it.

Was it him? Was it him?

It wasn't.

Then it was.

And yes, there he was: Gordon O'Hanlon in his charcoal grey trousers, teamed this time with a T-shirt. Catching my eye, he gave me a smile. 'Good morning, Ellen,' he said and then, slightly louder, 'Good morning, Ruby.'

Ruby leaned back on her chair. 'Hello, Gordon,' she said. 'Good weekend?'

'An excellent weekend,' he replied, his tone so buoyant I saw her lift an eyebrow.

'What did you get up to?'

'Well,' he said after a pause, 'on Saturday night, I saw a friend for dinner.'

That was me, I thought, now unable—completely unable— to stop myself from grinning. That was *me* he was talking about.

⸺

The following weekend, Gordon took me to Bondi Beach. Shamelessness lurked in places like this, home to the idle and barely dressed. I'd always been warned of that. But as we made our way to the shoreline, I was more struck by the sparkling water with its shimmering blue and thick foaming white.

'Ice-cream?' Gordon suggested, directing me to the road behind us; wide and winding and lined with haphazardly painted shopfronts.

'But it's winter,' I said.

He gave me a wink. 'Which means spring's on the way now, doesn't it?'

Then I just nodded, but later, when things were so awful, these were the words I'd murmur for comfort, repeating them over and over.

And so, on that cool winter's day, we ate ice-cream by the water. When the afternoon faded, Gordon took my hand and we made our way back to the car.

That's when he had the idea: *How about an early dinner?*

So we drove to a place Gordon knew in Leichhardt; the smell of tomatoes growing stronger and stronger the closer we came to the restaurant.

Inside, it was a small, cramped space, with saucepans hanging so low from the ceiling that I kept having to duck.

'Lucky you came early,' grumbled the waitress—a stocky woman with curly grey hair—when Gordon admitted we had no booking. 'Any later, darling, and you'd have nothing.' She found us a table right at the back, then brought us a basket of bread with the jug of wine Gordon had ordered.

For our meals, we both chose lasagne.

'My mum makes a great one,' he said, as he filled up my glass.

'Is she Italian?' I asked him.

He laughed. 'No, she's not. Irish. Bog Irish. And Catholic, of course.'

Catholic?

I tried not to sound shocked. 'Oh. Your father, too?'

'My dad?' he replied, a kink in his voice. 'He died four years ago. A heart attack, and all very quick. An enormous shock. For my mother, especially.'

'I'm sorry,' I said, very softly.

Enough now, I promised myself. *Just leave it. Don't ask him anything more.* But before I could stop it, the question was out. 'Was he Catholic, too?'

'Absolutely,' said Gordon and his eyes were dancing. 'If I'd become a priest, he'd have been delighted.'

'And you?' he enquired. 'Are you Catholic?'

I'd reached for my glass but was yet to raise it to my lips. This was just as well for I'd surely have spluttered the wine all over myself.

'No,' I said, as calmly as I could manage, 'I am not a Catholic.'

'Lasagne and lasagne,' called out a voice. It was our waitress, who'd returned with our meals. 'Enjoy,' she said.

And we did.

'My mum's is almost as good,' Gordon said through a mouthful. 'I'll get her to make it so you can see for yourself.'

So I can see for myself?

Was he asking me to meet his mother? His Catholic mother? Was that what he meant? I looked at him carefully, checking to see if I'd been mistaken.

'You'll love her,' he said, his smile wide, 'and I know she'll love you.'

'She will?'

'Oh yes,' he insisted, 'she will.'

'But why?' I pressed, surprising myself with such boldness.

'Because you're kind and clever and funny.'

Really?

'And beautiful,' he added, 'so beautiful.'

I shook my head to correct him. 'That's not right.'

'Sorry?' he replied, his voice softening.

'Beautiful. I'm not actually beautiful.'

Setting his elbows up onto the table, he leaned in closer. 'I disagree,' he said, his look so intent I had trouble meeting his gaze.

To cover my confusion, to busy my hands, to break from his stare, I picked up my glass—still half full—and gulped down the rest of my wine.

'Dessert?' he asked, and I nodded.

'Have the gelato,' he advised. 'It's fantastic.'

So I had the gelato—hazelnut and strawberry—and it was as he'd promised: fantastic.

Less so was my exit from the restaurant, for when I stood up, I lost my bearings and, my head strangely fuzzy, I needed to steady myself.

Gordon reached out to help me, his hand taking mine and, once again, a spark travelled through me, making me feel euphoric.

'Can I see you to your door?' Gordon asked once he'd driven me home. And when I didn't say no, he followed me up the stairs and into my apartment.

In the hallway he kissed me, a hand to my face, his lips pressing hard, as my body thumped too quickly. Still, I didn't pull back: not when his hand caressed my neck; nor when his hand moved lower until it was covering my breast, or when, for such a long time, he kept kissing me over and over again.

'Your bedroom,' he whispered, his breath on my neck, 'where is it?'

'Up the hall and on the left,' I said, as though giving a stranger directions. Yet it was he, not me, who led us there.

'Can I undress you?' he asked.

When I didn't reply—when I didn't pull back or shake my head—he unbuttoned my blouse and slipping it from my shoulders, let it fall to the ground.

Then my skirt came off, too, which left me in my underwear. And oh, oh, the confusion to be seen in such a state of undress.

'Give me a moment,' he whispered, his voice very low. He was wearing the bottle green pants I had made him and a shirt I had not. And right there in front of me, he took them both off.

Where, then, was I supposed to look?

Catching my hand, Gordon spoke gently. 'Are you all right?'

I nodded although I wasn't quite sure, for now a shaking had filled my body.

Running a hand over my shoulder, his finger caught on the strap of my brassiere. 'At the back or the front?' he asked.

Confused by the question, I stayed silent.

'Your bra,' he said. 'Does it open at the back or the front?'

What?

'Back?' he suggested, encircling his arms around me to check. When, then, my brassiere fell forward, I held my breath and stood very still, as it slid down my arms and, with his help, fell off me. 'You okay?' he asked then kissed me once more, his lips as dry as mine, even though, to my horror, unseen parts of my body were becoming wetter and wetter.

His hand, travelling to my now naked breast, brushed over my nipple, making it stiffen. With his free hand, he pressed into my back, the length of his body against me. Pulling me to him, he kissed me again, his lips soft on mine. But if his lips were soft, my own body felt hard and so moist it made me unsettled. And yet, I did not pull away. Not once.

'You're beautiful,' he whispered. 'You're absolutely gorgeous.'

Then, ever so softly, he murmured into my hair, 'I'm sorry but I don't have anything with me.'

I must have replied, although, to be honest, I didn't know what he was talking about.

'Next time, I'll be more prepared,' he promised.

14

IN THE MORNING, I WOKE with a jolt, startled to find myself naked. Slowly, the night came back, and when I turned my head, there was Gordon, sleeping beside me. Astonished, entranced, perturbed, I watched his head move every so slightly, in time with his breathing.

Then his eyes snapped open. And crinkled. 'Good morning,' he murmured, reaching an arm towards me.

I felt myself flinch. Eyes widening, he looked concerned. 'Are you okay?'

'I-I'm not sure,' I stuttered, as I watched his lovely face cloud over.

'Is it something I've done?' he asked, his voice now a whisper.

No, no, I wanted to tell him. *It's nothing like that.*

'I'm naked,' I said, beginning to tremble. 'I'm completely naked.'

His lips rose in the smallest of smiles. 'So am I.' Reaching out his arm once more, he stroked my cheek with the back of his hand. 'I need a shower,' he said, then gave me a smile. 'Should we have one together?'

A shower together?

A shower in broad daylight with both of us naked? My face flushed red, my scalp prickling with shame at the very thought of it.

I can't have hidden my horror, for quickly he added, 'How about this instead? Stay put and I'll bring you a hot cup of tea.'

I smiled as I pulled the bedclothes higher. 'Tea would be lovely,' I told him.

He stayed until late in the morning. When he was gone, and I was once more alone, try as I might, I simply couldn't stay still. I moved, instead, from room to room as if to locate something misplaced, although nothing at all was missing. And as I kept moving, I found myself humming—indistinctly, at first, no more than a trail of notes, coming and going, until it turned into Psalm 17, our Cantor's favourite. As I hummed, my steps marked time and soon I was skip-stepping all through my apartment, in what was sinfully close to dancing. Still, I didn't stop, so completely overtaken by that whirring, jumping elation inside me.

All day it lasted, all day I sang and smiled to myself. Only as the evening approached did I remember. The Sabbath. It was the day of the Sabbath and, for the first time ever, I'd forgotten it. I'd not gone to church, I'd not said even one prayer and I'd spent the whole day dancing.

But not only dancing, I reminded myself, as I considered just what I had done. I had allowed a man to lie beside me; we had lain naked together. I had allowed him to fondle my breasts and press himself up against me. And I had not stopped my hands from wandering over each part of him. Even that part. And how my face burned at the thought of it. How had I let that happen? How had I abandoned myself so completely?

A voice was filling my head now. A voice that began to get louder and louder. *You harlot, you hussy, you fool*, it shrieked. *No man wants a trollop.*

Well, yes, I thought. *Surely that is the truth of it.* I had succumbed; like a whore I'd offered myself up to him.

So I knew he wouldn't be back.

But if he wouldn't be back for me, he *would* be back at school the next day. How on earth could I possibly face him? And although this question plagued my sleep, by morning, I had a solution.

I'd leave early for school—that's what I'd do—to beat everyone else to our staffroom. Then I'd scoop up my books and take them straight to the classroom.

It was a good plan, I thought. A very good plan. And it would have worked well—surely it would have—if only I'd looked where I was going. For as I approached my classroom, I crashed into someone headed my way. And when I looked up, it was Gordon.

To soften the impact, he put out his hands and caught hold of my elbows. Lowering my eyes to the ground, I waited for him to release me; and kept waiting, until, confused, I glanced up, only to find him stifling his laughter.

'What?' I whispered before I could stop myself. 'What's wrong?'

'Well,' he said, his voice so low I needed to rise on tiptoes to hear it, 'I was scared you might try to avoid me—here at school, I mean—so imagine my surprise when, instead, you came running right for me.' His thumbs, gently pushing into my skin now, sent waves through my body and scrambled my thoughts together.

'No, I didn't,' I managed to get out. 'I didn't even see you at all.'

He was laughing now, properly laughing. 'You sure about that?' he asked, still cupping my elbows and when he finally let go, I found myself wishing he hadn't.

I was, that night, unsettled again, and, lying alone in my bed, chastised myself for thoughts I couldn't silence. Perturbing thoughts. Then more than thoughts: the urge—the overpowering urge—to throw off my nightdress, my singlet and, yes, even my panties, to touch myself the same way he'd touched me.

—

On Friday night, Gordon again took me to dinner and after driving me home, he followed me up the steps, one by one by one, through my front door and into my unit. Then, once again, he led me into my bedroom where first he undressed me before he undressed himself.

He was prepared that night, and this time I knew what he meant. And by the morning, I was no longer the maiden I'd formerly been.

Reverend Burnett would have been horrified; so, too, my parents and the rest of my Free Church community, Miss Habler included. I tried not to think about this; tried not to dwell on what they'd say should they ever find out.

I made, instead, a cocoon of the bed I'd now twice shared with Gordon. A cocoon from the world, a cocoon into which even God had no access.

Oh, the heresy, the arrogance of this; the mere contemplation of a world that excluded my Maker. But what else could I do? For how could I possibly welcome my God into this secret, fervent, baffling, unsanctified place?

And how could it be that I had succumbed to the sins of the flesh, unwed, unbetrothed as I was?

The answer—the only answer I had—was a shameful one. I could not stop myself. That was the truth of it: I simply could not stop myself.

And so it continued, still on the weekend but mid-week as well, when Gordon would come to my unit and lead me each time to the bedroom. And in the darkness of night, I was astonished to find what could happen; what could take place when I didn't shrink back, when I didn't say no, when, like a leaf unfurling, I'd open right up and let him explore me, the way I'd then explore him.

15

WHILE I DRIVE IN SILENCE, Gordon always plays music. And even though his is not a musical voice, that never stops him from singing along, both to the songs he knows, as well as those he doesn't.

So when he took me to lunch with his mother and sister—three months after our grocery store meeting—we drove to Gordon's singing, his notes mostly missing the mark.

As we crossed the city, Gordon kept singing while I kept listening, catching each note that fell flat, but never once correcting him.

Zigzagging our way through roads turning smaller and smaller, we finally stopped at the end of a cul-de-sac, beside a single-storey brick house, its front yard filled with flowers.

'Here we are,' said Gordon, his hand on my knee.

'So many flowers,' I murmured.

He smiled. 'My mum really likes gardening.'

I had imagined a woman not unlike our older parishioners from church. But to my surprise, the woman who came to the door was wearing no shoes and her toenails were brightly painted. She must have seen me glance at her feet because, wriggling her toes, she gave me a smile. 'Just a bit of fun.' These were her very first words to me.

She had bright blue eyes, short grey hair, her dress a shift with oversized pockets, like something an infant might wear.

'Well, hello,' she said, her smile growing broader. 'You must be Ellen.' Her Irish voice was light and lilting, and it made my name sound beautiful.

'Mrs O'Hanlon, hello,' I replied.

Her hand on my arm, she tutted a little. 'Call me Bernadette.'

'Come in,' she bustled us through. 'Come inside now, the two of you.'

We followed her through a small, tiled foyer and into a room with a sofa, two armchairs, a piano and bookcase. And three very large statues.

Bernadette ran a hand over the closest one. 'She's my favourite,' she whispered as if trusting me with a great secret. 'As far as the Virgin Mary goes, she's the most lovely.'

Unable to speak, I found myself nodding. All three statues were women; all three statues were Mary.

'Gordie thinks I go a bit overboard,' she confessed, 'and he might have a point. But whenever I see Mary, I just can't help it. I simply have to have her.'

Reaching into the bookcase, she pulled out a smaller Mary and handed it to me.

My fingers turned clumsy as I struggled to hold it, one hand on the neck, the other gripping both feet.

Pagans, heathens, idolators, Reverend Burnett hissed at me when I turned to Gordon for help.

'Ellen isn't Catholic,' he told his mother, as he whisked that idol away.

'Oh lovey,' she said, her eyes slightly widening, 'is that right?'

I cleared my throat. 'I'm from the Free Church. The Free Church of Kirkton.'

She looked at me blankly. 'I've never really heard of such a thing as the Free Church.'

'It started in Scotland—' I began to explain before a sound stopped me from finishing. And when I turned to check what it was, a woman was coming towards me.

'I'm Bridget,' she said. 'Gordon's sister.' And to my great surprise, she slipped her hand into mine. Ten years younger than Gordon, she was not quite twenty, and with her curly red hair and dancing green eyes, she made me feel strangely at ease. 'I've been desperate to meet you,' she said, her hand still in mine, her wide smile contagious.

Lunch was a roast, with potatoes, pumpkin, carrots and beans. And to drink, there was wine. *Wine*. At lunchtime! And while I had none, Bernadette, Bridget and Gordon must have had two glasses each.

Their conversation was loud, energetic and boisterous. How on earth, I wondered, could they make so much noise between them? It felt like a merry-go-round, a chattering classroom, an aviary of birds, and, to my surprise, I loved it.

'What do you think, Ellen?'

I started, lost in my thoughts. 'Sorry?'

Bernadette ran a finger along the stem of her now empty wine glass. 'About the power of the Virgin.'

I tried to keep my expression in check. 'I'm not sure,' I managed to say, desperate for Gordon to help me.

But he said nothing. Was she talking about me, I wondered. Was this her message to me: her admonition that Gordon and I were sinners; that what we had was unsanctioned and carnal. Was this what she was saying: that she knew the sort of woman I was, so unworthy of her son? My body began to wilt with the shame of it. Why, I wondered, had Gordon even brought me here?

Steeling myself, I did my best to focus on Bernadette's conversation.

'Well, I believe it,' she was telling us all. 'I believe in the power of the Virgin Mary. I believe she answers my prayers. I really do.'

With that, Gordon gave me a wink. 'I think the Protestants might have something to say about that,' he said. 'You don't go in for the Virgin Mary so much now, do you?'

The relief I felt was utterly monumental. This was not a conversation about me. This was not about my own sinful nature, my carnal behaviour. This was simply a chat about a woman who'd been dead for over two thousand years. It was nothing to do with me.

'Well, we don't pray to her,' I replied.

'I do,' said Bernadette. 'I pray to Mary. I feel close to her. Because she's a woman; a woman who lost her child, and I believe she hears what I say. And that gives me comfort. It does.'

Inside me, Reverend Burnett was hissing again, his voice harsh and angry: *Thou shalt not bow down to their gods, nor serve them, nor do after their works: but thou shalt utterly overthrow them, and quite break down their images.*

I shook my head, trying to dislodge him; trying to spell an end to his threatening words. *Be gone!* I commanded him. *Be gone!* And to my surprise, he quietened, although I couldn't be sure he was actually gone.

Beside me, Bernadette was smiling. 'I do so love the Virgin Mary,' she murmured. 'Really I do.'

—

That night, in my bed with Gordon, I began to feel anxious.

'What did she think of me?' I asked him. 'Your mother, I mean.'

'If she liked you?'

'Yes,' I heard myself whisper.

'With my mother, there's no mucking around. If she likes you, it's clear and if she doesn't, she's clear about that, too.'

'So she liked me?'

'I'd say she did. I'd say she really liked you.'

But still I felt worried. 'Does she know you stay here?' I whispered, my face turning warm.

He laughed. 'What's that got to do with anything?'

A current of shame surged through me. 'What must she think,' I began, my eyes prickling, 'when we aren't even married?'

Again he laughed. 'Well, that's easily fixed now, isn't it?'

16

AND JUST LIKE THAT, GORDON and I were engaged—and I soon had the ring to prove it. It wasn't a ring I'd chosen; nor was it a ring Gordon had chosen for me. The ring was one Bernadette's grandmother had given to her, that Bernadette then gave to Gordon to give to me.

But I didn't know that; not until Gordon took me back to our first, special cafe where, this time, we both ordered cake. And when they arrived—his chocolate tart and my sponge roulade—he pushed a small, wrapped package towards me.

'What is it?' I asked.

Shaking his head, he gave me a smile. 'Open it up and find out.'

So carefully, I opened my present. Inside, was a dark blue velvet box and inside the box was a ring. And oh, how lovely it was! A thin band around a circle of platinum, a diamond pressed into the centre with smaller ones dotted around it.

I stared at that beautiful box and at that beautiful ring and couldn't think what to say. Never but never had I ever seen something quite so exquisite. 'For me?' I asked, my voice a squeak.

That made him laugh. 'Well, it won't fit me. And if it doesn't fit you we can get it resized. I mean, an engagement ring needs to fit properly now, doesn't it?'

An engagement ring.

An engagement ring for me.

'It's beautiful,' I whispered.

—

I put it off for as long as I could, but once the date had been set for our marriage, I could avoid it no longer.

'How bad could it be?' Gordon blithely asked as, hand in hand, we walked up the straight concrete path that led to my parents' front door.

I didn't reply. I just rang the doorbell and waited.

And waited.

'Yes?' demanded my mother, when at last she arrived. She peered through the screen, puzzled it seemed, even though she knew to expect me.

'Can we come in?' I asked her.

Her answer was sharp. 'Just a minute.' A click, then another and finally the screen door swung open.

Tentatively I stepped forward. 'Hi, Mum,' I said. 'This is Gordon.'

He put out his hand. 'Pleased to meet you,' he said.

'Is Dad here?' I ventured.

'He'll be here soon enough,' was all she would say as we followed her into the lounge room.

We'd come for morning tea but I wondered if I should have brought it myself, for there was none to be seen. A moment later, as though I'd spoken my musings aloud, my mother gave me the answer. 'The biscuits are in the kitchen,' she said.

And they were. In the middle of the bench was a plate of Sao biscuits. No butter, no jam, no honey, no Vegemite. Just a plate of dry biscuits. Taking it into the lounge room, I couldn't bring myself to serve Gordon.

'Tea?' I asked him instead.

So I made us all tea, leaving my mother and Gordon alone in the lounge room. When I returned with the pot, all was quiet.

'Where's Dad?' I asked, if only to break the silence.

My mother's lips tightened. 'He's at an elders' meeting, and as you know, there's always a lot to get through.'

Then the room fell silent once more, and I couldn't think of anything else to say. Except, of course, what we'd come to tell her. And that's when I decided I wouldn't be—couldn't be—waiting even a moment longer. Keeping my back very straight, I took a deep breath and I gave her the news.

She didn't answer.

Hadn't she heard me?

'Gordon,' I started again, trying to speak slower, trying not to blur my words together, 'and I are going to be married.'

I watched her head tilt. 'That can't be right,' she countered. 'He hasn't asked for your father's permission.'

Before I could speak—but what would I say—Gordon stepped in to answer. 'I was hoping to ask him today,' he replied with a smile, his voice very calm and sincere.

But what he said was a lie and I was struck by how easily it slipped out of his mouth and into the room.

My mother did not return the smile. 'After my daughter's already accepted you?' she queried.

The smile stayed on his lips but did not reach his eyes. 'I must apologise,' he said to my mother. 'I should, of course, have waited.'

But before my mother could say anything more, there was a noise in the hallway. My father was back.

'Hello, Dad,' I said when he appeared at the door. 'How was the meeting?'

It was a stupid question: my father never revealed church business.

'This is Gordon,' I offered instead.

Gordon stood up from his chair. 'Gordon O'Hanlon,' he said.

And with that, any flicker of interest in my father's grey eyes disappeared.

Gordon must not have noticed, for on and on he continued. He wanted to marry me, he explained to my father, and was seeking permission to do so.

In answer, my father said nothing at all. He simply turned and walked out of the room, leaving my mother to answer for him.

Ignoring Gordon, her words were blunt. 'He's a Catholic, Ellen. Of course you can't be married.'

17

BUT WE WERE. WE WERE married. Not in the Free Church and not with my parents' blessing. Reverend Burnett himself had offered the choice: I could continue to be part of the Free Church or I could marry Gordon. I could not have both.

Did that upset me?

How could it not?

For what in my life did I know better, more deeply, than my Free Church: the scriptures, the Psalms and all our parishioners? To be banished from that—truly banished this time—well, I'd be lying to say it hadn't distressed me.

But was it enough to make me rethink my marriage to Gordon?

No, it was not.

Not for a moment.

—

Although I hadn't earned it, I did wear white to my wedding and, of course, I made it myself. Unlike my other frocks, however, it stopped at the knees.

Odd, I know, that my dress should be shorter than those chosen by brides, who on other days wore so little.

But if it is true that, for this one day, a bride can be a completely new person, I was no exception. And so, for the very first time, I made a dress that showed my legs and the shape of my body, in a fabric more glossy than I'd ever chosen before.

My hair, still very long, seemed so much shorter when braided and looped at the nape of my neck by Bernadette, who dotted tiny wired rosebuds in my braids.

I'll do your make-up, Bridget had insisted, refusing my protests that I never wore make-up at all.

'Well, for your wedding,' she vowed, 'you will.'

And I did.

Once my dress was on, my hair was done and my make-up ready, Gordon's uncle Joseph drove the three of us—Bernadette, Bridget and me—to the church where Gordon and I would be married.

Joseph was a bear-like man, with a very large head, broad shoulders and a round protruding stomach. His laugh was a chuckle and he chuckled a lot. And that day, he gave me away in place of my father.

With my hand on his arm, we walked down the aisle, Joseph and I. From time to time, he'd give me a smile, as mine became wider and wider the closer we came to the front of the church, with its paintings and statues and, of course, my Gordon.

And when the priest at this Catholic Church—Bernadette's church—asked if we'd take each other as husband and wife, we smiled and said that we would.

When the service was finished and Gordon and I were back in the sunshine, I had the urge to yell and yell and yell to the heavens, so great was the joy inside me. Instead, I threw my head back and I laughed, and Gordon, squeezing my hand, laughed with me.

Outside the church, our guests mingled and of those who greeted us with long embraces, most were strangers to me.

So when I saw a familiar face—such a familiar face—I couldn't help my loud exclamation. 'Miss Habler!' I called as she made her way to me, her beige felt hat shading her face, her long brown frock loosely tied at the waist.

Without thinking what I was doing, I copied those strangers who'd come to my wedding and reached out to embrace her. Instantly, her thin body stiffened and she pulled away, eyes wide with alarm and embarrassment.

Dropping my hands to my side, I tried again. 'I'm so, so glad to see you,' I told her. More than glad: I was astonished. For how could I have ever hoped to see her at my wedding? The risk of it all—to be found here with the Papists—was enormous.

'I can't believe you came,' I said. 'I just can't believe it.'

She gave a wry smile. 'Well, not quite,' she replied. 'I didn't make it inside.'

'Can you stay?' I begged. 'Can you come to the reception? It's not far, and it's just for lunch.'

Miss Habler shook her head. 'I'm sorry, Ellen,' she said. 'I really don't think so.'

I tried to smile, tried to swallow the urge to make her change her mind. 'What about tea some time,' I asked instead. 'Just the two of us?'

This time she nodded. 'Yes,' she said, 'I'd like that.'

18

OUR HONEYMOON WAS NOT A lavish affair. We'd married in winter so Gordon suggested a week in the mountains. It was, as it happened, the most perfect suggestion. Our hotel room was really two rooms: one a bedroom with a large ensuite; the other a living space with table and chairs, a sofa, a small kitchenette and a pot-belly stove for our heating.

We did venture out that week, but not often. Sometimes we cooked for ourselves; sometimes we called for room service and sometimes we ate in a restaurant.

And every morning, Gordon would wake me by whispering softly, 'Good morning, Mrs O'Hanlon.'

Mrs O'Hanlon.

Mrs Ellen O'Hanlon.

That was me. And I couldn't have been more delighted.

—

Throughout my teaching career, I'd followed Miss Habler's advice and carefully saved my money. And because Gordon had saved his, too, together we had a deposit to buy our own house.

The one we bought was not particularly beautiful; a small red-brick house with steps up to a landing leading to the front door and into our lounge room area. Beyond that was our kitchen, the sunniest place in the house.

The house itself had a dirty feel, even though it wasn't unclean. 'The paintwork,' said Gordon. For the white of the walls had a brownish tinge, which made for an unpleasant colour.

'Easily fixed,' Gordon promised. 'We'll just paint each room a completely different colour.'

Different shades of white or cream or beige: that's what I thought he meant. I was wrong about that. When he said he wanted each room to be different, that was exactly what he meant: yellow for the kitchen, orange for the living space, a light bright green for the bathroom and a soft sky blue for our bedroom.

I was both thrilled and alarmed by his suggestions. 'Isn't that all a bit bright?'

'Exactly,' he said. 'That's the whole idea.'

But never before had I lived in a house full of colour, and the idea felt somehow excessive.

'Come on,' said Gordon. 'It'll be fun. And we can try something else if we don't like it.' Sliding an arm around my waist, he kissed the top of my head. 'So what do you say?'

I leaned into the crook of his neck. 'Yes,' I whispered to him.

So Gordon and I spent our weekends painting the walls of our house in all those different colours. And once we got started, I never wanted to stop, delighted by how our house was transforming.

All Saturday morning we'd paint, and most of Sunday, too. This, I confess, had made me somewhat uneasy. I was no longer part of my Free Church—that was true—but I still felt the need to keep the Lord's Day holy. Which, I was sure, did not include painting our house in colours.

'Leave it to me,' said Gordon.

And the next Sunday morning, I woke not to an alarm, but instead to Psalm 91.

'On Saturdays, I'll put on the radio,' he said, 'but on Sunday we'll stick to the Psalms. That way we'll be able to paint and still keep the day holy.'

His eyes were dancing but his mouth was straight and I couldn't tell if he was joking or serious.

'Really?' I queried.

His eyes closed as he nodded, but I still wasn't sure.

'You really think so?'

Again he nodded and this time he added a smile. 'I do. Think of it as spreading the word.'

'Spreading the word? To whom?'

He drew me into his arms. 'Why to me, of course, my beautiful wife. And who knows, by the time we've got through all the Psalms, perhaps I'll be converted.'

My head to his chest, I drank in his heartbeat, and the longer I listened, the quicker it pulsed through my body. And when I relaxed against him, he wrapped his arms even more tightly around me.

'What do you say?' he murmured into my hair. 'Should we give painting to Psalms a go?'

So we did. On the Sabbath we painted and listened to Psalms and on Saturday mornings we continued to paint to the sound of the radio.

On Saturday afternoons, we did no painting at all. Instead, I'd change clothes to meet up with Miss Habler. We'd found a cafe both close to her house, while still a little bit out of the way; far enough, I hoped, not to run into anyone else from the parish.

Inside, the cafe had three wood-panelled walls and one painted white, with olive-green booths right along it. Miss Habler and I sat in the booth at the very far end.

Rhonda, the owner, would bring us a large pot of tea and a small jug of milk, then return with a tray of warm scones wrapped up in a tea towel, dishes of jam and whipped cream on the side.

It was, of course, an indulgence—all that jam and all that cream—and at first Miss Habler would allow herself no more than a sliver, while I wouldn't have very much more.

'Something wrong with my cream and my jam?' Rhonda finally asked us. She was a small, round woman with light brown hair, kind blue eyes and worry lines at her forehead. 'Most of my customers ask for more, but you two barely take any.'

I looked at Miss Habler and she looked at me but neither of us gave her an answer.

'I could do a different jam, if you like. Raspberry, say, instead of strawberry.'

'No,' I said, taking the lead, 'the jam is great, and so is the cream.'

That was the truth, but Rhonda still seemed to be waiting for some other explanation.

'Well, I—we—didn't want to seem greedy.'

'Greedy?' She laughed. 'Sharing a Devonshire tea between you isn't greedy. Three each, maybe, but one between you, I really don't think so.'

And that made Miss Habler smile.

From then on in, rather than having our usual scraping of jam and cream, we heaped them onto our scones. And what a difference it made to the taste, and how we laughed like children whenever a dollop of cream dotted the tip of our noses.

Over our Devonshire tea, we talked and we talked. Miss Habler told me about her Sabbath School lessons and how Hester Boyce was helping now that I no longer could. I smiled and nodded, but in truth it made me feel wistful. And so, to change the subject, I'd tell her almost my classes, my teaching, the books I'd been reading and how happy I was to be married.

Now I am a very punctual person, but after almost two years of afternoon teas, I arrived very late one Saturday.

When I rushed in, Miss Habler's eyebrows were knitted, her hands clenched tightly together.

'There you are!' she cried out in relief. 'I was so worried something had happened.'

Something had. Something too dreadful to tell her. For that was the week Gordon had been suspended from his new teaching position.

'Sorry I worried you,' I told her. 'Everything's fine.'

But that was a lie, for nothing was fine anymore.

Something awful has happened, I wanted to tell her. But how could I find the words to explain something so shameful?

So I let Miss Habler do most of the talking that afternoon. And while all I did was listen and smile, the pretence it required left me exhausted.

That was only the start of it. Three weeks later, and the police would shatter our morning when they came looking for Gordon.

In the days that followed that frightening morning, I was lost. All week I hardly managed to force myself up and get myself off to my classes. And when the weekend finally arrived, I wanted only to bury my head in my pillow and sleep the day away.

I didn't. Neither did Gordon. And that afternoon, I went to meet Miss Habler as usual.

I arrived early, which was as well, for once I'd parked, it took me such a long time to coax myself out of the car. 'A mistake,' I said to myself when I finally stepped out. 'It's all been a terrible, foolish mistake.'

I had spoken to no-one of Gordon's suspension; told no-one about the police and their visit. Instead, I kept my thoughts buried inside me, swirling around and around as my stomach churned and my heart raced and pounded.

That was the day I made my decision: I would tell Miss Habler exactly what had happened. For if I didn't tell someone, I'd explode with the pressure inside me. And of everyone I knew, Miss Habler was the one I most trusted.

Calmer now, I sat myself down at our favourite booth and, leaning against the wall, I waited for Miss Habler.

'Looks like you really need a cuppa today.'

Startled, I pulled myself up, for a moment unsure where I was. Blinking, I saw Rhonda in front of me and, rubbing my eyes, I gave her a smile.

'You must have dozed off,' she said. 'How about I bring you a cuppa to pep you back up?'

She returned with a pot of tea, some milk, a cup and saucer as well as the paper. 'Read that,' she said. 'It'll keep you awake while you wait for your friend to join you.'

It was the weekend paper she'd brought me, and idly I began to flick through it. Then I panicked. Could we have made the news? Could a reporter have somehow found out the police had been to our door? It was certainly possible, wasn't it?

But unlikely, I soothed myself. *That would be highly unlikely.*

And as I continued to look through the paper, it seemed I was right: there were stories of that American president and a shooting in Israel, but no mention of Gordon or me. Relieved, I made my way through the news section and on to the obituary pages, which I made a point of reading.

The first name on the list was Thomas Abel, who'd lived a long life, as had Rachel Bennett and Nina Carbone, both eighty-six at the time of their passing. Duong Thi Ngoc was younger at seventy-eight, as was Michael Evan Fuller, at seventy-three and Craig Jacob Fox, accidentally killed at fifty-seven.

Then I read this one.

HABLER, Edith—6 January 1935–16 July 2017—Late of Kirkton—Staunch and respected member of the Free Church of Kirkton—A service of thanksgiving will be held at the Free Church of Kirkton on Monday, 24 July at 10 am—By request no flowers.

HABLER, Edith.
HABLER, Edith

Over and over I read that name, that entry, my fingers becoming colder and colder until I could no longer feel them.

Miss Habler? *My* Miss Habler? But what on earth was her name doing there when we were about to take tea?

A mistake. That was all it could be. A ridiculous, unfortunate error.

Why, then, was I starting to panic?

Rhonda stopped on her way to a table of four who were now ready to order. 'Your friend,' she said, 'she's quite late today, isn't she?'

I nodded, coughed, then cleared my throat. 'I'll give her a call.'

The problem was this: Miss Habler had only a landline, which would be of no use if she was on her way, as she should be.

But what if she wasn't?

My cold, numb fingers made it hard to get the numbers right on my phone, and I tried three times before I heard ringing.

And as it kept going and going and going, I kept willing Miss Habler to answer.

'Hello,' she'd say, and I'd smile at the sound of her voice before revealing the colossal mistake they'd made in the paper. 'They said you were dead!' I'd exclaim. 'Can you believe it?'

And that would make us both laugh, before Miss Habler would explain that she'd misread the time and would leave right now to meet me.

Instead, the phone rang out.

19

BLACK IS A COLOUR I'VE never much liked and always try to avoid. I do have one black frock—patterned with small white flowers—and this was the frock I wore to Miss Habler's funeral.

'Is that okay?' I asked Gordon, so nervous my voice was shaking.

Stepping towards me, he cupped my cheek with his hand. 'Perfect,' he said. 'I just wish I could come with you.'

This, we'd decided, would be a mistake: alone I might manage to slip in unnoticed but not with Gordon there, too.

It felt strange to see my church after so long, first in the distance, then closer and closer until there I was at the entrance. I was not late to Miss Habler's funeral—nor was I early—and by the time I arrived, most people were seated. To keep myself well out of sight, I sat slightly slouched in the very back row.

The church, bare and silent, had one addition that morning: a plain wooden coffin, adorned with a thin white runner. Miss Habler's coffin.

Up in the pulpit, to the left of her coffin, Reverend Burnett stood tall. Looking out at everyone present—except me, I hoped—he lifted his hands. 'The Lord giveth, and the Lord taketh away,' he announced. 'Blessed be the name of the Lord.'

Then we sang Psalm 27.

There were words after that, from Reverend Burnett, to celebrate the life of Miss Edith Habler and her commitment to the Free Church.

I tried to listen—I tried very hard—but my mind wandered elsewhere, to another Miss Habler who'd found me a friend in Anne Shirley; who'd shepherded me back to the church that I'd lost; who'd been there for my wedding and the Saturdays that followed; who'd laughed as we slathered our scones with cream and jam; and who'd died in her home the day the police came in search of my husband.

Part two

Part two

20

*Look at thi*s.

One little comment, that's all it had been.

Afterwards, I wished I'd never pointed it out at all. *Look at this,* I'd said. So he had. Deputy Head of English at Grandborough College. That was the job being advertised. That was the job he applied for; and that was the job he got. A job just a short walk from our new house with all its sunlight and colourful walls.

Too good to be true, we'd laughed to each other.

Compared to what we were paid at Hopetoun Girls High, the salary there was extraordinary. An extraordinary salary for an extraordinary school, even if it did lack harbour views. Away from the coast, Grandborough College was nestled, instead, in a less tranquil part of town, not far from an industrial park. But because the campus was the size of a suburb— with a high black grille to keep out the world—none of this really mattered.

To celebrate my husband's appointment, a dinner was held in the old school hall—large and oak-lined—that was now mostly used for functions. I was seated to Gordon's left, his headmaster, Dr Malcolm, to his right. On my other side was someone called Richard Carmichael. Pinkish in tone, he was a large squat man with a small round head, dark eyes behind square-framed glasses. Barring a strip of brown hair at ear level, he was bald. His wife, Lisa, was at our table, too, and she, like her husband, was barrel shaped. Apart from that she had milky-blue eyes and layered brown hair that reminded me of a sparrow. Her light-coloured dress in camel and white—with elbow-length sleeves and a tight Peter Pan collar—did nothing to help her, so I tried to pretend it was navy. I may have been staring, for all of a sudden her eyes were on me and her face was starting to redden. Catching myself, I turned away.

Just as I did, the headmaster stood up, walked onto the stage, and readied himself to start speaking. He was a very tall man with hair turning silver and eyes too small for his very long face. He wore a well-made grey suit, that buttoned over his stomach and his voice was low and melodious. Ideal, I thought, to manage an orderly exit should, for example, the hall suddenly burst into flames.

'As staff members of this esteemed college,' he said, 'you are held high in the teaching fraternity. To be affiliated with Grandborough College is to be admired and respected, even envied.'

Zeroing in on my husband, Dr Malcolm gave him a smile. 'We, the family of Grandborough College, are delighted to welcome Mr Gordon O'Hanlon into our fold,' he said.

'Under your tutelage, we are confident our students will grow in wisdom and knowledge and ability. Here at Grandborough College, we employ only the cream of the teaching profession. Indeed, to be part of our college is to join the ranks of the elite.'

Applause filled the room and showed no sign of stopping until Dr Malcolm lifted a hand.

'On behalf of the students of Grandborough College,' he said, 'I call on Hunter Carmichael to say a few words. Hunter will be moving into Year 11 this term and is one of our most impressive students. Among other things, he captains the Firsts water polo team, and is, of course, a public speaker of some repute. Please welcome him to the stage.'

With enormous gusto, Richard and Lisa Carmichael were slapping their hands together. 'Our son,' mouthed Richard Carmichael when he managed to catch my eye.

But the lanky boy mounting the stage looked nothing at all like his parents. To begin with, he was at least a foot taller than either one of them. Unlike so many adolescents, this boy—this Hunter Carmichael—did not slouch. Instead, he held himself high: shoulders back, eyes straight ahead.

Standing behind a wooden lectern, he looked right into the audience, head turned to the left, the centre, the right, as if drinking all of us in. In all my years as an educator, I'd never seen a student with such extraordinary poise. Had he not been in school uniform, I'd have mistaken him for a teacher.

Long, thin hands clasping hold of the lectern, he leaned forward, a confident smile on his face. 'Dr Malcolm, Mr O'Hanlon, teachers, parents and students, I am humbled to have been chosen to speak to you tonight on behalf of the students of Grandborough College. I love being part of this school which, as Dr Malcolm so often tells us, really is just like a big family. I've learned so much in the four years I've been here and done so many things—water polo, drama, public speaking, basketball and so much more—and I'm looking forward to continuing them into the year ahead. In the meantime, I wish to congratulate you, Mr O'Hanlon, on your appointment and heartily welcome you to our school.'

Loud clapping came from his parents as the boy left the stage and made his way down the stairs.

'A great kid,' said his father. 'A really great kid.'

His mother also had something to tell me. 'I understand your husband has come from a public school,' she began. 'We don't normally recruit from public schools, you know, because the standard tends to be lower.'

A rebuke on my tongue, I opened my mouth to reply. But before I could, before I could get out a word, Richard Carmichael was being called to the stage. I watched him struggle out of his seat, a hand on the table to pull himself up, his face beaded with sweat.

'For the past four years,' said Dr Malcolm as Richard Carmichael hurried to join him, 'this man has worked tirelessly for the Grandborough Parents' Association, first as a committee member and secretary, and for the past two years as its president. Please welcome him to the stage.'

With that, Richard Carmichael took over the lectern, his face still sweaty. From his left trouser pocket, he fished out a creased piece of paper, opened his mouth to begin, then stopped. There was a problem. The microphone—a good height for his son and Dr Malcolm—was not a good height for him. As he struggled to lower it—no-one came to his aid—his face grew redder and redder. Then, at last, success.

With another quick cough, he lowered his eyes to his notes. 'It is a privilege to address you this evening,' he read, 'and I am humbled by this great honour. As GPA President, I'm excited to see what the new year will bring here at Grandborough College. The school play is always a highlight and I'm looking forward to seeing our young actors on stage in just a few months. As we all know, Grandborough's reputation is well established on the field and in the water and I'm eager to see all the trophies we'll bring home this year. But tonight, we are here to acknowledge our newest teacher, Mr Gordon O'Hanlon and, in welcoming him to the stage, I'd like to take the opportunity to congratulate him on his elevation to Grandborough College.'

Squinting into the crowd, he found Gordon and gave him a nod. 'Please join me on stage to say a few words,' he said, as the microphone started to echo.

Gordon was slow getting up, his limp more pronounced when he mounted the stairs, a hand on the wall to steady himself as he took the steps one by one. Willing him safely up, I held my breath until he'd reached the lectern. With one deft move, he raised the microphone stand and, looking out, gave me a wink. Then he spoke.

'My thanks to you all for being here this evening,' he said. 'I very much appreciate it. My particular thanks to Dr Malcolm, Hunter Carmichael and Richard Carmichael for your kind words. As a teacher, I have been a very lucky man. Most recently, I have had three tremendous years at Hopetoun Girls High where I was so pleased to teach an array of intelligent, thoughtful and creative students. I am looking forward to getting to know the students of Grandborough College and to imbuing them with a love of English literature and a delight in the creative possibilities it offers. Apart from my wife, Ellen, who is with me tonight, teaching is my great love and I'm looking forward to continuing my work here.'

21

AT GRANDBOROUGH COLLEGE, THE DRESS code for teachers was business attire, in short a suit. Gordon had one but it was years and years old so, for a surprise, I made him two more—one navy, one grey with a very light check, and each with two pairs of trousers.

To make him smile, I wrapped them up in a brown paper parcel and tied it with string, just like I had three years before when I'd made him those very first trousers.

At the sight of those newly wrapped parcels, Gordon gave a great laugh and reached out to hug me.

From that day on, Gordon would wear one of his two new suits to Grandborough College each day. Dressed this way, he'd carry his books and his marking and make his way there on foot.

He'd be teaching Year 11, Year 10, Year 9 and Year 8, and assisting with the school play.

'Doing what?' I asked.

'Directing.'

Really?

As far as I knew he'd never directed a play in his life. 'When's it on?'

'May,' he replied.

I gaped. 'But that's only three months away. Will it be ready on time?'

He gave me a wink. 'Just joking,' he said. 'They've got a professional director who's been working with the kids for most of last year. I'm there to make sure they all know their lines.

'A professional director?' I exclaimed. 'Are you serious?'

He nodded. 'Yep. And wait until you see the theatre. Unbelievable. Like being at the opera.'

I thought of the old wooden hall at Hopetoun High, used for drama, sports, music as well as our weekly assemblies. 'I can't believe the money they must have at that school.'

'Well, if you charge thirty thousand a year and you've got eight hundred and fifty students, that adds up to a lot.'

I tried to calculate. 'That's, what, more than two and a half million.'

He shook his head. 'Lucky you're English, not Maths. Try twenty-five.'

'Twenty-five million! That's unbelievable.'

'Uh-huh,' he said. 'That's how they get to build a super-theatre and employ some whiz-bang director.'

'What's the production?'

He pulled up straight as though on stage himself. 'This year, the students of Grandborough College will be performing *The Crucible* by Arthur Miller.'

I nodded. 'I really love that play.'

'Make sure you get good seats, then.'

'And how do I do that?'

He gave me a bit of a smile. 'Oh you know, pull some strings. Marry the Deputy Head of the English Department who also happens to be general assistant-in-chief for the theatre.'

'You'll get me a seat then?'

He leaned in to kiss me. 'The best in the house.'

—

While Gordon could walk to Grandborough College in fifteen minutes, mine was a forty-minute drive. But I'd still beat him home most days.

The paperwork, he'd tell me. The prep and the marking on top of everything else.

I understood that. Of course I did. These were issues I dealt with, too. And with a new job, in a new school, that would be even harder.

A couple of weeks into the term, Gordon was home later than usual. It was a Thursday evening and when, eventually, he walked in the door, he screwed up his face to apologise.

'Sorry,' he said, 'I got stuck. One of my Year 10s is having some problems so I stayed back after school. Then, I don't know, I must have lost track of the time.'

Her name was Laetitia and, from then on in, he'd be giving her a hand after school every Thursday.

'Are you getting overtime?' I asked, but it wasn't a serious question. There was, of course, no overtime at Grandborough College, not for sport supervision or lunchtime drama rehearsals or for making sure his Year 10 student kept up with the rest of the class.

'So what's she like, this Laetitia?'

He shrugged. 'Nice enough. Quiet. A bit on the outer, I think. Although she's in the school play so that's something.'

22

ON OPENING NIGHT OF THE Grandborough production of *The Crucible,* I had pride of place in row 3. And when the stage lit up, there we were in Salem watching Reverend Parris's sick daughter. The reverend himself mumbled and wept at the foot of her bed, his head bowed in prayer, before he suddenly sprang to his feet and screamed at his slave, a fearful woman called Tituba. And although I knew the play well, still I sat on the edge of my seat, so enthralled by the story that I failed, at first, to recognise Reverend Parris at all. The boy from Gordon's welcome dinner, that's who he was. The boy in one of Gordon's senior classes. A decent kid, by all accounts: bright and well spoken. But his name: what was it?

Hunter. That was it. Hunter Carmichael, completely transformed into Reverend Parris. *Well done*, I thought with some admiration.

Less impressive was John Proctor's spurned lover who stumbled onto the stage, a mere slip of a thing, too softly spoken for someone as dangerous as Abigail Williams.

Channelling his clergyman, Hunter was now in full flight. 'Abominations!' he bellowed, as Reverend Burnett might have done. 'I cannot blink what I saw, Abigail, for my enemies will not blink it. I saw a dress lying on the grass.'

The stick-like Abigail shrank back. 'A dress?'

He lifted a haughty chin. 'Aye, a dress. And I thought I saw someone naked running through the trees.'

Once more the girl pulled back. I leaned forward, watching harder. Something was happening. Something other than terror was crossing her face. But exactly what, well, that took a moment to dawn on me.

She was about to laugh!

In this moment, this crucial moment, the girl was about to giggle. Narrowing my eyes, I kept watch, waiting for her to dissolve.

She didn't. She took a breath and another, then, averting her eyes from Hunter's gaze, delivered her lines to the empty space behind him. 'No-one was naked! You mistake yourself, uncle.'

On the word *uncle* her voice seemed to teeter and her mouth began to twitch. But she didn't laugh. Who was she, I wondered, this girl who had only just managed to save herself? Squinting through the dim lighting, I scanned the program. *Abigail Williams,* I read, *played by Penelope Averill.*

When I looked up again, Hunter Carmichael had left the stage, replaced by an overwrought, thickset girl.

'What'll we do?' she cried out, rushing towards that ill-cast Abigail. 'The village is out! I just come from the farm; the whole country's talkin' witchcraft! They'll be callin' us witches, Abby!'

Her voice was strong and filled the hall. Apart from that, nothing about her spoke of self-assurance. Her shoulders rolled forward, slightly slumped, and her face was bland: round in shape with thick, peach-like skin. Befitting the servant she was pretending to be, she'd tied a scarf over her head, kerchief style, her straight light brown hair falling well past her shoulders. The smock she wore, loose and shapeless, was not flattering. And when, curious, my eyes dropped to the program, I was surprised by what I found. The girl's name was Laetitia— Laetitia Hartford. So she was the one Gordon had been helping after school. Sitting up straighter, I surveyed her more closely. What for, I wasn't quite sure. Signs of the struggles she had with her work? Signs that might somehow be there in the way she delivered her lines, in the tread of her feet across the stage, or the tilt of her head? But there was nothing. For in truth, beside the fey-like Penelope Averill, she was completely unremarkable.

When John Proctor walked on stage, I struggled not to smile. Instead of the strapping figure I had in my head, this John Proctor was tiny. Really tiny, except for his head, which was large. With thick metal glasses and a thin, reedy voice, he was an unlikely farmer from Salem and especially ill-suited to Abigail Williams' entreaties.

'We never touched,' he said, his voice just audible.

Soon after that, he fell silent. Completely silent.

A dramatic touch?

Well, no. At least not intentionally. He'd simply forgotten his lines. But I had not. I knew the words he could not recall. I knew them exactly, and now I was tempted to stand up from my seat and come to his aid by shouting them to him. I was, after all, close enough to do so.

I didn't have to. I didn't have to say a thing. For, suddenly, there they were, all his missing words, although the boy himself remained silent. The missing words—those forgotten lines, scene after scene of them—were ringing out in a voice I knew well: from the wings, my husband was prompting that boy.

'Is the accuser always holy now?' He was saying. 'Were they born this morning as clean as God's fingers? I'll tell you what's walking Salem—vengeance is walking Salem. We are what we always were in Salem, but now the little crazy children are jangling the keys of the kingdom, and common vengeance writes the law!'

They were big words and under my husband's command, so much more powerful than anything said by that thin-voiced boy. And in that vein, the play continued, with tiny John Proctor forgetting his lines and my Gordon throwing them back to him.

At the end of the night, John Proctor still got his standing ovation, as did everyone else. And once the applause had died down and everyone was leaving, I stayed in my seat, waiting for Gordon. The cast members were first to emerge from backstage, among them Hunter Carmichael—tall and blond and now make-up free—his arm draped around Penelope Averill who, in jeans and a T-shirt, looked even less like Abigail Williams.

They had my attention for a moment or two until I saw Gordon, walking behind them. And so wide was his smile and so handsome his face, I lost interest in anything else.

23

THREE WEEKS AFTER *THE CRUCIBLE* closed, that's when it happened.

I didn't know. Not at first; not until I'd arrived home from school to find Gordon had beaten me to it.

'Did you get an early mark?' I asked, my voice still bright.

He shook his head but said nothing.

'Cup of tea?' I tried.

Another shake of the head. So I made just one cup of tea— for me—and sat at the table beside him.

'A couple of the Year 9s tried it on today,' I told him.

He didn't react. Not at all, not even a nod or a murmur. He just stayed very still, his eyes on the table, hands clasped tightly in front of him.

Perhaps he hadn't heard, I thought, so I tried again. 'Some of the Year 9s,' I said, more loudly. 'They tried it on.'

This time he lifted his head. 'I'm finished,' he said, his face pale, eyes ringed with shadows.

My fingers curled more tightly around my tea cup as my body turned cold. What did he mean? What was he trying to say? Was he ill? Was he dying?

'Finished?' I echoed.

'They won't let me back.'

My mind raced on, faster and faster. *Because of an illness? What illness?*

'What do you mean?' I asked, my voice very high. 'What on earth do you mean?'

I would lose him, I thought, my heart in my mouth. I'd managed to find him and now I would lose him. How could I possibly bear it?

So when he said, 'Ellen, I've been suspended,' at first I relaxed. Suspended. Not ill. Not dead.

'Why?' I managed to ask. 'What happened?'

'A complaint. From a student.'

What student?

He didn't know; he hadn't been told. Couldn't be told. To protect the child, that was why. 'In case I approach her,' he said.

'Her?'

'It's a girl. The one who made the complaint. At least, that's what Philip implied.'

'Philip?' I heard myself echo.

'Philip Malcolm.'

Yes. Of course. Philip Malcolm. Dr Philip Malcolm.

'Oh,' I said.

'It's been referred to the police,' he added. Now he was crying, which shocked me as much as what he'd just told me.

For Gordon was not one for crying—not then, at least—and this was the very first time I'd ever seen him in tears.

'The police?' I whispered.

He was sobbing now, quietly though, very quietly. Soon, I would also master this close to soundless weeping.

For now, though, a slow dread had begun to roll through me. 'What sort of complaint?' I asked him.

When he didn't answer—when he couldn't—the dread overcame me and I struggled to catch my breath. Straining for air, I started to rasp while my heart beat faster and faster, pushing and pushing in time with the throb, throb, throb of my blood until I feared it would burst through my ribs.

24

SEXUAL ASSAULT. THAT WAS THE complaint the student had made against Gordon.

Who? We still didn't know.

When? We hadn't been told.

Where? No-one would say.

So how would we find out? We had absolutely no idea.

We knew only this: the investigating police specialised in crimes against children. But why? I wanted to scream. For my Gordon would not hurt a fly, let alone a child.

—

In the meantime, our lives continued. In a fashion, that is. We both got up, we both got dressed, but only I went to work. And there—and everywhere else—I stayed silent about what had happened to Gordon.

To stay silent had long been a forte of mine: there had always been topics I'd sidestep. As a child, I'd known my church had its critics, and I'd quickly learned to avoid conversations that might become heated.

So too, I no longer talked about Gordon after he'd been suspended. This, I knew, was the only way to avoid any difficult questions. For in those early days, we truly believed we'd be able to keep it secret: this private concern, this brutal misunderstanding. We would weather the storm together or, I dared hope, still it completely.

In my silence, I began to turn inwards, keeping the fear, the sadness, the confusion tucked tightly inside me. But the quieter I stayed, the more the pressure kept mounting: growing and growing and growing until my body, my mind, my very being threatened to buckle under the weight of it.

And if I couldn't speak to anyone about it—not even to Gordon, for fear of upsetting him further—if I couldn't let it out with my words, my cries, my indignation, how was I to keep myself together? How could I expel the fear from my body if I couldn't even say it out loud?

By going to church, I decided.

So that's what I did: I went to church. Not to my own Free Church or to the church nearest our house, which was said to be friendly and welcoming. For a friendly face, a welcoming place, can become a trap: an invitation to unburden all thoughts, to confess the weight being carried inside. And I couldn't afford to do that.

Instead, I put on my wide-brimmed hat and drove across town in search of another Free Church.

Once I'd found it, I stepped inside and slid into a pew on the side. I sat to sing the hymns, I stood to pray and I echoed the words of the minister who sounded just like Reverend Burnett: his Scottish burr loud and wrathful.

And it is the truth, the absolute truth, when I say that his angry words gave me comfort, as did the hard wooden pew, the blank white walls and the simple raised pulpit. So too there was comfort—such comfort—in those stern parishioners, who, intent on their worship, never once looked my way.

All these things relieved my pain and for the very first time since Gordon's suspension, I felt a kernel of calmness inside me.

It didn't last long. Moments later, the minister stepped into the pulpit and, catching my eye, attacked me with his sermon.

'A righteous man hateth lying,' he bellowed, 'but a wicked man is loathsome and cometh to shame. Righteousness keepeth him that is upright in the way: but wickedness overthroweth the sinner.'

My heart skipped a beat as his eyes bored into me. Were those words meant for me? Were his words my warning? And if they were, did that mean he'd seen right through me? Had he seen in me the shame and disgrace of a woman whose husband had been dishonoured? Or worse, had he somehow seen into the heart of my husband and found it that of a sinner?

25

A MONTH AFTER GORDON'S SUSPENSION, that's when the police first came to our door.

Two weeks later, and those same two women were back again.

'DSC Johnston,' the tall one said when I opened the door.

'DC Morrison,' mumbled the other.

This time they didn't ask to come in; they simply walked inside. And when they demanded to speak to my husband, I went to the bedroom to get him. I myself was still in my nightwear, my dressing gown on, the tie looped but not firmly knotted. Beside me, Gordon's hands were shaking as he tried to put on his trousers. I leaned in to button his shirt. I even tied his shoelaces. His hair was askance and, given the rush, I used my fingers to smooth it.

Then together—our hands grazing not clasped—we walked into our lounge room to join those two police officers. DSC Johnston stepped quickly towards us, reaching out to catch hold of my husband's right arm. With a curl in her lip, she uttered these frightening words. 'Gordon Patrick O'Hanlon, you are under arrest for the aggravated sexual assault of Laetitia Jane Hartford.'

Laetitia?

No, no, that couldn't be right. That couldn't possibly be true. How could it be when all he'd done was help her catch up on her school work?

Gordon would have to come to the station, DSC Johnston informed us, where he would be charged.

'Oh,' I heard myself cry out, 'then I'll need to get dressed. I can't go out like this.'

DSC Johnston turned from my husband and directed her gaze to me, dark, beady eyes fixed on mine. 'Not you, Mrs O'Hanlon,' she said, her voice condescending. 'We only need your husband.'

'But I'll take him,' I said, clearing my throat, 'and I'll wait while he's there.'

DSC Johnston looked unimpressed. 'It would be a lot better if we just took him with us.'

My husband agreed. 'Stay here, El,' he said, his voice very gentle. 'Please, stay here.'

I should have protested, I should have been more forceful. Instead, I deferred to my husband—I deferred to them all—and let him be led away.

What else was I to do?

'Oh Lord,' I cried out as the door closed behind them, 'please help me. And help Gordon, my love, my delight, my husband.'

Was it pride, was that the problem? For I was, indeed, proud of my Gordon. Very proud. Proud to be noticed, to be seen with him, held by him, and proud to carry his name.

Too proud? Had I been too proud? And was this how I was to be punished? For my pride, my hubris, my vanity?

As I huddled in my house of bright walls, from the depths of my mind came the words of Jeremiah: *Behold, I am against thee, O thou most proud, saith the Lord God of hosts: for thy day is come, the time that I will visit thee. And the most proud shall stumble and fall, and none shall raise him up: and I will kindle a fire in his cities, and it shall devour all round about.*

Was that now happening to me?

—

Time passed slowly as I waited for Gordon's return. *What are they doing?* I screamed to no-one. What had they done with him? Was he in prison? Is that what had happened? Surely not. Surely, surely not.

Do something, I chastised myself. Something of use; something industrious. For there was work to be done, and a lot of it. I simply needed to make a start: to make my way, for example, straight into the laundry and toil my way through the ironing.

I didn't do it. Nor did I attend to anything else. I did not wash, I did not clean, I did not tidy.

All I could do was sit at our dining room table, still as a statue. And that's where I waited all morning, all afternoon and into the evening. Only then did it occur to me: on his return he would be hungry and surely in need of some dinner.

This was the thought that finally set me in motion. Peering into the refrigerator, I tried to think what to make for my husband. Then a voice came from nowhere. *Prepare a feast*, it commanded. *Ready the table to bring him home.*

So I cooked a meal for my husband. A vegetable soup, that's what I made him. A vegetable soup with barley. And this, I believe—really I do—was what brought my husband back home to me.

For as soon as the soup was ready, I heard the soft jangling of keys. Cocking my head to the side, I stopped still. Was I imagining it? Had I hoped myself into trickery? My head turned around and my body did too as I stepped towards that familiar sound.

When I heard the creak of the door, I rushed to it. And there, oh there, was my husband, safely returned.

Looking at me with eyes that were sad and confused, he couldn't quite manage a smile.

Later, I knew what I should have done in that moment. Rather than waiting for him to step forward, I should have opened my arms out wide. Instead I stood still and asked if he felt like some soup.

But the answer he gave me had nothing to do with the question. 'Awful things,' he whispered, his voice croaky and muffled. 'She said such awful things.'

26

THAT NIGHT, I DID NOT rest well, my thoughts confused as I lay in bed, not quite asleep and yet not awake.

Beside me, Gordon's eyes were closed, giving me hope that he, at least, might be saved from staring the night into morning.

Nervous he'd wake, I kept myself still as I tried—but failed—to clear my mind of all the things making me fearful.

Accused.

Arrested.

Charged.

Each of these words drilled into my mind, tugged on my ear and tapped at the side of my head. *Tap, tap,* they went until finally they tapped me to sleep.

In the morning, I awoke with a start and a feeling of panic, before settling back into a blanket of sadness.

To settle myself, to comfort myself, I turned to watch Gordon sleeping.

He'd often wake slowly, a sleepy smile on his lips, a light in his eyes to see me. But that morning, his eyes sprang open. 'Court!' he cried out. 'What will I do about court?'

'We'll need a lawyer,' I murmured. But I didn't know where to find one.

Then I thought of someone who might.

—

Ian Stratford last came to see me shortly after Rosie had finished Year 12. I'd been shocked by his appearance. His bright eyes had dulled, his skin lacked lustre and his hand, when I shook it, was clammy. I took him across to the sewing room where we could have some privacy.

'How are you?' I asked once he'd taken a seat.

He tried to smile. 'Not great,' he said, before the next words came bursting out of him. 'I've been charged.'

I felt my brow furrow. 'Charged?'

He took a deep breath. 'With fraud. Bank loan fraud. They say I used fake documents to approve them.' He stopped, swallowed, then looked at me. 'So that's why they've charged me.'

I could only stare at him.

'I didn't do it. I swear I didn't do it,' he insisted, his voice high and strained. 'It's not true. None of it's true. Not a single word of it.' He swallowed. 'But the police still want to interview me.'

'Oh,' I murmured, not knowing what else to say.

'My lawyer won't let me. My lawyer said not to say anything to them.'

But why? I thought. *Why say nothing if there's nothing to hide? And if there's nothing to hide, why get a lawyer?*

His case was going to trial, and he needed a reference. A reference to say how I knew him and what I'd observed of his character.

Later, I heard he'd been acquitted, and after that we lost touch.

And now here I was, dialling his number. My hand shaking, the nausea rising, I held the phone to my ear, holding my breath when it started to ring.

'Hello?' he said.

'Ian Stratford,' I stumbled. 'I was hoping to speak to Ian.'

'That's right, that's me.' His voice, still familiar, was wary.

'It's Ellen,' I started, then stopped. *Ellen O'Hanlon*, I was about to say. But that was not who I'd been when I knew him. 'Ellen Wells,' I said instead, the words coming out in a rush.

For a time he was quiet. 'Ellen, hello,' he said finally. 'How are you?'

I paused to swallow the truth: *I am broken; I am destroyed; I am completely filled with despair.*

'I'm fine,' I said, then told him I needed a lawyer.

'A lawyer?' he echoed, sounding confused. 'What sort of lawyer?'

My lips were dry; so dry I had to lick them before I continued. 'A criminal lawyer.'

He went quiet. 'Yes,' he said. 'Yes, of course.' Then he gave me the name, a woman called Gillian Cooper.

He himself asked me no questions and for this I was grateful. But had he enquired about what had happened, I would have answered him simply. *It's not true*, I would have exclaimed. *None of it's true. Not a single word of it.*

27

GORDON AND I CAUGHT A bus to the city to meet Ian's lawyer, who wanted us there at four thirty.

'I'll be out of court by then,' she'd said on the phone, her tone unexpectedly friendly.

On the bus, Gordon and I were quiet. During the trip, I'd been feeling quite sick and, when we reached our stop, my stomach lurched and for a moment I feared I would vomit. Gathering myself, I checked the address then took Gordon's hand and headed for Gillian Cooper's office.

In the foyer, there were no flowers or paintings, and no window to look out on the city. This, I have to admit, did make me a little bit nervous. Where were the views and enormous foyer of that other law firm where we'd signed the contract to buy our marital home?

Gillian Cooper's office, by contrast, was on the second floor of a four-storey building that needed attention. The foyer was small: just three chairs and a small coffee table with a couple of old magazines. And instead of a reception desk, there was only a closed wooden door. Beside the door and affixed to the wall was a bell with a chain hanging down. *Please ring*, said the sign beside it.

Turning to Gordon, I tried to smile. 'Do you want me to ring?' I asked him. He was already pale so I kept my voice low in the hope it might soothe him a little. Still his face caved in—as though the question were simply too much to consider—so turning to face the door, I rang the bell myself.

Several moments later, the door opened up and a woman stepped out. She was, I thought, a curious sight, her hair tied up in a haphazard bun, her black woollen dress ill-fitting: too loose on the bodice, too tight on the hips. A quick alteration, that's all it would need, but this wasn't the time to offer.

'Hello,' said the woman, her eyes sharp and blue, 'I'm Gillian Cooper.' She extended a hand, first to me, then to Gordon before leading us into her office.

And what a mess it was! There were papers and folders all over the place—on the bookshelves that lined the walls and on the floor, too: all of it stacked in piles. And although she did have a desk, the only clear space was at the table and chairs in the middle of the room, so that's where we sat.

'Okay,' she began, 'what brings you here today?'

In answer, Gordon passed her the papers the police had given him at the station.

Gillian Cooper flicked through them, nodding then frowning then stopping. 'DSC Johnston, so she's the officer in charge?'

At the sound of her name, a stab of fear almost winded me.

'Yes,' said Gordon, his voice very soft, 'that's right.'

With a nod, Gillian Cooper took out her phone. 'I'll call her to say that from now on in, I'm the one she should contact, not you.' She gave us both a quick look. 'Is that what you'd like me to do?'

Overcome, no, overwhelmed with relief, I nodded. I nodded and nodded and nodded. For never, ever again, did I want to have anything to do with DSC Johnston.

Beside me, Gordon was clearing his throat. 'Yes,' he said, 'that would be good.'

Her phone on speaker, Gillian Cooper dialled while Gordon and I listened in. 'DSC Johnston,' we heard over a crackle.

'Good morning,' the lawyer replied, 'it's Gillian Cooper. I'm acting for Gordon O'Hanlon.'

At the sound of her words, my body relaxed and I began to exhale. We had a lawyer. We had someone to save my husband. And had I been just a little less shy, perhaps I'd have knelt down before her.

Once off the phone, she gave us a smile. 'Okay,' she said, 'that's done. Now let's talk about court next week.'

Court. The word alone made me sick.

The lawyer's voice softened as she leaned a little towards me. 'Don't worry,' she said. 'It's the first mention, that's all. We'll just get a date for the brief to be served.'

The brief?

'You know,' she said, 'the paperwork. The facts sheet, the statements, Gordon's record of interview. All of that. I'll do the talking. Gordon just has to be there.' Then she hesitated. 'There could be media,' she added, 'given the school's so well known.'

This took a moment to sink in. 'Does that mean Gordon will be on the news?'

She gave a small grimace. 'I doubt it,' she said, 'but you can never be sure. I suggest you warn your families, just in case. So it doesn't come as a shock.'

———

We'd planned to catch the bus straight home. Instead, we took the train to see Bernadette and Bridget.

The sun was setting when we got on the train and it was dark by the time we got off. My heart began to pound as we neared the house and I clutched on to Gordon for comfort. By the time we arrived it was tea-time and, unannounced as we were, Bernadette came to the door in her apron.

First her eyes widened, then she broke into a smile. 'Hello, luvvies,' she said. 'What a pleasant surprise.'

She kissed and hugged me then turned to her son and kissed and held him, too.

'Is Bridget here?' Gordon asked, his voice slightly shaking as we walked inside.

'Yes, dear, of course,' said his mother with the slightest of frowns, before she turned to call for her daughter. 'Bridget,' she said, 'it's Gordie and Ellen, they're here.'

When Bridget emerged—so young and so lovely—I couldn't help but smile. 'I didn't know you were coming for dinner,' she said.

Gordon didn't even try for a smile. 'There's a bit of a problem,' he said, his voice very soft.

I watched Bridget's brow furrow as Bernadette stepped forward to take her son's hand. 'What is it, honey?' she asked, her voice gentle.

Gordon tripped over the words, as though they were simply too much for him. 'I have to go to court,' he said.

Then he told them.

The room went quiet. It went deathly, painfully quiet.

'Oh love,' his mother said finally. 'Oh love.'

28

THAT FIRST TIME HE WENT to court, Gordon refused to let me go with him. 'There's no point,' he said. 'Go to school instead.' When I wavered, his voice became firmer. 'Please, Ellen.'

So I did what he asked, and didn't go with him. I ironed his shirt, I aired his suit, I packed him a lunchbox and, my heart palpitating, I made my way to work. My classes were long that morning as I tried to keep my focus, doing my best not to shake, and pretending everything was normal.

As I stepped into the staffroom at recess, I cowered, watching for sidelong glances or open-mouthed stares. Had my husband already been on the news? Had his face, his name been all over the television, the radio, and the internet, too, as I'd been teaching my classes? *Did my colleagues already know everything?*

In the staffroom, Ruby Chan was at her desk, head over her work, and when I walked in, she didn't look up. This might have meant nothing at all; she might not even have heard me. Or perhaps it was more than that: perhaps, having heard the news about Gordon, she could no longer stand the sight of me.

But Lori Reed looked up. Of all my colleagues, she was the one I liked the best. Sometimes we'd even walk over lunch to stretch our legs and clear our heads. Apart from Ruby, Lori was alone in the staffroom and when I came in, she gave me a very quick smile. *Why so quick?* I wondered. *Did she know? Did she already know what had happened to Gordon?*

I'd left my phone on my desk in the staffroom and now I flew to retrieve it. He'd promised to call once it was over. But when I checked the phone there was nothing—no calls, no voice message, no text.

Should I put in my earphones and play back the news? Should I search for his name or do nothing at all? *What on earth should I do?* I panicked.

Nothing.

Nothing.

That's what I needed to do.

So, with my head bowed, I sat at my desk and tried to prepare my next lesson. And when the bell rang, I went back to my classroom and did my best to pretend I wasn't completely crippled with fear.

Two hours later when the lunch bell sounded, I startled and jumped, adrenaline pushing me forward as I made my way out of the classroom and into the hallway. *Hurry, hurry, hurry!* a voice screeched inside me. *Don't run!* another one countered. *Just walk.* Battling these edicts, I found myself stepping out quickly, skip-tripping my way to the staffroom.

When I walked through the doorway, Ruby was making herself a coffee. 'Everything all right?' she asked with a crocodile grin.

I flinched and inwardly shook, before presenting her with a smile. 'Fine,' I said, coolly, before I walked across to my desk. Sitting down, I reached over to pick up my phone, trying not to pounce on it.

Bracing myself, I took a deep breath before I dared look at the screen.

A missed call. A missed call from Gordon. And then, as if by magic, a text message lighting the screen.

On my way home. Everything is fine.

—

But that wasn't quite right.

Six weeks later, Gillian Cooper rang to say the brief had arrived and she'd made a copy for Gordon. He picked it up the very next day and read it while I was at school.

'It's awful,' he said over dinner that night; a dinner he'd made but neither of us managed to eat. 'You don't have to read it,' he added. 'Perhaps you shouldn't.'

I nodded. The very thought of it made me feel like retching.

That night, with my husband beside me, I dreamed I was on an unlit stage. Reaching a hand into the blackness, I touched nothing at all. And when I stepped out, one foot feeling the way, I found only air, with no floor beneath me. *How could I move*, I questioned my still sleeping self, *if I had no idea what was before me?*

When I woke up, I knew what I needed to know; absolutely everything. Every claim, every allegation. I wanted to know every bit of it. And I wanted to know it immediately.

Tell me, my soul screamed out, eclipsing the fear of what horrible things I might find.

For up until then, we'd had an unspoken agreement: at home, we wouldn't bring up the case, discuss the charges or mention Laetitia's name. That way we hoped it would not swallow us up, destroy our home and ruin our marriage.

It was a good idea. But it didn't work. For although we could stop ourselves from discussing the case, we couldn't make it vanish. So instead of worrying about it together, I worried about it alone. And the more I worried, the more my fears festered, plaguing not only my days but more and more of my nights.

I broke down at dinner that evening. 'I need to know,' I told him. 'I need to know everything.'

One hand clutching his fork, the other his knife, Gordon closed his eyes but kept his head high. And like a blank-eyed statue he stayed there. Had I taken a picture, he might have simply looked thoughtful. But that's not how it was. For his heavy eyes and trembling lips betrayed an anguish so great it sucked the air from the room. I myself had two urges then: the first to scream and the second to close my eyes just like Gordon.

I did neither. For at that moment, Gordon opened his eyes and, without a word, stood up and left the table.

And me? Was he leaving me, too? Was he going to head for the door and leave me behind? This was my very first thought; a thought borne of panic and fright. That on top of the fear and the shame and the shock, I was about to lose him.

––

But I didn't lose him that night. Not that one.

For instead of walking out of our house, my husband walked into our bedroom. And when he returned, he had in his hands a thick wad of papers held in place by a bright metal binder. Placing it all before me, he took a deep breath. 'This is everything,' he said, before leaving the kitchen once more.

Pushing away my untouched dinner, I brought the papers closer. *Gordon Patrick O'Hanlon*, said the very first page, *Brief of Evidence.*

I took a breath and another, keeping one hand on my stomach. Then I turned the page.

Of the typewritten words that filled it, two lines stood out: *Court Attendance Notice*, and the words underneath, *Aggravated Indecent Assault (x 2)*. Bile threatened to rise from my stomach. Swallowing it down, I kept turning the pages until I reached the one with this heading: *Interview between Laetitia Hartford and Detective Senior Constable Vicky Johnston.*

Then I read what it said.

— *Laetitia, I'm going to show you a note—a typewritten note— which was sent to the principal of your school, Dr Malcolm, that I'd like you to read. Let me know when you've finished.*
— *Okay, I've finished.*
— *Thank you. Now because this interview is being recorded, I'm going to read the note aloud. This is what it says:* MR O'HANLON IS A PREDATOR WHO PREYS ON HIS STUDENTS. LAST THURSDAY AFTER SCHOOL HE GROPED LAETITIA HARTFORD IN THE STATIONERY

STOREROOM THEN HE FINGERED HER. Do you know who wrote that letter, Laetitia?

[No response]

— *Laetitia, did you write that letter?*

[No response]

— *Laetitia?*

[Response unable to be recorded]

— *Laetitia, did you write that note?*

[No response]

— *The recording can't pick up a nod, Laetitia. I need you to answer yes or no.*

[No response]

— *Did you write that note, Laetitia? Yes or no?*

— *Yes.*

— *And did Mr O'Hanlon take you to the stationery storeroom on 15 June this year?*

[No response]

— *Laetitia?*

— *Yes.*

— *And when you were there did he touch your breast?*

— *Yes.*

— *And did he slip his hand into your underpants?*

— *Yes.*

— *Thanks, Laetitia. I can appreciate how difficult this is to talk about but I need to get some more details. I want to take you back to that day, to Thursday, 15 June. Can you tell me what happened straight after school?*

— *I went to see Mr O'Hanlon.*

— *And why did you go to see him?*

— *I used to see him every Thursday after school.*

— *And why was that?*

— *For English tutoring.*

— *He was your English tutor?*

— *Well, no, I wouldn't say that.*

— *So what was he then?*

— *My English teacher.*

— *So he taught your English class at school?*

— *Yes.*

— *But he also taught you after school?*

— *Yes.*

— *Did he teach any of your classmates after school as well?*

— *Not sure.*

— *You don't think so?*

— *No, I don't think so.*

— *So why did he offer to teach you after school?*

— *He said it would be good for me.*

— *Good for you?*

— *To make my writing better.*

— *How long did they last, these after school lessons?*

— *About an hour.*

— *On 15 June, did the session last about an hour then, too?*

— *Yeah, I suppose.*

— *And when you went to the storeroom with Mr O'Hanlon, was that before the lesson or afterwards?*

[No response]

— *Before or after the lesson, Laetitia?*

[No response]

— *Laetitia?*

[No response]

— *When was it?*

— *[Pause] Afterwards. It was afterwards.*

— *And why did you go there with him?*

[No response]

— *Laetitia. Why did you go there?*

— *[Pause] To get some pens and stuff.*

— *And you went into the storeroom with him?*

[No response]

— *You went into the storeroom with him?*

— *[Pause] Yes.*

— *What happened then?*

[No response]

— *Laetitia?*

— *He closed the door.*

— *When you were both in the storeroom?*

[No response]

— *I need more than a nod, Laetitia.*

— *[Pause] Yes.*

— *And then what happened?*

[No response]

— *Laetitia?*

— *He did that stuff.*

— *What stuff?*

— *[Pause] Like, he touched me.*

— *How exactly did he touch you?*

— *He put his hand inside my bra.*

— *And what did you do?*

— *I didn't do anything.*

— *And then what happened?*

[No response]

— *Laetitia?*

— *Like the note said.*

— *Sorry?*

— *Like the note said.*

— *You mean he put his hand down your pants?*

[No response]

— *Laetitia?*

— *[Pause] Yes.*

I had to stop then. I had to turn away. *How could he? How could he do that?* My heart was hammering hard, so hard I thought it might even explode. My shoulders slumping, my body curled into itself.

Then I brought myself back. I gave myself a shake. I should have followed it up with a slap. *It was not true*, I reminded myself. Despite what I'd read, despite what she'd said, it was not true. It couldn't possibly be.

I felt my back straighten as I let my body unfurl. Then I gulped at the air, trying to breathe better, trying to breathe harder and deeper. *It was not true*, I told myself over and over. *None of it was the tru*th.

But why, a tiny voice whispered inside me, *would she lie?*

There was another interview in those papers. Another one with DSC Johnston. But this time my husband was being interviewed.

The time is 8.05 am, it began. *This is an electronically recorded interview being conducted at Morton Police Station on 27 July 2017 between myself, Detective Senior Constable Vicky Johnston and Gordon O'Hanlon.*

Then she gave him a warning. *You do not have to say or do anything if you do not want to, but anything you say or do will be recorded and could be used in court.*

It was a warning he had not heeded. A warning that still hadn't kept him silent. But why shouldn't he have spoken? Why shouldn't he explain what had happened? What, after all, did an innocent man have to fear?

— *On Thursday, 15 June 2017, where were you?*

— *During the day, I would have been teaching.*

— *What classes were you teaching?*

— *On Thursday I have Year 9 English, Year 7 English, Year 10 English—a double period.*

— *And was Laetitia Hartford in your Year 10 class that day?*

— *She's in the class so unless she'd been away, I imagine she would have been there.*

— *But she wasn't away, was she, because you asked her to stay back after school that day, didn't you?*

— *Um—I-I don't know.*

— *And when you were alone after school with her, you knew you'd be free to do what you liked, didn't you? And you planned to sexually assault her, didn't you?*

— I-I didn't do it.

— You didn't plan it?

— No, I didn't plan it.

— So it just happened?

[No response]

— Mr O'Hanlon?

— N-n-nothing happened.

— Did you or did you not ask Laetitia Hartford to stay back after school with you?

— I offered. [Pause] I offered to talk to her about an essay she was writing.

— And why did you offer to do that after school and not in school hours?

— Because there wasn't time. Because I had a whole class to teach.

— So you told her to stay back after school?

— I didn't tell her to stay. I said I had time to help her after school.

— And you saw her alone, is that right?

— [Pause] Yes.

— Was this a common practice: that you would see her alone after school?

— [Pause] Not really.

— And what do you mean by 'not really', Mr O'Hanlon?

— It wasn't my practice to do that.

— And yet you did it on that occasion.

[No response]

— There were other times you saw Laetitia Hartford alone after school, weren't there?

[No response]

— *Mr O'Hanlon?*

[No response]

— *You saw Laetitia Hartford alone after school at other times, didn't you?*

— *Yes.*

— *And when was that?*

— *A few times. I can't remember when, exactly.*

— *And why did you do this?*

— *To help her. To help her with her writing.*

— *And who else knew you were giving Laetitia Hartford extra tuition after school?*

[No response]

— *Mr O'Hanlon, who else knew you were giving Laetitia Hartford extra tuition after school?*

— *I don't know.*

— *Did you ask her parents for permission?*

— *[Pause] No.*

— *Did you ask the school principal for permission?*

— *No.*

— *Did you ask your head of department for permission?*

— *No.*

— *Why not, Mr O'Hanlon?*

— *[Pause] I don't know.*

Part three

Part three

29

THE TRIAL WAS HELD A year later, by chance in the middle of my holidays. Among all the horror, this was a fortunate thing: I could attend without asking for leave or explaining why I needed it.

Bernadette and Bridget were still the only ones who knew, for, to our relief, Gordon's case hadn't yet made the news.

On the first day of the trial—and the four days that followed—I did not go to court with Gordon. Unlike those wives I'd seen on the news, I did not enter the courthouse hand in hand with my husband.

Instead, Gillian Cooper told me to find a cafe and stay there until just before ten, then make my way to the courtroom. So I found a place nearby, ordered a tea, and somehow managed a smile for the waitress who brought it to me. She smiled in return, her eyes so shining with kindness it was almost too much to bear. Busying myself at the table, I reached out for the pot to fill my cup with tea. But my hands were shaking too much. When I glanced up, the waitress was watching. Meeting my eye, she inclined her head slightly. *You can do this*, she seemed to be saying. *You can get through it.* So I took a breath, a very deep breath, and even though my hands were still shaking, I reached for the pot and I poured myself some tea.

Just before ten, I left the cafe and I walked to what had once been a department store, but now was a courthouse; the courthouse where Gordon would be tried.

At the entrance I placed my handbag on a conveyor belt to be checked by a bored-looking officer who suddenly brightened. Plucking my bag off the belt, he fished out the small leather purse I took with me everywhere; the one holding scissors, two spools of cotton—one white, one black—and three sewing needles pressed into a piece of material.

'You can't take that in with you,' he told me. 'The scissors, the needles: they're a security risk.'

Sewing needles and that tiny pair of scissors, what sort of risk could they be?

But this was not the place to argue.

Hurrying now, for fear I'd be late, I made my way down the wide spiral stairs that led to court number 3.

The door to the courtroom was heavy and hard to open, but I managed it. Once inside, I gave a deep bow. This, Gillian had told me, was what I must do whenever I entered a courtroom: I must bow to the judge. But when I looked up, the judge's chair was empty. The courtroom was tiered, with two high benches: one for the judge, the other—a level lower—taken by a black-gowned young woman.

Built underground, in what had to have been the store's basement floor, there were no windows in my husband's courtroom, just three walls covered in a light-blue cushioned material.

Below those elevated benches was a very long table where Gillian Cooper was sitting. Next to her was Gordon's barrister, James Pierce, who, under his robes and his white horsehair wig, was a rather stout man with no hair.

At the far end of the table were two women I'd never seen before: one in robes and a wig, the other wearing a trouser suit.

Behind those women and facing the front of the courtroom were three seats, separate but fused together, surrounded by a small gate. That's where Gordon was sitting, alone. The gate was ajar, and slipping through it, I sat down beside him. Turning towards me, his eyes were gentle but he couldn't quite smile. Instead he placed his hand on my knee, and covering his hand, I gave it a gentle squeeze. And that's how we stayed.

But not for long. For suddenly Gillian Cooper was with us, speaking softly but with some urgency. 'You can't sit there,' she said. 'It's just for the defendant.'

I stared at her, unable to process the words until, in a rush, their meaning came crashing down on me. *You can't sit there. It's just for the defendant.* The defendant who was my husband, obliged to sit in a place where I could not even join him.

I felt myself sweating, the heat building inside me, rising so quickly, too quickly. *I cannot manage this.* These were the words that scrambled my mind. *I can't manage this at all.*

But you must, another voice whispered back. *You must.*

Keeping my body very still, I tilted my head towards Gillian Cooper. 'Of course,' I quietly murmured.

Lifting my hand from my husband's, I rose from the seat I should never have been in and, eyes smarting, moved quickly away. There were seats just behind him and when I turned to check if they were still free, I saw that two were now taken—by Bernadette and Bridget.

'When did you get here?' I mouthed.

'Just then,' Bridget mouthed back, as Bernadette waved me over to join them. Once I had, she reached for my hand and held it. 'I've got you,' she murmured. 'Love, I've got you.'

And for the days that followed, those words were my mantra. *I've got you, I've got you*, I'd tell myself over and over again, mostly to drown out the thought that kept me from sleeping: *Yes, but who's got Gordon?*

In front of us, there was movement: the young, gowned woman was now standing. 'All rise,' she said, her voice surprisingly low.

A knock then, loud enough to startle me. Then another and a third. From where though? Not from the door I'd come through, which was the only way into the courtroom.

I was wrong about that.

What I had failed to notice was this: a faint outline on the far wall that was, in fact, a door. And after those three knocks, from that door emerged a woman who was not only gowned but also wore a yellow-white wig of tightly rolled ringlets.

My eyes growing wide, I stared at her. Never had it occurred to me that Gordon's judge might be a woman.

Stopping in front of her judge's chair, she turned to us all and bowed. Gillian Cooper, James Pierce and the two women beside them bowed back. Gordon and Bernadette and Bridget and I did, too. Then we all sat down again.

Gordon's judge was tall and thin, with a long, thin neck and long, narrow face. She was, it struck me, as long and lean as a greyhound. And once that thought was with me, it stayed, and the rest of her became greyhound-like too: the outline of muscles along her jaw, the skin tight on her cheekbones. As I kept looking, I searched her face for something more—for signs of compassion or hope—but couldn't immediately find them. Still I hoped for kindness.

One of the women at the long table—the one in the wig—was standing again. 'Fiore,' she said. 'I appear for the Crown.'

I stiffened. So this was Gordon's prosecutor, the one who would have him convicted and jailed. And now that I knew who she was, I needed to see what she looked like. But, with her back to me, all I could glimpse were strands of dark hair peeping out from her wig.

'Pierce,' said Gordon's barrister, standing up as soon as Prosecutor Fiore sat down. 'I appear for Mr O'Hanlon.' He wasn't English, I'd just discovered, despite his strangely clipped vowels.

A man in blue stood by the entrance and, when asked, confirmed to the judge that yes, the jury panel was ready.

Five minutes later, a group of perhaps twenty-five filed into the room. And for the next hour, I watched in confusion as that black-gowned young woman dipped her hand in a bowl to pluck out the numbers to whittle those twenty-five people to twelve.

There were, in the end, six men and six women. Three women who were younger than me and three who were older. And of the six men, two were grandfatherly, three between forty and fifty, while one seemed little more than a teenager.

Then it all started.

'I call Detective Senior Constable Vicky Johnston,' the prosecutor announced and I cowered. For although I hadn't seen her in more than a year, DSC Johnston was still giving me nightmares.

So when a pale woman with mousy brown hair stepped into the witness stand, I was confused. This unremarkable woman in nondescript clothing—a black skirt and cream-coloured blouse—looked nothing like the woman who had so frightened me.

For here at the front of the court, she did not scream or shout or curl her lip in disgust. In fact, she didn't say much at all. *Yes, she had attended our house; yes, she had arrested my husband; and yes, she was the interviewing officer.*

And once she was done, instead of leaving the courtroom, she simply returned to her seat.

I soon realised why: my husband's accuser was about to give evidence.

But not in person. For instead of stepping onto the stand, Laetitia Hartford would appear by video, beamed onto a large television screen on the far side of the courtroom. When the screen lit up, I inhaled, fingers clenching the straps of my handbag. Bracing myself, I waited to see her face. *Would I know her at all?* Or, without the stage spotlight, stage make-up and tied-back hair, would she be a stranger?

One thing I knew for certain was this: nothing she said would surprise me. For hadn't I pored over her statement, trying my best, my hardest to make some sense of it? And now here I was, poised to see for myself. Sitting tall, I was a dog on alert, head cocked, body still.

That's when the prosecutor sprang to her feet, her voice loud and anxious. 'Your Honour,' she said, 'I understood the court would be closed for this evidence.'

The judge's brow creased, her eyes scanning the back of the courtroom, where they fixed on Bernadette, Bridget and me.

'The defendant's family should remain outside while the complainant is giving her evidence,' she said. 'Having them in the courtroom would be distressing for Miss Hartford.'

Back arched, jaw clenched, I waited for Gordon's lawyers to defend us; to assure the judge we'd cause no problems and promise to listen quietly.

'I have no objection to the court being closed,' was all James Pierce said in reply.

I was aghast. He may have had no objection, I thought, but I certainly did. *I will not leave my husband*, I wanted to scream, *I am his wife and I will stay here in the courtroom.*

But before I could open my mouth, Bernadette was slipping her hand into mine. 'Come on, darling,' she said with a tug to pull me up with her. And despite my outrage, despite my shock, I let myself be led out of the courtroom.

'I wanted to scream,' I hissed once we were outside. 'I wanted to scream at them all.'

Although Bernadette's lips lifted, her eyes were blazing and her pupils were small and angry. 'My word, Ellen, my word. But first I wanted to grab our boy and run away with him; to take him away from all this rubbish,' she said, her light, lilting voice turned menacing.

30

PATIENCE IS A QUALITY I'VE long possessed: my childhood had instilled it in me; the long hours listening to Reverend Burnett had demanded it and my parents had always expected it. Perhaps this is the reason I've always been good at waiting, provided I know how long the wait will be. It's the not knowing that tends to disturb me. And at the trial that day, no-one could tell me how long we might be left sitting outside that courtroom.

It was, as it happened, just after 1 pm when the courtroom door opened and the prosecutor stepped out. Turning towards her, I started to ask when she thought the girl's evidence might be over. But instead of stopping to consider my question, she headed straight for the stairs.

A moment later, the door opened again and Gordon and Gillian walked through it.

'Finished?' I mouthed but Gordon just shook his head so I didn't ask anything more. We ate lunch together—Gordon,

Bernadette, Bridget, Gillian and I—in Gillian's favourite cafe. Nobody spoke very much and Gordon said nothing at all.

At two o'clock, he and Gillian returned to the courtroom while we three continued to wait outside. All afternoon we waited, and it was well after four before Gordon finally emerged.

Hurrying towards him, I could no longer hold back my questions.

Are you all right?

Is it finished?

How was it?

'How was it?' he echoed, his voice sounding broken. 'It was terrible.'

⎯

Gordon and I retired to bed early that night, both so exhausted, I prayed that sleep would come quickly. Instead, with my husband beside me and my fears for the trial encircling me, I had the most peculiar sensation: my fatigue disappearing, I was suddenly strangely invigorated. Invigorated, alert and aroused. What I did next—considering the day, considering the stress we were under—seemed odd, even wrong. Yet I couldn't hold back. Straddling my husband's body, I pressed against him, feeling him harden while we both stayed silent. And when my head and my body filled with a rush of release, still I kept my silence. And when Gordon's body tensed then relaxed with a shudder, he kept his silence as well.

⎯

At court the next day, Gordon's headmaster was called as a witness. I knew he'd been asked to give evidence and that he had to comply. Still it felt a betrayal; still it charged my body with anger, dismay and confusion. *My husband is a good man*, I wanted to scream out as he sat himself down in the witness box. *How could you believe him capable of such a thing? How could anyone ever believe it?*

As if reading my mind, Bernadette pressed a firm hand on my knee to keep me silent. And while my insides boiled and bubbled, I stared at the man who had so ardently welcomed my husband to Grandborough College.

'Sir,' the prosecutor began, 'let me take you back to 19 June last year. What did you discover when you arrived in your office that morning?'

Philip Malcolm straightened before leaning forward. 'I found a piece of paper on the floor. It was folded in half and when I opened it up, I saw it had writing on it.'

'And how would you describe the writing?'

'It was typewritten, and all the letters were capitalised.'

'And was there any indication as to who might have written it?'

'No, there was not.'

Taking a step towards his witness, the prosecutor gave him a piece of paper. 'Do you recognise this?' she asked.

And even though I knew the words well, still they made me flinch.

MR O'HANLON IS A PREDATOR WHO PREYS ON HIS STUDENTS. LAST THURSDAY AFTER SCHOOL HE

GROPED LAETITIA HARTFORD IN THE STATIONERY STOREROOM THEN HE FINGERED HER.

Gordon's headmaster nodded. 'That's the letter,' he said.

The prosecutor seemed pleased with the answer. 'And what did you do once you'd read it?'

'I'm a mandatory notifier, so, of course, I informed the department.'

'And you're aware that Miss Hartford has since confirmed that she wrote the letter?'

He nodded. 'Yes, I'm aware of that.'

—

The fingerprint expert looked too young to be an expert at all. Yet, when he'd dusted that school storeroom, he'd managed to find fingerprints that belonged to my husband.

And?

My husband had never denied being in the storeroom that day, but swore he'd been alone. So it was no surprise that his fingerprints had been found in the room. The surprise was that Laetitia Hartford's prints had been discovered there, too.

And if ever my confidence had waned or my belief in my husband faltered, it had been on reading that young expert's statement. And now here he was, with his unblemished skin, his jet-black hair and his broad Australian accent.

I didn't want to like him. I didn't want to like him one bit.

But as he answered all of James Pierce's questions, he stayed calm and measured and affable. Could he have made a mistake? Could his statement be wrong? Laetitia Hartford's fingerprints hadn't actually been found in the stationery storeroom now, had they? And even if so, there must be an innocent explanation. Contamination, perhaps? Nothing deliberate, of course, just carelessness, in all probability. ·

To all of these questions, the young expert's answers were thoughtful, his manner polite. The dusting of fingerprints had been meticulous, he said. Laetitia Hartford's prints had definitely been found in the storeroom. There was absolutely no doubt about it.

Dismayed by his conviction, I ventured a glance at the jury. They were engrossed: all twelve absorbed by what he was saying. And how my heart sank to see it.

31

THAT AFTERNOON, A RECORDING WAS played to the jury. It was the video recording of Gordon's police interview, his face so gaunt, his mouth so slackened he was just about unrecognisable.

That's not him, I wanted to call out to the jury. *It's not him at all, not really.* But with Bernadette's hand heavy on mine, I stayed quiet.

Straight after that awful recording, it was Gordon's turn to appear in person. He was slow to reach the witness box, his limp more pronounced than usual. Closing my eyes, I willed him not to stumble; I prayed he wouldn't fall.

He didn't.

Once he was in the witness box but before he sat down, the black-gowned woman stood up, a laminated sheet in front of her. Looking at Gordon then down at the sheet, she read in her low rumbling voice: 'Will you swear to tell the truth, the whole truth and nothing but the truth?'

And Gordon swore that he would.

James Pierce stood up, stretched out his lips and adjusted his wig. 'Is your full name Gordon Patrick O'Hanlon?'

'Yes,' said my husband.

'And on 15 June 2017, were you employed at Grandborough College?'

He nodded. 'I-I'd been appointed deputy head of the English Department earlier that year.'

Forgetting myself and this place and the trial, I felt a brief stab of pride. Of all who'd applied, he'd been the one who'd been chosen. It was a momentary thing—that note of pride— and I swiftly rebuked myself for it. *You fool*, I snapped at myself, *you absolute fool. Just look where you are, just look where all this has got you.*

'And was that a teaching post?' asked James Pierce in his rich, rounded voice.

'Yes,' he replied, 'I taught English.'

'And was Laetitia Hartford one of your students?'

At the sound of her name, my heart beat faster and my fingers and toes grew cold.

'She's one of my Year 10 students,' said Gordon. 'I mean, she was.'

'And on 15 June 2017, was Laetitia Hartford in one of the classes you were teaching that day?'

'Yes, she was,' he agreed. His hands had been resting on the desk in front of him but were now out of sight. When I saw his arms moving quickly—up and down, up and down—I knew exactly what he was doing: to get rid of the sweat, he was wiping his palms on his trousers.

Use your handkerchief, I wanted to remind him. *It's in your suit jacket.*

All the while, as if to join him, as if somehow to help him, I'd been running my hands along my own skirt—up and down, up and down—until Bernadette reached out to stop me. Her touch at first was gentle but then she built up the pressure. Harder and harder she pressed on my hands until they were finally still again.

'Laetitia was in my last class for the day,' Gordon was telling his barrister.

'And after that class, the students went home, is that right?'

Again Gordon nodded. 'Yes.'

'All the students?'

My husband's face dropped. 'No,' he conceded, 'Laetitia stayed behind.'

'And why was that?'

'There was an essay due. She was having some trouble and wanted to talk it through.'

'And what was the essay about?'

Gordon looked blank.

I frowned. What was the problem? The question was clear and he knew the answer. Of course he did. It was in that long statement he'd written for Gillian Cooper. Even I could recite it word for word.

You know this! I wanted to shout. *To Kill a Mockingbird.* That was the book. *What does the mockingbird symbolise?* That was the question. And it took everything I had not to yell it out to him.

There in the witness box, my husband stayed silent while Bernadette kept gripping my arm. Together we watched as Gordon's face stayed blank before he finally brightened. '*To Kill a Mockingbird*,' he said. 'My Year 10 students were studying the book, but L-Laetitia was finding it difficult.'

'And she stayed after school to see you?'

He nodded. 'Yes, that's right.'

'And why was that?'

'So I could g-give her a hand. So I could help her out with it.'

'And how long did you stay to help her?'

His elbows up on the table now, my husband cradled his jaw in his hands. 'I don't know. I wasn't watching the clock. Half an hour, an hour, I'm not sure.'

'And did you go into the stationery storeroom that afternoon?'

'Yes,' he said softly, 'I did. I needed an exercise book and a couple of markers so I ducked into the storeroom to get them.'

'Did Miss Hartford go there with you?'

Gordon frowned at his barrister. 'No, she didn't. I went alone: I left her to work on her essay.'

'And then what happened?'

'I went back to the classroom, we checked what she'd done, then she left.'

'Mr O'Hanlon, are you certain you didn't enter the stationery storeroom with Laetitia Hartford that day?'

Gordon shook his head. 'I've already told you. I went to the storeroom alone. I got what I needed. I returned to Laetitia and when I'd helped with her essay she left. That's it.'

'Mr O'Hanlon, on that afternoon of 15 June 2017 did you, at any point, touch Laetitia Hartford's breasts?'

'No.'

'Did you place your hands down her underpants?'

Gordon lowered his head as his face creased in distaste. 'No, I didn't.'

'Did you touch her vagina?'

'No,' he whispered, lifting his head once more, 'I didn't.'

James Pierce turned to the judge. 'No further questions, Your Honour.'

That's when the prosecutor stood up, a pen in one hand, straightening her wig with the other. 'Mr O'Hanlon,' she said, 'before your suspension from Grandborough College, Laetitia Hartford was one of your students. That's correct, isn't it?'

Gordon's brow furrowed. 'Yes,' he agreed, with some hesitation.

'And she was part of your Year 10 English class?'

He nodded. 'Yes, that's right.'

'But you were not only her teacher, you were also her tutor, weren't you?'

As I watched his head tilt, I felt his confusion. 'Umm—well, not really.'

'Mr O'Hanlon,' continued the prosecutor, her voice turning slippery, 'did Laetitia regularly stay back after school to go through her English work with you?'

My husband's face reddened. 'Well, sometimes she did. She was having trouble with essay writing so I'd go through her drafts and give her some tips.'

'And did you charge for this work, Mr O'Hanlon?'

A pause. A small hesitation. 'I was paid my salary, if that's what you mean.'

The prosecutor clicked her tongue. 'No, Mr O'Hanlon, that is not what I mean. Let me be clearer: did you receive any recompense for tutoring Laetitia Hartford, separate to your salary?'

He shook his head. 'No, I didn't.'

'And how often did you keep Miss Hartford back to help with her schoolwork?'

In her tone was something I didn't much like: an imputation, a slur that made me want to reach out to strike her.

Stand up to her, I silently commanded my husband, *and tell her just how it was. It was the girl who asked for your assistance; you just agreed to help.*

'I don't know,' he said instead, beginning to stutter. 'Six, seven times, something like that.'

'How many other students did you help in the way you helped Miss Hartford?' The lilt in her voice was filled with suspicion, and how I hated her for it.

My husband's eyes widened with fright. 'I was new. I was just new to the school,' he stammered. 'Laetitia was the only one who'd asked me.'

'Asked you what?'

'For help. To help her.'

'And that's why you kept her after school, was it, to help her with her work?'

I waited for his answer. Everyone did. But my husband stayed silent.

'Mr O'Hanlon,' said the prosecutor, more loudly now, 'is that why you kept Laetitia Hartford after school, to help her with her work?'

I watched Gordon swallow. 'I didn't keep her,' he said. 'She came to me.'

'She came to you,' the prosecutor repeated, her voice beginning to curl. 'I see. But tell me, Mr O'Hanlon, on that particular day, did you inform anyone at all that you were keeping her after school?'

Gordon frowned. 'I don't know what you mean.'

'What I mean is this: did you inform the headmaster of Grandborough College that you would be tutoring her after school?'

'I wasn't tutoring her,' said Gordon, his voice very low. 'I was helping her.'

A hand to her wig, she gave a quick nod. 'Let me rephrase. Did you tell the headmaster of Grandborough College that you were *helping* Laetitia Hartford that afternoon?'

Gordon shook his head. 'No, I didn't.'

'Did you tell anyone else at Grandborough College that you were helping Laetitia Hartford after school?'

Again Gordon shook his head. 'I don't think so.'

'Did you get permission from Laetitia's parents to work with her after school?'

My husband's face was turning red now, violently red, the colour travelling down to his neck. 'No.'

'And on the afternoon of 15 June, where were you helping Miss Hartford?

'In my classroom.'

'And was anyone in the classroom with you?'

'No,' said Gordon, 'that was the point. To give her some individual attention; to check where she was having trouble.'

'And when you were giving Laetitia Hartford individual attention, was the door to your classroom closed?'

Gordon sat back in his chair and let out a sigh. 'I don't remember.'

That was the wrong answer. I saw it at once.

'So it's possible,' she said, her voice quickening, her tone now charged with excitement, 'that when giving Miss Hartford individual attention, you did so with the door closed?'

Gordon didn't answer. He simply shook his head, his eyes wide with disbelief. I waited for her to press him; to demand that he answer the question. Instead, she leaned towards the solicitor seated beside her, then lifted her head to the judge. 'My apologies, Your Honour. I need to locate a document.'

So we listened to the sound of rustling paper until the document— whatever it was—had been found.

'Are you familiar with this?' the prosecutor asked my husband, waving a bundle of sheets in her hand.

Eyes squinting, Gordon looked helpless, bamboozled. 'I don't know. I can't see what it is.'

The prosecutor turned back to the judge. 'May I approach?' she asked, before handing the sheets to Gordon.

'So' she said, repeating her question, 'are you familiar with this?'

This time, Gordon nodded. 'Yes,' he said, 'I am.'

'And do you agree that it's a document entitled *Grandborough College: Child Safety Guidelines*?'

Gordon gave a sigh. Had he been sitting back in his chair rather than craning to look at the document, no-one might have heard it. But because he was suddenly so close to the microphone, the sound of his sighing filled up the courtroom: loud, resigned, defeated.

'Mr O'Hanlon,' said the prosecutor, 'do you agree that the document now before you is a document entitled *Grandborough College: Child Safety Guidelines*?'

His sigh was softer this time. 'Yes,' he said, 'that's right.'

'Thank you Mr O'Hanlon. And if you could open the document to page 20 and read the first two paragraphs on that page.'

I watched as Gordon opened the document, located the page and, clearing his throat, began to read:

'It is a violation of the child safety guidelines to tutor a student of the school without the Headmaster's directions or knowledge. It is also a violation of the guidelines to be alone with a student outside a staff member's responsibilities and to single out a student for special favours or to encourage secrets.'

He stopped to look at the prosecutor. When she nodded, he continued.

'Activities between a student and teacher must be undertaken transparently and with the knowledge and consent of the Headmaster:
Make it public.
Make it authorised.
Make it timely.
Make it purposeful.'

The prosecutor drew herself up: head high, shoulders back. 'Your purpose wasn't really to assist Laetitia Hartford with her work, was it, Mr O'Hanlon? Your purpose was to groom her, wasn't it?'

Gordon's head reared back. 'W-what?' he replied. 'What?'

The prosecutor's voice lashed back at him, whip-sharp. 'It's my job to ask the questions, Mr O'Hanlon, and your job to answer them. Let me repeat my question. Your purpose wasn't to assist Laetitia Hartford, was it, but instead to groom her?'

Gordon's eyes were wild now, his hand on his head, scratching at his hair. 'She was having trouble with her essay. I was h-helping her with that. That's all.'

'Mr O'Hanlon,' she countered, 'I put it to you that after six or seven sessions helping Miss Hartford, you knew you had her trust and you knew she'd do just about anything you asked of her: including going into the stationery storeroom with you.'

Gordon's face was sinking now, his cheeks suddenly hollow. 'No,' he said, 'that's not true. None of it's true.'

'And once she was in the storeroom with you, you closed the door behind you and you reached out to run a hand over her breast, didn't you?'

Gordon stared at her, open-mouthed. *Close your mouth*, I wanted to shout out to him. *Close it*. For with his mouth hanging open like that, he did not look like my kind, clever husband. Instead, he looked like a fool; a fool who had just been caught out.

'Didn't you, Mr O'Hanlon?'

Gordon dropped his head, closed his mouth then looked across at the prosecutor. 'No,' he said, very softly, 'I did not.'

'Then you placed your hand through her blouse and under her bra and you rubbed her breast and pinched her nipple?'

Again Gordon shook his head, again he whispered, 'No.'

'And you put your hand inside her underpants, didn't you?'

'No,' he said, 'no, I didn't.' The tears had begun now, tears that fell down his face and onto the *Child Safety Guidelines* in front of him.

—

Next, Tony Jackson, still English head at Hopetoun Girls High, told the jury of his enormous surprise to learn of my husband's arrest on charges he simply didn't believe could be true. And my gratitude to him for saying those things only just outweighed the shame that he should be part in these awful proceedings.

The following day, the judge and the lawyers did all of the talking and, when that was finished, the judge sent out the jury to determine my husband's fate.

They didn't take long. They didn't take very long at all. They needed less than three hours to bring back a verdict of guilty.

—

He would not be sentenced that day. That's what the judge informed us. The case would instead be adjourned and my husband remanded in custody.

I stayed very quiet, very correct. Lifting a hand as my only farewell, I kept still while they took my husband away. And when, as he left, I tried to give him a smile, I couldn't. Stone-like I sat in my chair, as Bernadette and Bridget wept on either side of me.

When, together, they stood to leave, I followed them out of the courtroom. And once they'd recovered enough to catch the train home, I left them there and kept walking. I kept walking and walking until I reached a small square of grass that wasn't really a park. And making my way to the edge of the grass— my back to the street—I closed my eyes and I yelled from the bottom of my belly to the top of my throat. I yelled hard then harder and harder. I yelled like my body was being destroyed, like my limbs had been pulled apart.

'Why?' I yelled to the sky. 'Why have you forsaken me?'

32

THEN I WENT HOME.

Inside, the house was different. The air had thickened, darkening the rooms and turning them sticky with sadness. So I did as my mother had taught me: I started to clean. I cleaned out the thickness, the misery, the darkness of that day. With anger I cleaned it all out; an anger I sent to those twelve people who with just one word had ruined the life of a good man. My good man.

And oh, what a powerful agent I found in my anger, that pushed into benchtops and tables and vanities, and thwacked at the floors with a mop. In a frenzy I whirred through our house, and I cleaned it with zeal and vigour and fury.

And not until my arms and my legs had become numb with exertion did I finally sit down to rest. Only then did I feel it: even though the house was now spotless and fresh, still the air was heavy.

The anger, by contrast, had left me. Not for good. Not for long. But it did leave me. And once it was gone, it left my body empty and hollow, making space for more sadness to slowly seep inside me.

And laying my head on my hands, I started to weep.

I feared I might weep all night but, to my surprise, my tears dried up and I suddenly found I was hungry. So I made myself toast, scrambled some eggs and ate in front of the television.

I should never have watched the news that night.

For that was the night Gordon first became famous. That was the night he made the news: another paedophile teacher uncovered, unmasked and convicted—and soon to be sentenced.

I should have turned it off.

Instead, I watched it all; I watched every bit of it. I watched the footage of Gordon, his gait ungainly as he made his way into the courthouse. And I watched the footage of Grandborough College as the camera panned around the school's wide steel gates and a young reporter told the world what Gordon O'Hanlon had done.

'But it's not true,' I cried out at the screen. 'None of it's true. Not a single word of it.'

—

That weekend, Gordon's face covered the newspapers and the following week, when school resumed, I went back to work.

When I arrived, Lori Reed and Ruby Chan were alone in the staffroom. Ruby kept her head down but Lori gave me a smile. Without saying a word, she stood up and came over, a biscuit tin in her hands. Giving it to me, she murmured an apology. 'I baked too many,' she said. And when I opened the tin, I found it filled with three kinds of homemade biscuits.

As the staffroom filled, some of my colleagues did not greet me at all, while those who did had strangely pitched voices: too high or cheery or mumbled. To try to relieve the panic inside me, I fled to my classroom well before the bell had rung.

First up that morning, I had my Year 12s and this was a blessing, for they were my favourite students. The class was small, I knew them all well, and we were comfortable working together. But things that day were different: the girls were unusually silent, and some wouldn't meet my eye.

Perhaps I should have just said it. Perhaps I should have started the class with this announcement: *My husband, my innocent husband, has been taken to prison.* Would this have cleared the air; would this have broken the silence?

I don't know. For I never did utter those words, not then or any time later. And so they hung there between us, my unspoken reply to the news they'd surely already heard.

Next were my Year 10 girls: my rowdy, fidgety Year 10 girls who, that day, were unusually quiet. For this, I admit, I was grateful: grateful to be able to focus on staying dry-eyed and stopping my voice from shaking.

And when I managed these things, satisfaction momentarily fluttered inside me.

Less so, the following day when I woke to such desolation and sorrow, I was not at all sure I'd make it out of bed.

So what now? I despaired, as I lay in the bed that was too big without Gordon. *What now?*

Now you fight, said a voice, small but determined inside me. *Now you fight against your anguish and sadness.*

First, I took out the notebook I kept in my handbag, then I wrote down all the things I needed to do in order to make it to school.

Get out of bed
Put on dressing gown
Go to the bathroom
Take a shower
Make the bed
Boil the kettle
Make some toast
Make tea
Drink tea and eat toast
Wash up the breakfast dishes
Get dressed
Leave the house
Lock the front door
Check all books for school are packed in the car
Drive to school

My list would have made Gordon chuckle.

Why write any of that stuff down? he'd have asked me. *There's nothing you'd actually forget.*

And had he been here, I'd have laughed and agreed.

But because he was gone, my answer was different. *Without such a list*, I whispered to no-one, *I might forget to wake up at all.*

Helped by my list, I made it to school that morning; by ten past eight I was stepping into the staffroom.

'Hello,' I called out when I saw Ruby there, willing my voice not to falter.

Instead of a greeting, she asked me a question. 'How could you have married him?' That was her question.

I thought, at first, I'd misheard her. 'Sorry?'

'How could you have married such a monster?' she asked, her voice high and shrill. 'Did you really have no idea?'

As though slapped in the face, I felt myself reel. 'No idea about what?' I stammered.

That's when her face contorted. 'That he was a paedophile.'

A paedophile? My husband is not a paedophile! These were the words that roared through my head—how they roared and screamed and tumbled—while I myself stayed quiet.

For what was the use in engaging at all, when it would only encourage her further? Instead, silent and blinking, like some startled animal, I lowered my eyes and turned to sit at my desk.

I dragged myself through my classes that morning—I did manage that—but by the time lunch finally came, I wanted to sink to the ground and collapse. Instead, I did what I did every Wednesday: I headed to the sewing circle. But as I got closer, I became anxious. What if no-one came? What if they all stayed away? What if when I arrived, the room was completely empty?

But the room was not empty.

They were all there. My seven girls were there.

Beth Lander, usually quiet, was the first to greet me. 'Hello, Mrs O'Hanlon,' she said, her voice little more than a whisper. She was the youngest—small and bespectacled—and I was especially fond of her.

'Hello, Beth,' I replied, my voice almost as soft as hers.

Josie had brought in some brownies. This was not so very unusual: the girls might bring in cake for a birthday, or even the end of term. But there were no birthdays that day and the term had only just started.

'Lovely,' I said, with a catch in my throat. 'How very lovely of you, Josie.'

But the girls did not smile as usually they did. Instead, they were quiet and watchful. And this made me nervous. What were they thinking? What might they ask me? And how oh how, would I answer their questions?

Lead, came a voice in my head. *You must lead. They are watching for guidance and strength, and this is what you must give them.*

Closing my eyes, I took a deep breath then one more. Drawing myself up, I looked at my girls and I gave them a warning. 'But girls,' I said, trying to sound stern, 'absolutely no eating while you are sewing. The last thing I want to see today is sticky finger marks on your beautiful work.'

In front of me, each of those faces relaxed. Josie even smiled.

'Yes, Mrs O'Hanlon,' they murmured, before we got started: Gina and Laura on the machines, the rest of us working by hand.

I'd been making a shirt for Gordon and had started to hand-stitch the buttonholes.

'Oh,' said Charlotte, looking up from her work, 'it's almost finished.' But before I could say, *Yes, it is*, she kept talking. 'Are they allowed to wear normal clothes?' she asked me. 'Because, well, you know, I thought they all wore a uniform.'

Charlotte had a very loud voice—often unpleasantly so—and now it filled the room. Open-mouthed, the other girls stared at her then at me.

I felt my face flush as my resolve began to crumble. *Strength,* came the whisper inside me, *and guidance.*

'It's for afterwards,' I replied in a cheery tone, putting an end to any more questions.

33

GORDON WAS IN JAIL FOR over two weeks before I was able
to see him. At first, I didn't even know where he was. They'd
taken him somewhere, I just wasn't sure where. There are many
jails in New South Wales and he could have been sent to any
one of them. No-one sent me a message to confirm where
he was or to tell me not to worry. No-one sent me anything.
There was an information number I could ring, but only on
weekdays, between 9.30 am and 4.30 pm.

Gordon had been taken to jail late on that Friday; the information number rang out when I tried on the weekend, and
for the rest of the week I had classes to teach. And even if I
managed to call in a break, what if someone overheard me?

I needed to ring from home, and before four thirty. So I
sped home on Monday, making it there by 4.24 pm. My heart
racing, breath catching, I dialled the number and waited for
it to answer. 'My husband,' I said when finally it did. 'I need
to know where he is . . . so I can visit him.'

The woman at the end of the phone was not warm. 'MIN number,' she said, her voice flat.

I was confused. 'Do you mean mobile number?'

There was a silence. 'Are you trying to be smart?' she asked, her voice rising.

I felt myself shrink. 'No,' I said, 'I'm not.'

'His prisoner number,' she continued, 'what is it?'

His prisoner number?

'I don't know.'

'Then you'll need to ring the switch and sort it out.'

In front of me, the kitchen clock ticked over to 4.28 pm.

'What time does the switch close?' I asked although I knew what the answer would be.

'Four thirty.'

'And when does it open?' I asked, my voice hollow.

'Nine thirty.'

The next day, I made it home even quicker, and by 4.15 pm, I was through to the switch.

This time, a man answered my call. 'Corrective Services,' he said.

Mustering up courage, I cleared my throat. 'I need a number,' I said, then stopped, the words stuck in my throat, 'for a prisoner.'

'Name?'

'Ellen O'Hanlon.'

There was a silence. Were it not for a slight background buzz, I'd have thought the line had gone dead.

Eight minutes passed before he was back. 'No prisoner by the name of Ellen O'Hanlon,' he said.

My body gave a jolt. 'No.' I stumbled. 'That was my name.'

The clock clicked. It was 4.25 pm.

'So what's the prisoner's name then?'

I swallowed. 'Gordon O'Hanlon,' I said.

'Right-o.' Then he was gone, before returning with a question. 'Full name and date of birth, please.' A pause. 'Not yours, his.'

'Gordon Patrick O'Hanlon. 7 June 1985.'

Through the phone came a whistling. A soft, flat whistling. 'Yep,' he said, 'here he is. Got a pen, love?'

MIN 673914. That was the prisoner number for Gordon Patrick O'Hanlon.

'And do you know what prison he's in?' I asked, my voice cracking.

'Sorry, love. You'll have to call prisoner locations for that.'

But it was already 4.36 pm.

It was 4.21 pm when I rang prisoner locations the following day.

'MIN number?' The voice at the end of the phone was familiar. It was the woman from Monday.

I gave her the number and when she said, 'I didn't get that,' I gave it to her again.

He was at St Martin's, she told me. 'In the SPC at St Martin's Correctional Centre.'

'SPC?'

'The SPC Unit. Special Purpose Centre.'

But I still had no idea what she meant.

'Special—Purpose—Centre,' she said, drawing the words out as though addressing a very young child, 'where all the kiddy fiddlers go.'

For a moment I went blank. Then my stomach contracted. 'When can I visit?' I managed to whisper.

'You'll need to call prisoner visits,' she said. 'Monday to Wednesday they take bookings.' She paused. 'But it's already late, so you'll have to call next week.'

The following Monday at 4.13 pm, I rang through to prisoner visits.

'Hello, visits.' The woman on the phone had an Irish lilt and a friendly tone.

'Saturday?' she asked once I'd spoken. 'I'm so sorry but we're all booked up. Can I give you a tip, love? You really need to get in early on a Monday: it's first in, first served here.'

I cried then, yes, I'll admit it. There on the phone, I cried to a stranger. To a stranger who tried her best to soothe me.

'Shush, love,' she said. 'Let's see what we can do, will we? How about you come on Sunday instead? On Sunday morning we should be able to squeeze you in. At eight—but there'll be a queue so do try to come early.'

—

I was ready well before seven, my bag packed with the books I'd chosen for Gordon: books I'd taken from home. That had not been the plan. The plan had been to buy him three new books. I'd even gone to the bookshop to get them. But once there, the choice had been overwhelming. For the stakes were so high and there was so much I needed those books to do: comfort my husband, soothe him, cheer him and also keep him safe. In short, I needed those books to look after him when I could not. And standing there in the bookshop, surrounded by all the choices I had, I just couldn't make a decision. So I left empty-handed.

Instead, from our own collection, I picked out three books to lift his spirits. For adventure, there was *Huckleberry Finn*; for magic, *The Lion, the Witch and the Wardrobe*; and to still the mind, that very slim volume about one old man and the sea.

—

A line of high fences. That's how I knew I'd reached the prison. Where earlier there'd been shops and houses, now there were buildings set back from the road, a grass strip the width of a moat and lengths of barbed wire fencing, beyond a large parking area. And although it wasn't yet half past seven, it was still hard to find a spot. Once I had, I stayed in the car for a minute or two, uncertain what to do next. Ahead of me was the entrance: boom gates blocking a roadway beside a narrow path that led to a glassed-in office. From the car park, a stream of people were heading towards the entrance. I took a deep breath and followed them.

Standing outside that glassed-in office were two prison guards.

'Name,' said one, and I knew he didn't mean mine.

'Gordon O'Hanlon,' I replied, trying to keep my voice low, trying not to be heard.

The guard put a hand to his ear. 'You're going to have to speak up a bit, love.'

So I raised my voice a fraction.

As he scanned his list, he clicked his tongue. 'Gordon Patrick O'Hanlon, yes, here he is.'

He looked me over. 'And you are?'

I swallowed. 'I'm his wife.'

He looked impatient. 'Your name, love, that's what I need. And your driver's licence.'

I nodded. 'Ellen,' I said, 'Ellen O'Hanlon,' as I fumbled for my licence.

Taking it from me, he looked at it closely then examined me even more carefully. 'SPC,' he said, returning the licence to me. 'It's up there, to the left.'

Following the trickle of people ahead, I came to a red-brick building, then walked through a sandstone archway. Beyond the archway was a concrete courtyard and at the end of the courtyard, a heavy steel door. Attached to the door was a sign, the word *VISITORS* in heavy black lettering. Below it were pictures, each framed by a circle and struck through with a line. The first was a mobile phone, the next a hat, then a pair of thongs, some sandals, a watch, a bracelet, a necklace, a ring and a packet of cigarettes. None of these things could be brought on a visit, nor could visitors wear any revealing clothes. There was little about this place I found cheering, but those last words made me smile. For one thing I could confidently say was this: with my knee-length skirt and long-sleeved shirt, I would not be in breach of that particular rule.

To my surprise, the heavy steel door was not locked, and no-one was there to stop me from walking right through it. Once I had, I found myself in a small waiting room, a glass-secured reception on one side, lockers and a vending machine on the other.

In the middle of the room were two rows of seats, welded together and back to back so they all faced outwards. And although there were other people around— twenty at least— none of them was seated. They were all lined up before the reception, each holding a slip of paper.

What was it?

Searching around for a clue, I discovered a shelf affixed to the wall. On the shelf was a pen tied to a string with slips of paper strewn across it; each slip a form requesting the visitor's name and the inmate to be visited. So I filled in the form then joined the end of the line.

'Finger on the machine,' said the woman who served me. She wore a blue prison guard uniform, her left arm a mess of tattoos that ran all the way to her wrist.

When I looked at her, distracted and puzzled, she let out a sigh. 'I need to fingerprint you.'

To my right was a white plastic cradle that lit up in green when I pressed my finger on it.

'First visit?' she asked.

I nodded.

'All right,' she said, 'that explains it.'

I tilted my head, confused.

'Why you aren't in the system.' She scribbled onto a piece of paper then slid it under the counter. 'That's your VIN number—your visitor number. Don't lose it. You'll need it.'

But we weren't finished yet. 'Driver's licence,' she said.

Again?

'My driver's licence?' I queried.

'Put it this way,' she snapped, 'you won't be getting a visit until I've got it.'

Stifling the urge to call out her rudeness, I gave her my licence, then waited for her to return it.

But instead of my licence, she gave me a key. 'Put all your stuff into the locker,' she said. 'You'll get your licence back once you return the key.'

'Thank you,' I said, my voice very crisp, 'but I'll take my bag with me: I have books to give to my husband.'

The woman gave a great laugh. 'Well, you won't be taking your bag in, love, I can assure you of that. Everything goes in the locker, including your bag. Ten dollars in coins, that's all you're allowed to take with you.'

I shook my head. 'He doesn't need coins—he needs books.'

Her face hardened. 'I'll tell you one thing for free: there's no way you'll be taking in books. No way on earth. Coins, that's it.'

Behind me, there was muttering and movement. 'What's the problem?' someone called out.

'Coins,' the woman repeated, 'for the vending machine. That's it.'

The fight gone out of me now, I nodded. And into the locker I placed Gordon's books and everything else I had with me. Everything except the eight dollars I'd managed to scrape up in change. As I tried to work out how to carry the coins—I had no pockets—I heard my name being called. So I joined the queue near a large steel door, and when it clicked open, I followed everyone through it. None of us got very far: less than two metres ahead the second steel door wouldn't open. The door we'd come through had locked behind us so now we were stuck—no, trapped—between those two doors. *Don't panic*, I counselled myself. *Whatever you do, don't panic.*

Because I'd been at the end of the queue, I was closest to the first door.

'You might want to check the door's properly shut,' advised a grey-haired man just in front of me, and when I did as he said, the door gave a click and the second one promptly opened.

Once we were through, I craned my neck, looking for Gordon. But instead of my husband, I saw two guards and a scanner. Apart from that, the room was empty. Following the rest of the SPC visitors, I stepped through the scanner, then out the far door, across a courtyard, through a steel door and into a room where, once again, we were kept waiting. Our strictly two-hour visit was rapidly seeping away.

Guarding the room was a guard who seemed too young for the job. His skin looked soft, his cheeks were red and when he called out the name of my husband, his voice was thin and high as though it hadn't yet broken. Motioning me forward, he led me into a large open area with a raw concrete floor and sickly green concrete walls. Even the furniture was concrete: concrete stools around concrete tables, all cemented to the ground.

Seated, one by one, at each of the tables were men in white cotton jumpsuits. One of these men was my husband.

Gordon! I wanted to shout when I saw him. *Oh Gordon.* Only the weight of the room—its bleakness, its strangeness—kept me silent. But as soon as I reached him, I became tongue-tied, overwhelmed by all the people around me.

Gordon stood up and cupped my face with his hand. 'Hello, darling,' he whispered, bringing me to him, one hand on my face, the other stroking my arm. Gently he kissed the top of my head while I rested my head on his chest.

'I'm so glad you came,' he murmured. 'I even dressed up,' he added, stepping back to show me just what he was wearing. And although he gave me a lopsided smile, his eyes did not sparkle and his face did not light up.

'It's very strange—' I began, for in truth, never had I seen such a garment: such an odd coverall without any zips or clips. But before I could finish, a shrill whistle sounded.

When we turned, that young guard was pointing straight at us. 'You'll need to take a seat,' he said. 'No standing for visits.'

And while Gordon immediately sat down, I took a little bit longer.

Why? I wanted to argue. *Why must we sit? Why can't we stand?* As if reading my thoughts, my husband gave a very small shake of his head, and—not wanting to create a fuss—I nodded and sat down beside him.

'This thing,' he said, pulling at his outfit, 'is a non-secretion suit.'

A what?

'No pockets. No place to secrete anything inside it.'

Still I was puzzled. 'Like what?'

'Contraband: drugs, cigarettes, anything like that.'

'Or books,' I said, my voice beginning to crackle. 'I wasn't allowed to bring books.'

'That's a shame,' he said, with a gentle smile. 'I could do with something to read.'

'I'll send them,' I said. 'Surely they'll let me do that.' I'd been trying to keep my voice cheery, trying so hard until, all of a sudden, I found myself crying.

Stop! I told myself. *Gather yourself.* But I couldn't.

'I'm sorry, my love,' Gordon said softly, 'I'm so sorry you've been dragged into this. So, so sorry.'

'I can't believe it,' I said, my voice very low. 'I can't believe they found you guilty.'

His face reddened. 'I shouldn't have been alone with her,' he berated himself. 'I shouldn't have let her stay back after school. It was stupid. So stupid. But I swear to you, Ellen, I never, ever touched that girl.' His eyes searched mine. 'You believe me, don't you?'

I nodded. 'Yes,' I said, 'yes.' Then I swallowed and said it again.

34

ON THE MORNING MY HUSBAND was due to be sentenced, I couldn't get out of bed. I simply could not. And when the alarm went off at 6 am, I just lay there, as though strapped to the bed, unable to lift my head, unable to reach over and stop the ringing.

Yet somehow I did it. Somehow I rose up to meet the day, murmuring words of encouragement, as a carer might for an invalid. For every task, I gave myself credit. Showering myself was a triumph. As was dressing plaiting my hair and protecting my face with sunscreen.

Bernadette called me at seven. 'You all right, my love?' she asked, her voice strangely cheery. It was a false note, a forced note, I knew that. Still it lifted my spirits, making me hopeful that maybe we'd manage the day.

'Yes,' I lied, 'I'm fine.'

There was relief in her voice. 'Good,' she said. 'I just wanted to check you were up and about, and that things were going okay.'

She'd asked me to stay over, so we could all go to court together.

'Thanks,' I'd replied, 'but I'd prefer to get ready at home.'

This had been partly the truth. The rest I found hard to explain. Simply put, it was our bed—the bed I shared with Gordon—that stopped me from staying away. For although I now slept alone every night, I half-believed I wouldn't wake up that way; one fine morning, I'd simply open my eyes to find Gordon back there beside me. That's when I'd know what I'd always suspected: the whole thing had never been real; it had only ever been a nightmare.

This was why I couldn't stay over, not even just for one night.

Instead we met on the steps of the courthouse and entered the courtroom together.

When we arrived, the lawyers were gathered around their long table. Gillian Cooper smiled to see us and I tried my best to smile back. It wasn't her fault that the jury had found Gordon guilty, of course it wasn't. But my teeth still clenched at the sight of her face and my hands refused to unfurl.

Gordon was already there in the dock, wearing his suit and a dark grey tie, a prison guard seated beside him. Stifling the urge to hurry across and hold him close, I sat quietly behind him, and Bernadette and Bridget sat beside me.

And that black-robed young woman—the judge's associate— entered the courtroom. 'All rise,' she said, so we did.

We all rose to wait for the judge to arrive. When she did, her eyes met mine for a second. And in that second, I sent her a silent message. *Give him back*, I ordered her. *Give me back my husband.*

All morning the lawyers kept speaking: James Pierce extolling my husband's good character while the prosecutor completely denounced him.

You are mistaken, I wanted to cry out to that nasty woman. *You are badly, badly mistaken.*

Tell them more, I silently urged James Pierce. *Tell them more of my husband's goodness.*

But he didn't.

Instead, the court adjourned and we were told to come back at three.

Bernadette's hand, clammy and sweaty, clutched onto mine. 'What now?' she beseeched me.

'Now,' I said, my voice slightly shaky, 'we should eat.'

So we went to that cafe I'd found at the start of Gordon's trial. And the waitress who took our order was the same one who'd served me then.

To pass the time, I played with my food, and after our plates had been taken away, Bernadette and Bridget asked for coffee while I ordered tea. And when theirs arrived with a chocolate perched on the saucer and mine came with two, I almost managed a smile.

At a quarter to three we returned to the courtroom and at three fifteen, the judge delivered her sentence.

Looking over at Gordon, I gave him a nod and tried to look relaxed. His face was pale and his lips were white but he gave me a very small smile.

Be kind to my Gordon, I willed that judge.

But she was not.

'On 7 September 2018,' she read from her notes, 'the jury found the offender guilty on both counts on the indictment. The counts relate to offences committed against the victim who was his student. At the time of the offences, she was sixteen years old.'

His victim? The words felt like a blow to my body. *No, no, no!* I wanted to shout at that judge. *My husband is innocent, so please stop speaking like that.*

But she didn't.

'Both counts are offences of aggravated indecent assault,' she continued, 'for which the maximum penalty is imprisonment for ten years. The circumstance of aggravation for both counts was that the victim, being under the age of eighteen years, was under the authority of the offender, who was her teacher. The facts surrounding the offences—which I am satisfied the evidence establishes beyond reasonable doubt and which are consistent with the verdicts of the jury—may be summarised as follows. Both offences took place at the school where the offender was a teacher and the victim was his student. The first offence involved the offender reaching into her bra to fondle her breast. The second offence occurred when he touched the victim's vagina.'

I shook my head. I shook it so hard that Bernadette caught hold of my arm and squeezed it until I stopped.

From her elevated seat, the judge kept on reading. 'An anonymous letter was addressed to the principal of the school where the victim was a student and the offender a teacher. The letter, which was slipped under the principal's door, set out the details of the offending behaviour. In keeping with his responsibilities as a mandatory reporter, the principal informed the authorities. He then interviewed the victim who initially denied the allegations but subsequently confirmed them.

'The offender was arrested on 27 July 2017 before being released on bail. Upon his conviction, bail was revoked and the offender placed into custody. Apart from that, his criminal history is clear. Although no victim impact statement has been tendered, I accept the evidence before me that the victim felt anxious and violated.'

I frowned. I breathed hard. *No, no, no. That's not right.*

For how could that girl have felt that way when none of it actually happened?

It's not true, I longed to yell out, *so stop all of it now.*

But that judge did not.

'On behalf of the offender,' she continued, 'I have a report from the forensic psychologist Mr Yeo and one from the offender's general practitioner. There are also three character references detailing the offender's expertise as a teacher.

'The offender was born on 7 June 1985. He was, by all accounts, a talented school student and studied at university to become a high school teacher. His wife is also a school teacher. There are no children of the marriage.

'Although in good health generally, the offender suffered a stroke some ten years ago—while still a young man—which has left him with a pronounced limp affecting his mobility.

Both the psychologist Mr Yeo and his general practitioner also record a history of depression and anxiety, dating back to the time the allegations were made, and worsening since his trial and subsequent conviction. In his report, Mr Yeo was unable to discern any indication of psychological issues or deviant behaviour and is not of the view that the offender exhibits paedophilic tendencies.

'I accept that the effects of the offender's stroke and his mobility issues will make any custodial term more onerous and I have taken this into consideration.

'In addition to the evidence given at trial by Mr Tony Jackson, the letters provided by the offender's colleagues at his previous school detail his prior good character and expertise as a teacher. Each letter expresses shock at the allegations made against the offender. I have taken into account the offender's prior good character and lack of previous convictions. In matters involving sexual offences committed under authority, however, such factors carry little weight. More emphasis is given to matters of general deterrence and the need to protect children against sexual molestation. The sexual preying on a child under the offender's authority is a deplorable act and sexual predators must be punished accordingly.'

That's when I knew I needed to vomit. But I couldn't, not here of all places. Controlling myself—completely controlling myself—I kept my hands in my lap as the judge kept destroying my husband.

'As to the issue of recidivism, the psychological report of Mr Yeo is of assistance,' she said. 'Mr Yeo conducted a number of tests upon the offender and interviewed him at some length. As for general recidivism, Mr Yeo found the offender had a low risk. In relation to sexual recidivism, he concluded that the offender was also of low risk.

'Overall, Mr Yeo considered the offender has good prospects for rehabilitation which would be enhanced if he could undertake the appropriate prison-based sex offender treatment programs. I note, however, that these programs will not be available should he maintain his innocence in relation to the offences. I accept the offender has a low risk of recidivism. Despite this, there is no doubt in my mind that the current offences are very serious. Only a term of imprisonment would be appropriate in the circumstances.'

The words had started to jumble, all of them rolling and merging together. All except for that very last sentence, which stood alone and stark and clear.

It should not have shocked me so much. Gillian Cooper had given me no reason to think that Gordon would return home that evening. She'd offered me not the slightest assurance. And yes, I had listened but I had not believed her. I simply could not.

Even now, as that judge kept on going, still I harboured a sliver of hope.

'For each offence, the offence is convicted and sentenced to imprisonment,' she pronounced. 'For each of the two counts, a non-parole period of two years and six months is set. The total term of the sentence imposed is four years commencing on 7 September 2018 and expiring on 6 September 2022. The non-parole period expires on 6 March 2021, which will be the earliest date the offender may be released.'

Pushing her notes away, the judge glanced up. For a moment, she looked straight at me before shifting her gaze to the lawyers. 'Have I made any mathematical or other mistakes?' she asked.

'No,' said the Crown Prosecutor.

'No,' said James Pierce.

Yes, I screamed to myself, *you have made a terrible mistake!*

35

ONCE MORE, GORDON MADE THE news; once more, his name was splashed everywhere; once more he was the subject of public discussion and so many awful words. My own computer even threw up the filth, the one time I typed in his name.

For solace, I turned to Bernadette, and from her I sought refuge whenever I needed to hide. And each time she would be there, just waiting. That's where she'd hold me, before she'd take me inside.

'You're okay,' she'd whisper. 'My little love, it will all be okay.' And while I no longer believed this to be true, for that small moment I'd trust her.

'How do you cope?' I asked her once Gordon was sentenced.

She'd shrugged and given the ghost of a smile. 'Well, my love, this is what I think to myself: if my boy can cope there where he is, then surely I can cope here in my home, with all of its comforts. And I have Bridget and you—and the Virgin, of course, who's always here to protect me.'

'From what?' I asked.

'Oh,' she'd replied as her smile had faltered, 'all sorts of things really. It used to be fury but these days it's mostly despair.'

—

The day after Gordon was sentenced, I went back to school.

I'd prepared my lessons, I'd done my marking and had in the car the box of materials I needed. I was ready—completely ready—for the day.

Except for one thing: once I arrived, I couldn't get out of the car. The car was not locked and the door wasn't stuck. It was me. I was the problem, for I simply couldn't stop shaking. *Be still!* I commanded myself, but my body kept trembling.

What now? I thought, beginning to panic.

It was pride, in the end, that catapulted me out of the car and into action. Pride that I'd never been late to a class, pride that I'd never let anything stop me from being on time. And so, still shaking, I'd opened the door, taken my bag and my box of materials and, swallowing hard, headed straight for my classroom.

Once I was there, I took a deep breath and waited for my Year 9 girls, who were sometimes over-exuberant.

Of all the girls in Year 9, Sophia Peckham was the most beautiful. Everyone agreed, especially Sophia herself. She was particularly proud of her strawberry blonde hair, her blue-green eyes, her lightly tanned skin and her small button nose.

Midway through the class that morning, Sophia put up her hand and curved her lips into something I thought was a smile.

'Yes, Sophia?'

Raising her chin, she looked straight at me. 'Is your husband in jail for being a paedophile?' she asked, her voice light and musical.

She might have slapped my cheek, such was the shock of her words. The stinging, smarting shock of that horrible question.

Say nothing, I counselled myself. *Turn away and say nothing at all.*

But that was not what I did. Meeting her gaze, I yearned to grab at her hair and pluck out those taunting eyes.

I didn't do that either. Taking a breath, I kept my body in check, while only my mouth escaped me. 'That's not true!' I bellowed.

All eyes were on me; all mouths were open. For I had bitten. Instead of ignoring the question, I'd given them all a reply.

And with that, my power was gone. All the power I'd harnessed over my teaching years was gone. Finished. Over. And right there before me, my classroom collapsed into chaos.

'Quiet!' I commanded them. 'Be quiet!' But my voice sounded feeble and my body just wouldn't stay steady.

'It was in the newspaper,' said Jasmine Adler, her flat voice a foghorn from the back row. 'He got four years in prison.'

'For raping his students, that's why.'

Whose voice was that? For a while I struggled to place it. When I did, I felt myself slump even further. Could that really have been gentle Anne Cohen, who rarely said a thing?

'So disgusting,' said Melanie Li, the words bouncing all over the classroom.

No, No, NO! I wanted to scream. She lied, she lied, she lied. Laetitia Hartford lied.

But why on earth would she lie? that small voice once again asked me.

—

I made it through the day. Somehow, I did all I needed to do and managed to get myself home. Once there, try as I might, I simply could not rouse myself to make dinner. So, I ate a raw carrot, some bread and butter, and I took myself off to bed.

For a long time now, my sleep had been poor. Most nights, I'd awake with a start in the darkness—mind spinning, heart racing—before dozing off again. In the morning, on instinct, I'd feel for my husband, reaching further and further into the space beside me until, finally alert, I'd remember. And once I'd remembered, I found it hard to get out of my bed; sometimes almost impossible.

I did, though. Each day, I did and, Monday to Friday, somehow I'd make it to school.

And slowly, so slowly, I inched my way to the end of term.

It would be, I'd decided, my last term there: my very last term at Hopetoun Girls High. For how could I stay when everyone knew about Gordon?

I needed to leave; I needed to find a place where nobody knew me. So, I needed a transfer. And I needed one quickly.

Part four

Part four

36

FOR THREE YEARS I HAD been Mrs Ellen O'Hanlon. With pride, I'd worn my name: the name of a happily married woman. With so much pride.

Too much? I could hardly say I hadn't been warned. *Pride goeth before destruction.* I knew that.

And now my name, my beautiful name, needed to be destroyed. For how could I take it with me, the name that marked me as his, that teacher in prison?

I could not. I simply could not.

I'd have to discard it. Despite my marriage, I'd need to revert to the name I'd given away. I needed to be Ellen Wells once again.

As Ellen Wells I'd become a teacher, and it was to Ellen Wells that my payslips were all still addressed. For upon my marriage, I'd requested only one thing from the Education Department: a change of my email address. One day I was ellen. wells3@education.au, the next ellen.ohanlon1@education.au.

And what a delight this had been! For the sheer thrill of seeing my new name on screen, I'd even send myself emails, my heart swelling each time I saw ellen.ohanlon1@education.au in my inbox.

And now I'd have to give it all up, and that made me sad. It also made me worried, for how could I explain my position? What would I say? How could I possibly do it?

That's when I had an idea, but to check if it worked, I'd need to send myself an email. Not this time to the self I'd become; instead to the self I'd once been.

TEST, I wrote in the subject line before I sent it to ellen. wells3@education.au.

And *ding*, just like that, a message was there in my inbox.

TEST2 was the second message I wrote, and I addressed it once more to ellen.wells3@education.au. Only this time I sent it from her as well: a brief note from ellen.wells3@education.au to herself.

And *ding* there it was.

I had done it.

I was ellen.wells3@education.au once more, and I was pleased to have done it so easily.

But I quickly saddened again.

Gone.

'The dishonour is unwarranted,' I burst out in despair. 'The shame undeserved.'

But the voice would not be silenced. *Who will believe you?* it prodded me. *Who will believe the wife of a criminal?*

The wife of a criminal.

And oh, how these words found their mark! Needling and goading until my mind filled with pictures of people pointing and bellowing, *There she is, the wife of that criminal.*

And that's why I did what I did.

37

IT TOOK ME SOME TIME to build up the strength to go in. I loitered outside for a while, peeking in through the glass when I fancied myself unobserved. And just when I thought I could do it, I'd baulk once more.

Just do it, I scolded myself.

And finally I did. Steeling myself, I walked up to the entrance, pushed the door open, then I went inside.

It was the first time I'd been into a salon. As a child, my mother cut my hair—just the ends to stop them from splitting—and since then, I'd cut it myself.

But now I needed more than a trim. I needed to become unrecognisable, and for this, my hair, which reached to my waist, would have to go.

The hairdresser was alone in the shop. 'Hello,' she said, her mouth wide, her face kind. 'I'm Kaye.' She had very short hair and was dressed like a man. 'It can take a bit of courage, can't it?' she said. 'To actually come inside, I mean.'

'It's my first time,' I confessed, touching my plait. 'How much would it be?'

For a moment she carefully surveyed me. 'Five hundred dollars,' she said finally.

My eyes widened. Perhaps my lips even trembled. 'Five hundred dollars?' I repeated. 'That much?'

'For that length, that quality.' She tilted her head to the side. 'Tell you what, I'm even feeling a bit generous, so let's make it five hundred and fifty.'

I felt my brow knit. 'Five hundred and fifty?'

She nodded. 'That's right. Five hundred and fifty for the plait. You might get more in the city, but, well, you're here now aren't you?'

That's when I saw the sign on the counter: *WE BUY HAIR*.

'I pay cash,' she continued, 'and the price includes a tidy-up.'

'A tidy-up?'

'To give it some shape.'

It had all begun to sink in. 'You'll buy my hair,' I said slowly. 'You'll pay me five hundred and fifty dollars for my plait.'

She nodded. 'And then I'll tidy you up.'

So I took a seat and, looking through the wall-length mirror before me, I let her sever my plait.

For a moment I fancied I heard Reverend Burnett bemoan the loss of my feminine glory. But where once I would have cowered with shame, now I just smiled at myself in the mirror. And oh, the lightness I felt without the weight of the hair that had anchored me down from my childhood.

Draping my plait over her hands, Kaye took it across to the counter, wrapped it up, then tucked it into a drawer.

'Tell you what,' she said, returning to where I was seated, 'I'll throw in a wash for free.'

She took me to a row of chairs in front of a long, metal basin. Behind each chair was a plastic board cut into a C-shape.

'Sit down,' she said, directing me to the first of the chairs.

'Lean back,' she continued, so slowly I did, jerking back up as a great gush of water shot into the back of my neck.

'Relax,' she murmured. 'Just relax.'

And so, with some hesitation, I dipped my head back into the water. That's when she placed her hands on my head and began to massage my skin. Startled by her intimate touch, I froze. Then I gave into it, letting my shoulders collapse, my head loll back and my eyes gently close over.

That's when something dissolved inside me. And although I tried not to, I couldn't stop crying. And the more her fingers dug into my skull, the more I kept weeping.

Sorry, I wanted to say to this stranger. *I'm so sorry.* But because I didn't think I could form the words, I kept my eyes closed and stayed silent.

⎯

After the massaging and the washing was finished, I returned to my seat in front of the mirror, and Kaye styled my hair. When she had finished, my hair ended at the nape of my neck, short wisps of it framing my face.

I looked . . . I looked . . . for a moment, I couldn't think how I looked.

Kaye was frowning into the mirror, a hand on her hip, head tipped to one side. 'Yes,' she said, as her frown disappeared. 'Yes.'

Yes?

'Very chic—that's how I'd describe it.'

'Very chic?' I repeated.

She nodded. 'Absolutely. It really brings out your features, especially those beautiful eyes.'

Then she had a question. 'How about a bit of a touch-up?'

'A touch-up?'

'Give me a minute,' she said as she headed to the back of the shop, returning with a box filled with bottles and brushes and plastic containers.

'I'm just going to match up your skin,' she said, swivelling my chair away from the mirror to face her. Now her fingers were on me again, but this time all over my face. 'Bit of foundation works wonders if you're feeling washed out,' she murmured.

Her face too close to mine, she tickled my cheeks with a brush and drew on my eyes with a pencil. Stepping away, she turned me back to the mirror. 'Take a look at yourself,' she said.

I took a look. But instead of myself, what I saw was a stranger: a stranger with short sharp hair, pink-red lips and stiff eyelashes.

'Look at you!' she exclaimed. 'You're transformed!'

—

I still needed to sort out my clothes. For my sturdy skirts and my well-buttoned shirts—that had done me such good service—would no longer do. To complete my new look, my new self, my new life, I would need something different to wear. That's how I came to be in a department store, bamboozled by all the choices.

As I began to fluster, a gentle voice addressed me. Turning around and blinking a little, I saw a young woman in a black dress with a name tag that said *Jess*. 'Can I help you?' she asked me.

It wasn't a difficult question but the answer I gave her was garbled and made no sense. Not even to me.

But Jess just smiled. 'Are you looking for something special?'

I took a deep breath. 'I need to change my style,' I confessed.

She took in my outfit—my long brown skirt, my high-necked shirt—and nodded. 'Something more modern, perhaps?'

Something to make me new, I wanted to say. *Something to make me completely unrecognisable.*

'Yes,' I told her instead, 'something more modern.'

38

THAT WEEK, I SECURED A late morning visit for Saturday. I slept in a little, ate breakfast in a leisurely manner and took my time in the shower. Then I went to the wardrobe to take out the clothes Jess had selected. Laying them out on the bed, I couldn't decide which to wear. In the end, I picked out the fun frock.

'This one's great,' Jess had assured me. 'Really fun. You can make it formal with a jacket and heels or keep it casual with flatties.'

My fun frock had stripes. Horizontal stripes in orange and red and yellow and aqua, against a navy background. With a stretch to the fabric, the frock was straight and fitted. It had a boat neckline, sleeves that stopped at the elbow and a belt to gather it in at the waist. Never before had I worn anything like it. Slipping it on, I felt bold, even brazen. But when I caught sight of myself in the mirror, I felt a spark of excitement. For I was unrecognisable, truly I was, even to myself.

I arrived at the prison in plenty of time but was, as usual, left waiting. I waited and waited, my head cocked in the air as I listened for Gordon's name to be called. 11.03, 11.09, 11.12, 11.18 and still I waited.

It was 11.23 am when I thought I heard his name, although the speaker was muffled so I could well have been mistaken. Standing up, I went to the door, not wanting to lose any more time.

'You here for O'Hanlon?' a guard asked me.

When I nodded, the steel door clicked open and with one small push I was in: back in that room of concrete tables and chairs and men in non-secretion jumpsuits.

I looked around for Gordon's raised hand showing me where he'd been seated. But everyone's hands were down. Nervousness crept into me. Why was he not here? Why had he not come?

'My husband's not here,' I said to the guard. 'Do you know why?'

The guard gave a frown. 'O'Hanlon?'

I nodded.

He glanced at his list, then scanned the room. 'He's here, all right. Table 15.' Then he laughed. 'You sure he's really your husband?'

I followed his gaze and saw he was right: Gordon *was* at table 15.

As I hurried over, I watched his eyes widen. 'Your hair,' he whispered.

Clapping a hand to the side of my head, I gave him a nervous smile. 'I sold it.'

'You what?'

'I sold it. To the hairdresser. For five hundred and fifty dollars. Just for my plait.'

His face, drawn and thin, creased up into a smile. 'Your plait was worth five hundred and fifty dollars?'

I nodded. 'I might have got more in the city, she said, so she cut my hair for free.'

Now he was shaking his head. 'You look so different,' he murmured. 'The hair, the dress, everything.'

Reaching out across the table, I gave his hand a squeeze. 'It's for the new school,' I explained, 'so I don't look the same. So I look completely different.'

I hadn't yet told him the news: against the odds, I'd managed to get a transfer. To Salisbury High, a girls' school not far from our house.

Gordon rested his hand on the top of our intertwined fingers. 'That's good,' he said, his voice very soft. 'Well done.'

39

WHEN I FIRST ARRIVED AT Salisbury Girls High everything was quiet. It was a staff development day and none of the students were present.

For the English and History teachers, the development day took place in the library, with an opening address by the principal, Mrs—no, Ms—Sara Henson.

'Welcome back,' she said, with a business-like smile. 'I hope you've had a chance to re-energise over the break.'

'We are especially lucky to welcome Ellen Wells to the school,' she continued, 'who'll be taking over from Randa Habib.'

There in the library, we were seated on chairs placed in a circle and, after the principal's introduction, smiles came at me from all directions. To my left was a blonde-haired woman with eyes of a startling blue, and whose smile was so broad, it made her face fall into creases.

'I'm Valerie,' She gave my hand a squeeze and, still holding on, let out a small cry of delight. 'Oh,' she said, 'your engagement ring! It's so beautiful. Did you pick it yourself or did your husband choose it for you?'

My stomach dropped. *You idiot*, I chastised myself. *You fool.* I'd changed my name, my hair, my clothes, my face and yet, in less than a minute, I'd been caught out as a liar. My rings: why hadn't I thought of that? Why hadn't I kept them off?

I did my best to think quickly. 'No, no,' I said, shaking my head, 'that's not my engagement ring. It was my mother's. The wedding band, too. They both belonged to her.' I stopped for a moment and, stomach churning, pushed myself even further. 'I've never been married myself,' I told her.

The window behind us was open and the breeze tickled the back of my neck as a shiver passed through my body.

'Oh,' she replied, 'so you're single?'

I nodded. 'That's right. I'm single.'

As I spoke, there came through that window a most unlikely sound. Cocking my head to the side, I listened. 'It's a rooster,' Valerie explained. 'One of the neighbours keeps chickens. And at least one rooster.'

A rooster?

My heart sank. I knew something of roosters. Of denial and disloyalty, too.

For had not Peter himself denied Jesus, not once or twice, but three times?

Three times Peter denied him; three times I'd denied my Gordon. And how I wanted to weep out my shame and, with it, all of my sorrow.

275

Instead, I smiled. I smiled hard at Valerie Booth, just as hard as I could manage. And when I got home, I took off my beautiful rings and hid them away.

—

The students were back the next day, and I began with my new Year 12 class who, like Year 12 students throughout the state, were starting their final year in Term 4.

The class was a small, cosy group of sixteen, who appeared to have chosen one of their cohort, Kara-Jane Stewart, to speak on their behalf.

'We chose our texts with Mrs Habib so we've already got what we need.' Kara-Jane's voice, husky and nasal, rose at the end of the sentence, as though challenging me to an argument.

Well, she wouldn't get one from me. 'I know,' I agreed. 'Mrs Habib left me her notes, and I'm happy with everything you've chosen.'

More than that, I'd been relieved by my predecessor's efficiency; relieved that the texts had all been selected, and I wouldn't have to choose them myself. As it was, ever since Gordon had been taken, choosing anything at all—even groceries—had become an ordeal. So many brands, so many products, all crying out with their colours, their value, their size. *Pick me*, they'd scream, and I'd start to panic. Closing my eyes, I'd force myself to breathe and breathe and breathe. Only then, when my heart had slowed and my breathing had steadied, would I open my eyes and quickly reach out for the very first thing I saw. And by the time I'd ticked off my list and was back in the car, I'd be perspiring.

What sort of idiot are you, I'd ask myself, *if you can't even do the shopping?* My hands in a fist, I'd push my fingernails into the flesh of my palms then squeeze my eyes tight to stop myself from crying.

Catching myself, I returned my attention to Kara-Jane Stewart and the rest of my new Year 12 class. 'Don't worry,' I said, 'I'll take good care of you all.'

—

By the end of the week, I knew all the names of all sixteen of my Year 12 students. It helped that they sat in the same place each lesson: Kara-Jane in the front row, Anneke Janssen to her left, Anouk Mason to her right. Anneke Janssen was a pretty girl, with large navy-blue eyes, a narrow face, long fair hair and a certain brittleness. Certainly, her smile was wary. Anouk Mason, by contrast, rarely smiled at all. Broad-shouldered with a very deep voice, she wore her dark hair like a helmet.

Beside Anouk, but at some distance—with a space between chairs—sat Tia Brown. She was a pallid girl, with thick spongy skin and hair a biscuity colour. Unlike Anouk, she'd often give me a smile.

'Let's begin,' I said at the start of our first Friday lesson together. On my desk was one of the texts the class and their old teacher had chosen. I'd found it hard to re-read, I'll be honest, for try as I had to put it out of my mind, still it kept sending me back to that college.

With a deep breath, I brandished the book in front of me. '*The Crucible* is a play by Arthur Miller,' I said. 'It's a play about the Salem Witch Trials of 1693 and the effects they had on the town's community and political structure. And because it's a play—not a novel—it's best to read it aloud.' I stopped, I swallowed, I gave what I could of a smile. 'So let's have a reading.'

I chose Kara-Jane to play Abigail. Of course I did. So intent had she been, so forward had she leaned, what could I do but select her? She was, as it happened, a very good choice: loud, feisty and passionate. I was hardly surprised that she threw herself into the role.

I could not say the same for Tia Brown who delivered her lines in a voice that was scarcely audible, and sounded nothing like Reverend Parris. Nothing like him at all. For nowhere in her words was the confidence needed to be that man, and certainly not the arrogance.

To play the servant girl Mary Warren, I chose Anneke. Throughout the reading, not once did she lift her voice, not once did she quicken the pace. Instead she garbled her words and let her lines fall flat.

'The whole country's talking witchcraft! They'll be callin' us witches, Abby!' She droned on. 'Abby, we've got to tell. Witchery's a hangin' error, a hangin' like they done in Boston two years ago! We must tell the truth, Abby!—you'll only be whipped for dancin', and the other things!'

The words called for passion and fear but Anneke showed none of these things. In truth, her reading was close to the dullest I'd heard.

Not that it mattered. No, it didn't matter at all. Still the words pierced into me, still they made me flinch. For with those words, I was there once more in that vast auditorium, Laetitia Hartford on stage as that cowardly Mary Warren. Laetitia Hartford who, less than eighteen months later, would secure my husband's conviction.

Stop! I wanted to scream at Anneke Jansson. *Stop, stop, stop! I cannot bear one more word of it. Not one.*

I did not scream out. I did not slide through my chair and hide under my desk. I did not run out of the classroom weeping. I did not say a word. I just let the reading continue. And once my Year 12 students had reached Scene 2, Act 1, I praised them for their efforts.

Then I asked them all a question. 'From this short reading, what do you think Arthur Miller is trying to explore in this play?'

Anouk did not hesitate. 'It's about misogyny,' she said.

Kara nodded. 'And how bad religion is.'

'What about you?' I asked, turning to Tia Brown. 'What do you think?'

The girl's sallow face flushed a brilliant red and at first she didn't reply.

'Tia,' I insisted, 'what do you think it's about?'

Her voice was soft, very soft, and I had to lean forward to hear her answer. 'It's about a lie,' she murmured.

40

IT DIDN'T TAKE LONG TO settle into Salisbury Girls High. There was much I liked about the school: it was small, the grounds were well kept and the girls were, in the main, nicely behaved.

The staff were also pleasant, although I tended to keep my distance. I wasn't looking to make new friends, I wasn't looking for any attention. I just wanted to stay unnoticed. So rather than getting to know the staff—who, like Valerie Booth, might ask me difficult things—I put my energy into the students, whose questions I could simply refuse to answer. That was the merit of being in charge: I could set the agenda, the conversation, the tasks. In the classroom, there could be order. And during those hours I spent with my students, I could try to forget how much my life had unravelled.

And so the classroom became my haven—yes, my sanctuary—a place to turn the attention away from myself and pour it into my students, especially my Year 12 group.

'Have you always been in the same English class?' I asked them one morning. 'As a group, I mean.' They seemed, for the most part, close-knit, and that had made me curious.

It was the start of the class, the girls were taking out their books and their pens and my question was lost in the shuffling. Tia Brown was the first to settle, so repeating myself, I directed the question to her.

But instead of Tia, it was Kara-Jane who answered. 'Don't ask Tia,' she said. 'She won't know: she's new.'

No-one had told me that. 'Oh,' I said, returning my attention to Tia. 'How new?'

The girl reddened. 'Just this term,' she replied.

I was surprised to hear it. 'So you're just as new as I am?'

Her head dipping down, she gave a quick nod.

'Where did you come from?' I asked her. 'I mean, what school were you at before?'

She took a moment to answer. 'Morton High,' she said finally.

I felt my breath catch. I knew the school. Not well, but a bit. It was less than a kilometre away from our house and across the road from Grandborough College.

That was close. Too close. Too close to everything. I felt my face flush. *Did she know?* I wondered. *Had she heard about Gordon?*

I caught myself mid-thought. What was I thinking? Of course she'd know, of course she'd have heard! Everyone had. His face had been splashed all over the news and his name—and that of the school—had been absolutely everywhere.

Then I had another concern. *Had the girl seen me?* On one of the many times I'd been to Grandborough College, had she watched from the gates of Morton High and seen me there with Gordon? And if she had, would she recall it now?

I checked her face more carefully, trying to discern some slight recognition or a gradual dawning: any sign she could name me as the wife of that teacher and, in so doing, completely unmask me.

Only then did I remember. Of course she wouldn't recall me. For gone were the hair and the clothes that had once made me so distinctive. With all of it gone, even my husband hadn't spotted me. And if he had been fooled, then how on earth would this girl know who I was?

My anxiety subsiding, I took a deep breath as Anouk's deep voice boomed out. 'So, Tia, why did you leave?' she asked. 'Why didn't you stay there for Year 12?'

Having returned to its normal pallor, Tia's face was once again burning bright red. *I needed a change*, was all she would offer.

This, I mused later, was actually a very good answer. One I could also use to explain my own situation.

I needed a change, that's all.

It was simple. It was truthful.

And, from now on, it would be my answer to any curious questions.

———

After that, my affection for Tia Brown grew. We were both new. We were both getting to know the school and its people. In this way, our shared situation drew me closer to her. It even made me feel protective. Outside of class, I found myself checking that she was all right: not on her own; not left to fend for herself; not being excluded.

In class one day, the conversation turned to knitting: an interest shared by a group of my Year 12 girls. And while I don't knit quite as much as I sew, I still like to do it.

When I confessed this to my Year 12 class, the girls became excited.

'You should come to the knitting group,' said Kara-Jane.

'The knitting group?' I hadn't known there was such a thing.

'It's on every Wednesday,' she said, 'at lunch, in the library annexe. You should come.'

'Oh,' I said pleased, even flattered, 'I'd like that.' And for the first time in so very long, I felt a spark of excitement. Was it a sign—a good sign—that this group also met on a Wednesday? A sign that, like my sewing circle, it might also give me some pleasure?

I'd started a jacket for Bernadette—deep red wool with three wooden toggles—and this, I decided, was what I'd take to the knitting group.

When the lunch bell rang on Wednesday, my stomach gave a flip of anticipation. Popping my knitting bag under my arm, I made my way into the library and through to the annexe room at the back.

There I found a small circle of students: four I knew—Kara-Jane, Anouk, Anneke and Tia—and two I did not.

'Esther and Georgia,' said Kara-Jane, introducing them.

'Hello,' I said, suddenly shy. Was the group just for students, I started to fret. As a teacher—and a new one at that—would I be unwelcome; would I feel out of place?

I looked over at Kara-Jane. 'Are you sure?' I asked, gesturing loosely in front of me. 'I don't have to stay.'

But the girl clicked her tongue and gave me a smile. 'We'd love to have you,' she said.

I returned her smile, then took a seat next to Tia. She'd been knitting herself a green jumper, and was holding it up to show Esther.

I was glad to see that she'd been making friends. And when I asked if she missed her old school, she shook her head. 'Not at all,' she said. 'I really hated it.'

Curious, I lifted an eyebrow. 'Why was that?'

'Because it was strict,' she said with a grimace.

I was surprised to hear this, for that had never been my impression. In fact, I'd have said that the students of Morton High could have done with a fair bit more discipline. For me, they'd seemed a rowdy, motley group, many not even in uniform. But perhaps things had changed; perhaps there'd been a new principal.

'Who's in charge there?' I asked her. 'The principal, I mean. Who is it?'

But Tia gave no reply.

Perhaps she hadn't heard me, I thought. Or perhaps she'd not understood. 'At your old school,' I clarified, 'at Morton High. Who's the principal there now?'

Her head had lowered but now it bobbed up again. 'Sorry,' she said, her face growing red, her voice slow and careful. 'I really can't remember.'

'No matter,' I said.

But later I thought about this again. Wasn't it just a little bit odd, I mused, for a student to forget their principal's name?

41

THE FOLLOWING WEDNESDAY, WHEN THE bell rang for lunch, I hurried across to the library to take my place with the knitters. I'd been making good progress with Bernadette's jacket and was keen to keep going on with it.

Sitting beside me, Tia leaned over to take a look. Her jumper was practically finished: a band for the neckline, cuffs for the sleeves, then she'd be done.

'What's next?' I asked her.

Her pale face quickly lit up. 'I'll show you,' she said, holding onto a phone with a grubby blue cover. *1111*, she typed in before scrolling through dozens of photos.

'My mum knitted me this really great jumper,' she said. 'It was loose and super comfortable. I thought I could knit one for me in a different colour. Maybe yellow.'

I stopped myself grimacing. Yellow, on such a complexion? But I held my tongue said nothing.

Beside me, Tia kept scrolling until she suddenly gave a grunt. 'Here it is. Here's the jumper Mum made me. That's the pattern I'd like to copy.'

Taking her phone, I looked at the photo she wanted to show me. It was a slightly fish-eyed picture of Tia in front of a tree and wearing a baggy blue jumper.

Sitting beside me was Kara-Jane, who held out her hand for the phone. 'Can I have a look?' she asked.

But when I passed it to her, she hardly glanced at the picture, and began to scroll through other photos instead.

'God, this one's hot,' she said. 'Who's he?'

Standing up, Tia made a grab for the phone.

Laughing, Kara-Jane held it up high, away from her grasp. 'Send me his number then you can have it.'

But Tia wasn't laughing with her. A red spot had formed on each of her cheeks and they were spreading across her face.

'Give it back,' she said, her voice rising. 'Just give it back.'

Her mouth had tightened and her eyes were starting to glisten.

'Kara-Jane,' I said, putting my hand out. With a shrug and a laugh, the girl pressed the phone into my palm. 'Take a look at him, miss, and see what you think.'

I should have chastised her. I should have rebuked her for not giving Tia her phone. Instead, I stopped to look at the photo. It was of a young man, chin up, eyes straight to the camera, his hair very blond, his eyes green, cool and confident. And, I thought, strangely familiar, although I couldn't work out why.

In bed that night, it came to me.

Reverend Parris, that's who he was; that's who he'd played in that newly built auditorium.

And his name? *His name.* For a moment I floundered. Then I remembered. His name was Hunter Carmichael. Of course it was: Hunter Carmichael, my husband's former student.

42

'STRANGE,' I SAID TO GORDON when I visited him that weekend, 'don't you think?'

He didn't seem concerned. 'Do I think it's strange that one of your students has a photo of Hunter on her phone? Not really. The kids send photographs all the time. And anyway, just because he's on her phone doesn't mean she actually knows him,' he said, his voice reassuring. 'She might have just seen him around and taken a photo. It could be as simple as that.'

'You should see the photo,' I said. 'I can't remember seeing a boy his age looking so poised and so confident.'

Gordon laughed. 'Yes, he never seemed to lack any confidence. And given his talent for self-promotion, I wouldn't be surprised if he ends up in politics.'

'Self-promotion?'

'To be school captain. The moment the nominations were open, he spent most of his time campaigning for votes in the playground. Absolutely driven, he was.'

'Did he get it?' I asked. 'Did he get made captain?'

He shrugged. 'Not sure. I was gone before the voting took place. But if doggedness counts for anything, he'd have easily been the winner.'

'And was he like that in class, as well? Just as tenacious, just as driven?'

Gordon moved his head from side to side as if to better consider the question. 'Not really,' he said. 'If anything, I'd say he was patchy: his writing was sometimes mediocre, at other times outstanding. I'd even started to wonder how much of it was his own work. I'd been planning to chat to him about it.'

'And?'

'And, well, nothing. I was suspended before I could raise it.'

Suspended: once again, the word made me flinch and then it filled me with fury.

But I couldn't let that spoil the rest of our visit, so I changed the conversation.

I'd spoken to Gillian about the appeal, I told him.

He lifted his head. 'What did she say?' There were many notes to his tone—despair, wariness, fatigue—and hope.

'She's still waiting to hear from the barrister.'

Gillian was not alone in this: we were all waiting to hear his opinion on Gordon's appeal. To run an appeal, Gillian had told us, the barrister needed to find at least one error of law. Without an error, there was nothing to argue.

But he's innocent, I'd wanted to argue. *They've sent an innocent man to prison. Isn't that error enough?*

I already knew what her answer would be. It was not enough to believe in his innocence, we had to be able to prove it.

—

'The Great Debate,' I said to my Year 12 students the following Monday, 'that's what we're doing today.'

Anneke stretched up her hand. 'You mean a debate about politics?'

I shook my head. That was not what I meant. 'A debate about *The Crucible*.' I'd taken four questions from past examinations, written each down on strips of paper, folded them up and put them all into a bowl.

Once they'd formed into groups, I called for a delegate to come to the front, dip into the bowl and pull out a strip of paper. 'On it will be the question I'd like you to discuss in your groups,' I said, circling the room with my eyes. 'Now, who's going to start us off?'

Kara-Jane's hand shot straight up. 'Me,' she said.

Once she'd come to the front, I held the bowl high, making her reach on tiptoes.

Her fingers scrabbled around in the bowl before she pulled out a strip of paper. '*Mary Warren deserves our pity rather than our contempt*,' she read out.

'Right,' I said. 'You've got twenty-five minutes to prepare a group answer.'

My own opinion was clear, although I said nothing: I did not like Mary Warren. She was weak, and she was a liar. And the lies she'd told were not small ones. They were lies that had sent a good man to his death; lies that had led John Proctor to the gallows. And for this, I had contempt rather than pity.

In Anouk, it seemed, I had an ally. She'd been grouped with Kara-Jane, Tia and Anneke, and was addressing them all, her voice sharp with conviction. 'Mary Warren is clearly to blame for John Proctor's death. Without her accusation, he'd never have been arrested. Without her lies, he'd never have been hanged.'

'She didn't have a choice,' Tia retorted, her soft voice wavering. 'If she hadn't accused him, she would have been hanged herself.'

'Of course she had a choice,' said Anneke. 'She could have been honest. And if she'd told the truth from the beginning— that Abigail had put a curse on Elizabeth Proctor—she could have stopped the whole thing from happening.'

'That's not right,' Tia cut over her. 'That's just not right. I don't understand why Mary Warren should be getting the blame for everything Abigail started.'

Her voice was loud now, surprisingly loud for someone who was usually so quiet. 'Abigail was the one who got Mary involved in the first place. So why should Mary Warren be the one everyone hates?'

A hush fell over the group; everyone, it seemed, as surprised by the outburst as I was. To be frank, I was happy to see such passion. For wasn't that my job as a teacher: to inspire my students and rouse them from their silence?

In front of me, Anouk was shaking her head. 'Mary Warren is weak as piss.'

The language was vulgar and this made me wince but I held my tongue and said nothing.

'And she's a coward,' Anouk continued. 'She doesn't stand up to Abigail—she says whatever Abby tells her to say—then she turns on John Proctor as soon as she feels threatened. That's weak. That's piss weak.'

'No, it's not!' yelled Tia. 'That's not weak. That's frightened. Abigail was really dangerous. People were being hanged because of Abigail's lies. Mary had no power: she was a servant. What was she expected to do?'

'Be brave,' said Anouk. 'She should have been brave. How could she live with herself otherwise?'

'Because it wasn't her fault. That's how she could live with herself. Because it wasn't her fault. She was forced into something she couldn't get out of.'

Anouk gave a snort. 'Well, she should have tried harder.'

43

THE FOLLOWING DAY, I RECEIVED a message from the school office. Emma Brown had called. She was the mother of Tia and she needed to come and see me.

When I called back at recess, she picked up on the very first ring.

'Can I see you today?' she asked me. 'Perhaps if you're free at lunchtime?'

Then she'd hesitated. 'Please don't mention this to anyone.'

My stomach lurched at her words. *Why the urgency? Why the secrecy?* Had I done something wrong? Was she coming to make a complaint? Worse still, had she found out who I was? *Did she*—I swallowed—*did she know about Gordon?*

In the two lessons between recess and lunch, my heart raced and my temper threatened to fray. And when, finally, the lunch bell rang, my fingers were icy. Taking a breath, then another, I made my way to the school foyer where I'd arranged to meet Tia's mother.

She was already waiting for me. Dressed in tailored trousers and a short-sleeved knit, Emma Brown looked nothing like her daughter. Where Tia's shoulders were broad and her hips were wide, her mother was as slight as a sparrow. Only her blonde-brown hair reminded me of my student.

I had booked a small meeting room and, after showing her in, went to make her a cup of tea.

'Tell me,' I said on my return, trying to keep my voice steady, 'how I can help you.'

At first, she just surveyed me.

'It's my daughter,' she said finally. 'She's been so happy here; really so happy. But yesterday she came home in a state. She didn't want to tell me what had happened although I managed to get it out of her. It was your English class. That was the problem. To be honest, it was the first time I've seen her so upset since, well, since all the kerfuffle.'

'The kerfuffle?' I asked.

Had there been a kerfuffle at school?

'It was at her last school,' Tia's mother explained, 'but she doesn't like to talk about it. She got away from it all and now she's trying to forget about it.'

Forget about what?

She wouldn't tell me. 'My daughter doesn't want me to say. So I'm in a bit of a spot. But she likes you—of all her teachers she likes you the best—and I thought I needed to say something; tell someone. Then when she came home so upset, I thought, well, perhaps we could have a quiet word. In confidence.'

Relief coursed through my body. I had not been discovered. I had not been found out. I was safe. I was still safe here at Salisbury Girls High.

I nodded. 'Of course.'

The woman's eyes filled with tears. 'I just thought it might help if I told you why she might be, you know, emotional at times.'

Once more I nodded.

'There was a court case,' she said. 'Laetitia was involved in it.'

At the sound of that name, an electric shock coiled through me. 'Laetitia?' I queried, as my pulse began to race.

The woman's face reddened. 'I mean, Tia. Laetitia's her name but she insists on being called Tia. I've been trying, but sometimes I still forget.'

I tried to keep my voice from rising. 'There was a court case, you said.'

She nodded. 'It was one of those teachers. One of those paedophile teachers. He preyed on her.'

'Oh,' I said, my throat so dry I found I couldn't swallow. 'I didn't know.'

'No-one does,' she replied. 'Like I said, I wasn't supposed to say anything. She'd kill me if she could hear me now. Her father would, too. Putting it all behind us, that's what we're supposed to be doing.'

'I see,' I whispered. It was all I could manage.

'Because they got him, didn't they?' Her voice was high now, high and rushed. 'He was found guilty and now he's in jail, and we thought that would be the end of it. But it wasn't, was it?'

'It wasn't?'

'At school there were problems. At her old school, I mean. Problems with some of the students. The teacher—' Here her voice faltered. 'The teacher who did those things to her, some of the students still liked him. They said, well, they said they didn't believe her, that he wasn't the type.'

Now the woman was looking straight at me, her face beseeching. 'But that's exactly it, isn't it? No-one can really know just what a person might do.'

She didn't wait for an answer; she didn't wait to see if I had anything to say. She just kept on talking. And now that she'd started, it seemed she couldn't stop.

'I couldn't understand it. How some of those students— students she'd known for years—could be so awful. Especially after the trial and everything that went on beforehand. None of it made any sense. In the end, we had to change schools. All that saving to get her into such a good school—all those fees, year after year—all of it gone, all for nothing.' She was crying now, wiping her tears with the back of her hand as they spilled down her face.

I tried to speak, but I couldn't. Clearing my throat, I tried again. 'I thought Tia came from a public school; from Morton High.'

Shaking her head, she looked away. 'That's just what she tells her classmates, to stop any questions. If she'd told the truth, people would know who she was. And that was the last thing we wanted.'

My heart was hammering so loudly, I feared Emma Brown would hear it. 'So what school did she come from?' I asked, trying to keep my voice neutral.

'I don't like to say, if you don't mind,' she apologised. 'They kept her name out of the paper, which was an enormous relief, and we've taken our own steps to make sure she won't ever be linked to that school. I'm sure you can understand that.'

But no, I could not understand it, not now that a ball of hot lava had lodged in the pit of my stomach. *Tell me!* I wanted to yell. *Tell me the name of the school!*

But I forced myself to stay quiet.

'You can't imagine the toll it's taken on our family,' she continued. 'Especially my husband. He's so protective, you know. Laetitia—I mean, Tia—she's our only one and my husband's always been very strict. No boyfriends, no going out, nothing like that. Because we needed to keep her whole. Not running around half-dressed like some of those other girls you see. Protecting her innocence: that's always been his priority. Mine too, of course.'

Her voice faltered. 'Then this. They say that's what happens, you know. It's men like him—like that paedophile teacher— who prey on the innocent ones like Laetitia.'

Leaning back on her chair, she took a deep breath. 'She'd have my head if she knew I'd told you so much. To be honest, I didn't mean to say any of it. I just wanted to let you know she's a bit fragile, and could do with someone to talk to. Someone outside the family, I mean. Not about all that kerfuffle, just day-to-day things, when she's feeling a bit lost. And, as I said, she likes you a lot so I'm hoping you might keep an eye on her. To check she's going okay.'

I managed to nod. And I promised to look after her daughter.

When school had finished that day, I headed straight to the office. I needed to get into the system, I told the assistant, to check some student details. My hands were cold and my stomach was jumping, but somehow my voice stayed calm.

'No problem,' she said. 'Just let me set you up.'

And just like that, I was in. I typed, then I scrolled. I typed again then I scrolled until I found the record I needed.

Student's first name: Laetitia
Student's preferred name: Tia
Student's last name: Brown

Moving down, I searched for more. And I found it.

Mother's name: Emma Brown
Father's name: Anthony Hartford

It was her. My student—the student I'd sworn to look after—was Laetitia Hartford, my husband's accuser.

44

I SLEPT POORLY THAT NIGHT and, when I awoke in the morning, was filled with trepidation. How could I face her? How could I even look at the girl who'd said all those things about Gordon?

I could have stayed home. I could have claimed sickness. Maybe I should have. Instead, I forced myself out of bed. I boiled an egg, I toasted some bread and I made sure I ate it. Then I showered, I dressed, I drove to work and when it came time for my Year 12 class, I did my best to contain the dread that was building inside me. Perhaps she'd be absent, I caught myself thinking. Perhaps she wouldn't turn up. But this, I knew, was unlikely. For the girl who was and was not Tia Brown was never away from school.

When she walked into class, her smile was so dazzling, it caught me off guard and I found myself smiling back.

Behind her were Kara-Jane and Anneke.

'My God, Anneke,' exclaimed Kara-Jane, 'do you text your whole life?'

For as usual, Anneke's phone was there in her hands, fingers tapping as she headed to her seat.

'Phone away, Anneke.' I told her. 'Books out,' I said to the rest of my class, averting my eyes from Tia.

When it was lunch and time to head to the knitting group, I baulked. I couldn't go. I just couldn't go. And had I not seen Esther there in the corridor, I'm sure I'd have stayed away.

'You coming, Miss Wells?' she asked me, her face so earnest I could only nod and follow her.

When we arrived, the others were already there.

'Miss Wells,' said Tia, tapping the free seat beside her, 'I want to show you how much I've done.'

So I sat down beside her, and Kara-Jane sat beside me.

When Tia unfurled her work to show me, I had to agree: she'd progressed extremely quickly.

'You'll be finished before you know it,' I said.

Pride brightened her face and she smiled as she kept on with her knitting.

I did not, for my thoughts were growing darker. *How could this possibly be?* I asked myself over and over.

How could this girl, this affable girl, be the cause of my life's ruination? How could she have denounced my husband for something he hadn't done? For if my husband was indeed honest and truthful—and I was certain he was—then the girl knitting beside me could only be a liar.

Yet, in all the time I had known her, I had found Tia Brown to be nothing but kind and caring. And that was a problem. For it was impossible, simply impossible, to fit all these things together.

Stopping my thoughts—stopping all thoughts—I focused instead on keeping my hands very busy. And so lost did I become in my knitting, I jumped when I heard the bell ring.

Unlike the students, I did not have a class immediately afterwards. So rather than hurrying to pack up my knitting, I decided to work a bit longer.

'You go,' I told the others. 'I'll pack up the chairs when I'm finished.'

So I settled back down with my knitting and tried to push back the thoughts that would otherwise send my mind spinning. I knitted and knitted until soon I'd just about knitted my free lesson away. Only then did I pack up my wool and begin to stack the chairs.

That's when I saw it: a mobile phone lying under my chair. A phone that wasn't mine, but whose grimy blue cover I knew. It was Tia Brown's phone. It was most definitely hers.

And now I'd have to find out where she was so I could give it back.

That, at least, was my first thought. A second thought followed, taking form as Kara-Jane's words came back to me. *My God, Anneke, do you text your whole life?*

At the time, they hadn't meant anything much, but now, with Tia Brown's phone in my hands, they had me thinking.

Did Anneke really text her whole life? And what did it mean if she did? That I'd know everything about her, so long as I read her texts?

As I thought about this, my grip on Tia's phone tightened. That's when I made the decision: I wouldn't be returning the phone, after all.

Not yet, at least.

And switching it off, I slipped it into my handbag.

45

ONCE I WAS HOME, I turned on the phone, then punched in the password, praying it hadn't been changed.

It hadn't. It was still just the same.

1111 and I was in.

Sitting down on our sofa, I tapped on Messages. Then I scrolled back to the previous year until something caught my eye: a name—*Hunter C*—with a circular photo beside it. The photo was small, that was true, but immediately recognisable. It was him. It was Hunter Carmichael. I was sure of it.

And when I pressed on the picture, a new screen appeared, filled with a long string of messages.

I scrolled up. Up and up until I couldn't go any further. Only then did I lean back and start reading.

4 APRIL 2017, 3.20 PM
U want to hang out?

4 APRIL 2017, 3.21 PM
Okay

303

4 APRIL 2017, 3.22 PM

4pm behind the toilet block

> **4 APRIL 2017, 3.23 PM**
>
> Okay

5 APRIL 2017, 8.20 AM

You were so hot last night.

U free after rehearsal today?

> **5 APRIL 2017, 8.21 AM**
>
> Maybe. 6pm at the park?

5 APRIL 2017, 8.30 AM

Ok

> **5 APRIL 2017, 6.10 PM**
>
> Where are you?

5 APRIL 2017, 9.05 PM

Soz, I couldn't get away.

And Penel was there so I couldn't text.

11 APRIL 2017, 8.36 AM

You want to meet after training?

> **11 APRIL 2017, 8.37 AM**
>
> What time?

11 APRIL 2017, 8.40 AM

4.30

> **11 APRIL 2017, 8.41. AM**
>
> At the park?

11 APRIL 2017, 8.52 AM
How about your place?

11 APRIL 2017, 8.53 AM
My mum will be there.

11 APRIL 2017, 8.59 AM
Park 445 then.

18 APRIL 2017, 10.30 PM
Send me a photo? I'm super horny.

18 APRIL 2017, 10.40 PM
Come on, just your tits then.

18 APRIL 2017, 10.43 PM
I dunno

18 APRIL 2017, 10.44 PM
You frigid or something?

18 APRIL 2017, 10.50 PM
No

18 APRIL 2017, 10.51 PM
Come on then. Give me something.

18 APRIL 2017, 10.54 PM
Please.

The next screen wasn't a message. It was a photograph. For a moment I baulked then I clicked to make it larger.

A pair of breasts, that's what it was. Nothing else: no face, no neck, no belly, just breasts. And the sight of them there on the screen so shocked me I almost dropped the phone. They were large, pale breasts, tear-drop shaped, with nipples the size of saucers. With shaking hands and a hurried tap, I reduced those breasts and swiped them away.

But this was just the beginning. For those breasts kept on coming and soon there was more than that. Soon the pictures were even more private; so private they made me flinch.

Scrolling away from them, this was the message I found:

18 APRIL 2017, 11.04 PM
Makes me so hard I want to fuck you right now.

'Oh,' I cried out, appalled, my voice loud in our empty house.

And what had she sent in reply? No rebuke, no censure; no remonstration. No words at all, in fact. Just a face. A yellow smiley face.

I was floored, speechless, horrified.

Scrolling on, I waded through more and more of that girl's flesh. I scrolled past April and when I reached May, there was Tia looking into the camera, her large breasts uncovered, her lips slightly pouting.

I'd only just got to June when a message took my attention.

1 JUNE 2017, 3.01 PM
What's up?

1 JUNE 2017, 3.01 PM
English lesson

1 JUNE 2017, 3.01 PM
WTF?

1 JUNE 2017, 3.02 PM

With Mr O

My heart quickened. Mr O. That was Gordon's nickname; the name lots of students had called him.

1 JUNE 2017, 3.02 PM

He got the hots for you or something?

1 JUNE 2017, 3.03 PM

Doubt it.

1 JUNE 2017, 3.05 PM

Bet he does. 😝😝😝😝😝

As I flinched at those lascivious faces, the thought of that boy—that impudent boy—filled me with fury. And if he'd been there before me, oh, how I'd have wrung the impudence out of him.

Instead, I scrolled further.

15 JUNE 2017, 8.39 AM

Meet up when I'm done with Mr O this arvo?

15 JUNE 2017, 8.40 AM

Yup—bottom gate 5pm.

15 JUNE 2017, 8.41 AM

Ok

That was it. That was all. There was nothing else for that day: the very day my husband was accused of assaulting that duplicitous girl.

I scrolled down, and kept scrolling until I reached 19 June. There were many dates that troubled me now: this was one of them. For it was the day of my husband's suspension.

And on that hideous day, the girl had only this to say:

> **19 JUNE 2017, 11.32 AM**
> Free period—Mr O away.

Nothing more. Not a word of the awful things he was said to have done; not a word of those accusations. Not one.

Raging, confused, perplexed, I read on.

> **21 JUNE 2017, 8.39 AM**
> Today 4pm?

> **21 JUNE 2017, 8.43 AM**
> Your place?

> **21 JUNE 2017, 8.44 AM**
> 😉

Then this.

> **21 JUNE 2017, 2.39 PM**
> WTF have you done?

> **21 JUNE 2017, 2.40 PM**
> Meet me after training.

And this.

> **22 JUNE 2017, 10.20 PM**
> I'm going to tell Dr M the truth.

22 JUNE 2017, 10.30 PM
Then I'll have to tell your folks the truth too. I think
you know what I'm talking about. I swear I'll tell
them everything.

Working well into the night, I catalogued my discoveries. Screen by screen, I photographed those messages, printed them out, then clipped them together. After that, I left a message for Gillian Cooper, requesting a legal appointment.

—

At school the next day, I had a surprise for that girl who now called herself Tia Brown. With a smile I tried to make warm, I handed her the phone. 'Are you missing this?' I asked her.

Her eyes lit up and she gave me a smile. 'You're the best,' she told me.

And you are not, I seethed, as I smiled in return.

46

AFTER SCHOOL THE NEXT DAY, I didn't drive home. I parked in the city then walked to Gillian Cooper's office.

'Your hair,' she said when she saw me, her gaze slipping down to my clothes. 'And, well, everything. You're unrecognisable.'

I nodded, smiled, then took a seat in her office. 'These might help the appeal,' I said once I passed her the printouts.

With a frown that gradually deepened, she worked her way through the papers. Once she had finished, she gave me a very odd look. 'How on earth did you get hold of these?'

I felt myself blink: I'd not prepared for this question.

I could, of course, have told her the truth. But what then? Who would let me stay in a job teaching my husband's accuser? And I could not afford to lose my position. I needed the work; I needed to work. With Gordon in prison, I had to meet all the household expenses, including the mortgage repayments. So no, I would not be telling Gillian Cooper just how I came to have those printouts.

Struggling to think of something to say, my gaze fell to the mess on her desk. There were piles of papers: some loose, some clipped and some stapled. There were also documents still sealed in their envelopes, most stamped and one with a personal message: *Att: Gillian Cooper*, it said, followed by the words: *Delivered by hand*. And with that, I had my answer.

Clearing my throat, I began. 'Well,' I said, not quite meeting her eye, 'when I arrived home yesterday, a large envelope—folded in half—was sticking out of my letterbox.' I shot another look at the mess on Gillian Cooper's desk. 'Blank,' I clarified. 'The envelope itself was blank: no name, no address, no stamps. It was just a sealed envelope. And when I opened it up, I found the mobile phone records inside.'

I'd begun leaning forward, further and further with each word I spoke, my head jutting out, my spine badly curved. And as soon as I'd finished, I fell back in my seat, fatigued by the lies I'd just told her.

Her head cocked to one side, Gillian Cooper held the screenshots towards me. 'So they appeared in your letterbox, did they?' She clicked her fingers. 'Just like that?' Then she looked straight at me, eyes wide and disbelieving.

For a moment, I felt myself crumble: the urge to confess so strong it was almost overwhelming.

But not quite.

'That's right,' I heard myself tell her. 'In an envelope left in the letterbox.' My voice stayed steady but I lowered my eyes.

When I looked up again, Gillian Cooper had become thoughtful. 'Fresh evidence,' she murmured.

'Fresh evidence?' I echoed.

She nodded. 'If we can prove it's fresh evidence, it could help the appeal.' Using only her thumb, she flicked through the papers. 'But first, we should tell the police.'

47

THAT WEEKEND, WHEN, WORD FOR word, I told Gordon what I'd explained to Gillian Cooper—that an envelope had been left in the letterbox, filled with Laetitia's phone records—his jaw had dropped and his eyes had widened. But he hadn't questioned my story.

'Who would have done it?' he mused instead. 'Who on earth would have left them there for us?'

But I just shrugged and shook my head then spoke about other things.

—

I was not alone in the staffroom when Tia Brown came to the door. It was before class on Monday and Valerie Booth got up to see what she was after.

'She wants to see you,' she came back to tell me.

The girl's face was drawn and downcast. 'Can I see you after school?' she asked me. 'In private?'

No! I wanted to scream at her. *No, you cannot. And certainly not in private.*

Instead, I mustered a smile of concern and said, 'Of course, Tia, no problem.'

We met after school and I took her into the staffroom. It was empty now and we took a seat in the corner. Her eyes, I saw, were red-rimmed. 'What's wrong?' I asked, trying to keep my voice gentle.

'Everything,' she whispered as her face crumpled. 'Just everything.' Turning to me, she looked deep in my eyes before lowering her own to the floor. 'I've done something bad,' she murmured, 'and now I don't know what to do.'

My heart gave a nervous jump. 'If you tell me,' I said, trying to keep myself steady, 'perhaps I can help.'

And with that, it all came tumbling out.

'I got a call from the police,' she said, 'from a detective I know: Vicky, Vicky Johnston.'

As always, the sound of her name made me flinch but I managed to keep my face neutral.

'I was part of a trial,' my student continued, her voice very low. 'Vicky was the officer in charge and I was the primary witness.'

'Oh?' I replied, a rasp in my voice. 'Were you really?'

She swallowed, nodded then kept on going. 'The trial finished months ago, but now Vicky says there's a problem and she needs me to come in to see her. It's urgent, she said, quite urgent.'

The girl was starting to cry now, tears rolling down her cheeks and onto her chin.

'The thing is, Miss Wells, because I'm not yet eighteen, Vicky told me to bring someone with me. A support person, that's what she called it.'

She looked at me then, her eyes very wide. 'Will you come with me, Miss Wells? Will you be my support person?'

I gaped. 'What about your parents?' I replied with a stammer. 'Shouldn't you ask them instead?'

Her tears kept falling. 'I can't, Miss Wells. I just can't.'

Lowering my eyes, I thought for a minute. *Click-click*, and then a decision. 'This detective,' I said, 'when does she want to see you?'

We locked eyes then, my student and I, her face lit with relief and gratitude.

'Tomorrow,' she said, 'after school.'

48

I DRESSED CAREFULLY THAT MORNING, hoping I wouldn't be recognised. And that afternoon, once the bell had rung and the school grounds had emptied, I drove Tia straight to the station. I was nervous, of course, but not like the girl, who couldn't stop shaking.

I left the car in a narrow side street and from there we walked to the station. On the other side of the entrance doors was a counter, sheets of perspex guarding the policeman sitting behind it. With my head slightly lowered, I followed Tia over.

'Detective Vicky Johnston told me to come here,' she told the officer, her voice so quiet he asked her to say it again.

Then he wrote down her name and told her to take a seat. So we took a seat and we waited.

Now this might sound unlikely but I swear it's true: I sensed DSC Johnston well before I saw her. And when she came into view some moments later, I held my breath, fearful of being caught out. But if she gave me even a cursory glance, I must have missed it.

'Laetitia,' she said, with an edge to her voice, 'thanks for coming in.'

The girl nodded. 'Miss Wells is m-my teacher,' she stuttered, 'and she's come with me.'

DSC Johnston nodded. 'As a support person?'

'Yes,' I murmured, 'that's right.'

We were led down a corridor and into a room with three chairs: two on either side of a desk and another—the one for me—up by the wall.

DSC Johnston sat behind the desk and asked Tia to sit in front of her. On the desk was an electronic machine with buttons and lights and switches. Beside it lay a thick grey folder, the word *Hartford* written in black marker pen.

'Do you know why I asked you to come in and see me?' asked DSC Johnston as my student's pale face slowly reddened.

When the girl shook her head, the detective took a wad of papers from the grey folder.

'Gordon O'Hanlon's solicitor sent me these,' she said. 'You'll need to read them carefully.'

Unclipping the bundle, one by one Tia considered the pages, laying each face down after she'd read it. When she'd gone through them all, her hands were shaking and her back had begun to slump forward.

'I'll need to ask you some questions,' said DSC Johnston, 'so why don't we start straightaway?'

Turning to me, Tia's eyes became wide, her face red and confused.

In that moment, I knew exactly what I must do to properly counsel my student. *Think carefully before you say anything*, I needed to warn her. *Ring your parents and tell them you need a lawyer. In the meantime, say nothing at all.*

These were the things I knew I should tell her; and I knew I should say them now.

But I didn't. I didn't say a thing.

In the meantime, Tia agreed to answer the questions DSC Johnston had for her.

'Good,' said the detective, 'let's get started then, shall we?'

Another police officer entered the room and once she'd given her name—Detective Constable Chen—she said nothing more.

'Laetitia,' DSC Johnston continued, 'you're under eighteen so, before we begin, I need to know if you'd like to talk to a lawyer.'

'I don't know any lawyers,' the frightened girl said, her voice not much more than a whisper.

'That's not a problem,' the detective assured her. 'I can give you the name of a couple.'

I watched Tia swallow. 'Does that mean my parents would have to find out?'

DSC Johnston gave a shrug. 'I couldn't say,' she admitted.

Turning towards me, the girl looked perplexed. *What do I do?* her eyes were asking me. *Tell me what to do.*

But, once again, I said nothing, and once again Tia swallowed. 'I'll just get it over and done with,' she whispered.

Squinting into the machine that sat on her desk, DSC Johnston cleared her throat before she pressed a large green button. 'The time is 4.13 pm,' she said, her voice slow and clear. 'This is an electronically recorded interview being conducted at Morton Police Station between myself, Detective Constable Sarah Chen and Miss Laetitia Hartford. Miss Hartford is being supported by her teacher, Miss Wells, who is also in attendance.'

Her next words were directed to Tia. 'You do not have to say or do anything if you do not wish to, but anything you say or do will be recorded and could be used in court. Do you understand this?'

Her voice had stayed loud but her tone was so flat it took me a moment to understand a question had come at the end of it. Perhaps Tia had been confused, too, for, offering no answer, she simply stayed silent.

'Laetitia?' prompted DSC Johnston, her voice slowly rising. 'Did you understand what I said?'

The girl's face reddened once more. 'Yes,' she mumbled.

'And do you agree,' the detective continued, her voice getting quicker, 'that you were asked if you wanted a lawyer but declined the offer?'

Tia shot me a look—her face florid and fearful—and opening my lips, I was tempted to give her a warning. *Run, Tia, run.* This was what I would have told her. *Run, run away now.*

Instead, I stayed silent. I even lowered my head.

'Laetitia?' repeated DSC Johnston. 'That's right, isn't it?'

'Yes,' said the girl, her voice now resigned, 'that's right.'

And with that, DSC Johnston got started, asking first about Hunter Carmichael and how exactly she knew him.

The girl took a moment to answer. 'He was at school,' she said, 'one year above me. We took part in a play together.'

DSC Johnston let out a small grunt. 'And was he your boyfriend, this Hunter Carmichael?'

Shaking her head, the girl's eyes started to fill with tears. 'Penel was his girlfriend, not me.'

'Penel?' the detective asked her. 'Penel who?'

'Penelope Averill. She and Hunter were both the school captains.'

I tilted my head: that was news to me.

To DSC Johnston as well, it appeared. 'Really,' she said, 'and are they still going out, those two captains?'

The girl shook her head. 'I really don't know,' she whispered.

'And why don't you know?' shot back DSC Johnston, her voice suddenly sharp.

Tears spilled down Tia's face and ran down her neck. 'Because I don't speak to him now.'

'And why is that?'

Wiping her face with the back of her sleeve, she murmured something I couldn't catch.

'What was that?' asked DSC Johnston. 'What did you say?'

The girl kept crying as she tried to reply. 'Because of the court case,' she said between sobs. 'Because of Mr O.'

'Mr O?' queried DSC Johnston.

'Mr O'Hanlon,' my student replied, and oh, how my body reacted to that; how my skin tingled and sparked to hear the name of my husband.

'I see,' said DSC Johnston. 'So tell me this then, Laetitia, am I right to infer that your relationship with Hunter was sexual?'

Curling herself away from me, the girl slowly nodded her head.

'And when did it start, this sexual relationship with Hunter Carmichael?'

'April,' she murmured. 'In April last year.'

'And if he had a girlfriend, did this mean your affair was a secret?'

She nodded.

'So how did you manage to see him and still keep it secret?'

'We'd go to his house, if his parents weren't there. Or my place, when my parents were working. Or sometimes we'd meet in a park.'

Nodding a little, the detective stretched back in her chair. 'I want you to focus on 15 June last year. Do you remember that day?'

I watched the girl flinch. 'Yes,' she said very quietly.

'Do you remember your last lesson that day?'

She nodded. 'I had English.'

'And who was teaching you?'

'Mr O'Hanlon,' she said very quietly.

'And what did you do after his lesson had finished?'

'I stayed in the classroom.'

'Why was that?'

'Because he was helping me with an essay.'

'Was this an unusual thing for Mr O'Hanlon to do?'

The girl bit on her lip. 'No,' she replied, 'he'd often stay back to help me.'

'Laetitia, you gave a statement that on that day—on 15 June—Mr O'Hanlon assaulted you in the stationery storeroom.'

Now the girl was shaking her head. 'What I said wasn't right. What I said wasn't true.'

She needs a lawyer, I thought to myself, and she needs one right now.

Stop! that's what I should be yelling out now. *Stop the questions and get that girl a lawyer.* As her support person, that was my job. That was what I should have been doing.

Instead I let DSC Johnston continue.

'Laetitia,' she said, 'let's go back to that afternoon when Mr O'Hanlon was helping you with your essay. What time did you finish?'

I watched the girl consider the question. 'It would have been around four,' she ventured.

'And then?'

'Well, then Mr O'Hanlon left.'

'And where did he go?'

'I don't know. He just left.'

He left.

He just left.

Then why, I wanted to cry out, *did you lie about that?*

DSC Johnston paused before she asked her next question. 'Tell me, Laetitia, that afternoon, did you see Mr O'Hanlon go to the storeroom?'

'No, I didn't,' she said. 'He must have been there before though,' she added.

'And why is that?' asked DSC Johnston.

'Because his keys were still there.'

His keys were where?

The detective's head also shot up. 'His keys were still where?'

'Still in the storeroom door, like he'd forgotten to take them back with him.'

'And they were Mr O'Hanlon's keys?'

'Yes.'

'How can you be sure?'

'Because they had his ID on them.'

'And when you say keys, how many keys would you say were there?'

I watched the girl put a hand to her cheek as if trying her best to remember.

Don't stop, I wanted to scream as the weight of her words sank in. *Keep going. Say more. Tell the detective everything.*

'Only two,' she replied. 'One to the storeroom and one to the English staffroom. They were on a cord, I remember. That's how I knew they were Mr O's keys, because he'd wear them around his neck.'

'And when you saw the keys sticking out of the storeroom door lock, did you give them back to Mr O'Hanlon?'

'How could I,' she replied, 'when he was already gone?'

'Gone where?'

'I don't know. Home, I suppose.'

'And did you go home, too?'

She shook her head. 'Not straightaway.'

'What did you do instead?'

'I stayed at the front of the school.'

'Why was that?'

'Because I was waiting for him.'

'Waiting for who?'

'For Hunter,' she said very softly. 'He was at training— basketball training, up at the hall—and I told him I'd wait at the front.'

'At the front of the school?'

She nodded. 'Not at the hall, in case somebody saw us together. So I stayed at the front of the school and Hunter said he'd come down once he'd finished.'

The detective's mouth tightened. 'And did he?'

Again she nodded. 'We were supposed to be going straight to his place because his parents wouldn't be home.'

'And is that what happened?'

'No,' she replied, 'it wasn't. We were about to leave when I remembered I'd left my hat on a hook outside Mr O's classroom, so I went back to get it, and Hunter came with me. That's when we saw Mr O's keys in the door to the stationery storeroom.'

'And?'

'Well, Hunter was, like, really excited about it. Students were never allowed into the storeroom and Hunter wanted to take a good look inside. So he turned the key and walked in.'

'Did you go, too?'

'Not at first. But Hunter kept calling me in to see what he'd found. Exercise books and pens and highlighters and things like that. I was scared to enter, in case we got caught but Hunter wouldn't let up. So I took the keys out of the lock and kept them there with me, just in case the door slammed behind us. That's when Hunter grabbed the keys and started mucking around.'

'What do you mean by mucking around?'

'He put the keys around his neck and pretended to be Mr O'Hanlon, who had this weird way of walking, like he had a dead leg or something. Hunter started walking like that, sort of limping and dragging his feet, and swinging the keys around his neck.'

When she said that, I wanted to spring to my feet and scream the place down. And if Hunter Carmichael had also been there, I would have smashed him into the ground. Instead, I kept my face composed, my rage confined to a twitch at the side of my mouth.

'And then?' continued DSC Johnston, her voice impassive.

Tia took a deep breath and leaned back in her chair. She looked exhausted 'He closed the door right behind me and switched off the light so it was completely black. Then he, like, kissed me and stuff.'

The detective's next question was icy. 'Could you be a bit more precise, please Laetitia? What, for example, do you mean by, *and stuff?*'

The girl's face turned a purply-red as she bit down on her lip. 'Like touching me up and that.'

'I see,' said DSC Johnston, 'and when you say, "touching you up", which parts of your body are we talking about?'

Once more, my charge bit down on her lip. 'My breast,' she said quietly. 'He slipped a hand through my shirt and inside my bra.'

'Is that all?'

Lifting her head to the ceiling, the girl gave a sigh of despair.

I could still protect her, I thought. I could protect her from any more questions. *Enough!* I could shout. But if I did that, then how would I save my husband?

With a turn of her head, Tia looked at me in some desperation.

I gave her a smile. Just a smile, nothing more; I wasn't trying to make her continue. Not really.

But she did continue. 'He wanted to finger me, too,' she mumbled.

I winced at the vulgar expression; DSC Johnston didn't flinch. 'When you say he wanted to finger you,' she replied, 'do you mean he wanted to insert his finger into your vagina?'

'Yes,' the girl mumbled.

'And did he insert his finger into your vagina?'

She shook her head. 'I was scared we'd get caught and really just wanted to go. So when he put his hands down there, I started to push him away.'

'Did he touch your vagina?'

'Well, yes,' she replied, her face a bright pink.

'So he put his hand inside your bra and touched your breast, then he put a hand inside your underpants and touched your vagina?'

She nodded.

Having unwittingly slumped in my seat, I suddenly straightened.

For that's what she'd said about Gordon. All those things she'd described: they were the very same things she'd sworn Gordon had done to her.

Ask her about that! I silently roared. *Why don't you ask about that?*

'What happened then?' the detective enquired instead.

'Nothing much,' was the girl's reply. 'He just turned on the light, opened the door and we both walked out.' She swallowed. 'That's when I said we should put back the keys.'

Leaning back in her chair, DSC Johnston lifted her head up a notch. 'Put them back where?'

'In the staffroom. There's a hook by the door where Mr O would hang them. It was better putting them there, I thought, than leaving them where we'd found them. The staffroom door was locked so we used Mr O's keys to let ourselves in. That's when Hunter decided to check the place out a bit.'

'Sorry,' said DSC Johnston, 'I didn't quite get that. What do you mean by "check the place out a bit"?'

'You know,' she replied, 'to have a look for anything interesting.'

'And what did he find?'

The girl lowered her eyes. DSC Johnston waited a moment then repeated her question.

'He looked at the stuff Mr O had on his desk,' Tia admitted.

What stuff?

'What do you mean?' asked DSC Johnston.

'Essays,' she said. 'There were a pile of them on his desk. For Hunter's English class. Mr O had already marked them and Hunter wanted to see what he'd got.'

'And?'

Her shoulders lifted a fraction. 'Nothing,' she said. 'He didn't get a mark. There was a Post-it note stuck to the cover instead.'

'What did it say?'

The girl's answer was hard to make out. 'Something about plagiarism,' she mumbled. '*Check if plagiarism*, or something like that.'

All at once, Gordon's words came back to me. Words about Hunter—throwaway words—that, at the time, seemed to hold little importance: *I'd started to wonder how much of it was his own work.*

Was the boy a cheat?

'When Hunter saw the note,' my charge was explaining, 'he started to swear.'

DSC Johnston's nod was encouraging. 'And what exactly did he say?'

Her brow creasing, Tia shot me a look: we both knew I couldn't abide bad language. But today I would make an exception. A quick blink at my student, and she had my permission to repeat that horrible boy's bad words.

Still she turned away from me before she answered the question. 'He said, "If that dickhead tells Big Mal, I'm fucked."'

'Big Mal?'

'Dr Malcolm, the school's headmaster.'

Despite everything else that had happened, everything else I'd heard, a smile twitched on my lips.

Big Mal. I didn't know they called him that.

'And why did Hunter say that, do you think?'

'Because he wanted to be captain and if he got done for cheating, he couldn't be nominated,' said Tia, the words spilling out in a rush. 'That's why he got rid of the essay.'

'Oh?' said DSC Johnston.

'He took it out of the pile and put it into his schoolbag.'

'But when Mr O'Hanlon gave back the essays, he would have noticed Hunter's was gone, wouldn't he?'

Tia didn't answer this question. She just sucked on her lip, flipping it in and out of her mouth.

'Laetitia?' DSC Johnston prompted.

The girl was looking more and more uneasy. 'Hunter had English on Tuesday,' she said, 'and by then, Mr O was gone.'

'Gone?' The detective's voice was icy again.

Tia dropped her head. 'I mean suspended.'

DSC Johnston was shaking her head. 'Because of the letter,' she murmured, as though to herself. 'The letter,' she repeated, more firmly, 'the one that you sent to the headmaster.'

Now the girl was red-faced. 'I didn't do it,' she said, her eyes filling. 'That wasn't my idea.'

The room fell quiet as DSC Johnston looked through the grey folder before, she pulled out a page. 'Is this the one you mean?' she asked, sliding the paper to Tia.

'Yes,' the girl murmured, 'that's right.'

From where I was sitting, I could just make out the words of that typewritten letter. It was not the first time I'd seen it, but, still, how its contents burned right into me.

MR O'HANLON IS A PREDATOR WHO PREYS ON HIS STUDENTS. LAST THURSDAY AFTER SCHOOL HE GROPED LAETITIA HARTFORD IN THE STATIONERY STOREROOM THEN HE FINGERED HER.

Those ghastly words brought everything back all at once: the trial, the conviction, the sentence, the prison. It hit me so hard that my head started spinning. *Breathe*, I told myself. Now was not the time to be fainting.

So I breathed in and breathed out and, once I'd recovered, turned my attention to DSC Johnston's next question.

'Well, if you didn't send it, who did?'

That was when Tia slumped, and crumpling into her chair, she stayed silent.

I, on the other hand, was sitting bolt upright, eyes sharp, ears pricked, intent on her reply.

Not now. I itched to rebuke her. *Don't go quiet on me now.* But still she stayed silent.

Answer! I raged. *Answer that question!*

DSC Johnston leaned forward. 'Who wrote the letter, Laetitia?' she asked, menace creeping into her voice.

My student startled but still wouldn't answer.

'The letter,' growled the detective. 'Who wrote it?'

Closing her eyes, the girl's breaths were quick and jagged. 'Hunter,' she said. 'Hunter wrote it.'

'But what he said wasn't true now, was it?' Gone was the menace as DSC Johnston became gentle once more.

Was that why Tia began to cry? Harder and harder she cried, and soon she was weeping. Then she started to speak. 'No', she murmured, 'none of it was true.' Lifting her head, she tried to explain. 'I didn't know he'd done it. He only told me later.'

The detective's voice stayed gentle. 'And did he say why?'

Tia wiped at her tears. 'It was about the essay. He'd paid someone to write it and he thought that would get him suspended. Then he'd never get to be school captain. And he wanted that more than anything.'

'But why write the letter?' asked DSC Johnston, her voice beginning to cool again.

'To spark an investigation. That's what he told me. And while the investigation was happening, Mr O wouldn't be allowed back at school. So he wouldn't be there to hand back the essays or notice that Hunter's was gone.'

'And is that what happened?'

Shell-shocked, I could only watch on, too perturbed even for anger.

'Mr O got suspended before he could give back the work—just like Hunter said. And when all the essays were returned later on, Hunter told the new teacher that his had gone missing. So she let him re-submit it.'

'And the old essay?'

The girl looked blank. 'I suppose he chucked it.'

'And what about Mr O'Hanlon?'

'Hunter kept saying it would all blow over; or else the school would find him a job somewhere else. That it would all be fine.' She was faltering now, and starting to trip on her words. 'It wasn't fine, though. It wasn't fine at all.'

'And why wasn't it fine?' asked DSC Johnston.

But the girl couldn't answer because now she was trembling.

I didn't care. I was simply impatient. Impatient to hear what she had to say next. *Tell me all that you know*, I wanted to hiss. But she was shaking so much she could hardly have managed.

So how could I keep her talking? First, I needed to hide my impatience, then I needed to comfort her. Steeling myself, I approached her. 'It's okay,' I murmured, my voice very gentle. 'It's okay.' I put my hand on her shoulder and left it there until she'd stopped shaking.

Then with a short nod to DSC Johnston, I let the questioning continue.

'Why wasn't it fine?' the detective repeated.

The girl closed her eyes before she started to answer. 'Because Dr Malcolm called me back in to see him again, only this time with the school counsellor. And the counsellor kept asking about the letter and whether I'd written it, and if there was anything more I could tell her. Especially about Mr O. I kept saying no, no, there wasn't, but she kept pushing and Dr Malcolm kept pushing me too. And they both kept on pushing, both kept saying how much they wanted to help me.'

She took a deep breath then continued. 'But there was nothing they could do because the letter wasn't true. And I didn't know how to explain it, so I stayed quiet. But I felt really bad. So I went to see Hunter after school that day and told him I wanted to tell them the truth.' Now she was crying again, her face turning red and blotchy.

Keep going, I willed her. *Keep talking*.

'And what did Hunter say about that?' asked DSC Johnston.

'Not much,' she said, her eyes on the floor. 'He just got out his phone and started to show me his photos.'

She stopped for a moment and when she continued, her voice had fallen. 'I'd forgotten,' she murmured, 'how many he'd taken.'

DSC Johnston leaned forward. 'What were the photos he showed you?'

But the girl wouldn't answer. She just buried her face in her hands.

'Laetitia,' DSC Johnston said softly, 'just what sort of photographs were they?'

Slowly, she lifted her head. 'They were of me,' she whispered.

'And what were they like?'

Instead of giving an answer, she started to cry again. 'He said they'd just be for him and that nobody else would see them.'

'Tell me, Laetitia,' said DSC Johnston, 'what were you wearing in the photos he took?'

But the girl just pressed at her eyes, pushing harder and harder, as though trying to rub them right out of existence.

At first, we just watched her, we looked on together, until DSC Johnston did what I should have done. Standing up, she walked across to my student and, placing a hand on each of her arms, gently, but firmly, she told her to stop it.

And she did. She stopped rubbing her eyes. Then she answered the detective's question. 'I wasn't wearing anything,' she told her. 'I was naked in all of the photos.'

'And why do you think Hunter wanted to show them all to you?'

For a very long time, Tia did nothing but chew at her lip. *Stop it and answer the question*, I wanted to say. But she would not stop chewing her lip and she would not answer the question.

So DSC Johnston asked it a second time.

This time the girl gave an audible sigh. Keeping her head down, she began to speak, her voice little more than a whisper. 'So I'd know he still had them and could send them anywhere he liked.'

'And where did you think he might send them?'

The girl stayed very still, except for her hands: these she clasped then unclasped then clasped together once more. 'He said he could easily print them out for my parents and he could also post them online.' Here her voice wavered then fell. 'For people out there to enjoy.'

DSC Johnston's face remained impassive. 'And why did you think he said this?'

This time the answer came quickly. 'So I wouldn't talk about the letter. So I wouldn't say that he'd done it and that nothing he'd written was true.'

'What did you do?'

I watched her face slowly crumple. 'I agreed not to tell Dr Malcolm about the letter. I promised not to say anything.'

'But what about Mr O'Hanlon?' asked DSC Johnston, as the back of my neck grew tighter.

'Hunter said it would be all right. That nothing would happen to Mr O'Hanlon because it was just an anonymous letter.' She stopped. 'But then it got out of control.'

'And when did it get out of control?'

At that, the girl tilted her head and stared straight at DSC Johnston. 'When you came to school and started asking me all of those questions. That's when I really freaked out, when everyone kept asking and asking if I'd written that letter. I couldn't say no, I couldn't tell the truth, so in the end, I just said yes. "Okay," I said, "I admit it, I wrote it." Then I couldn't take it back and the whole thing got out of control. Even when I was signing the statement, I wanted to say, *Stop there's been a mistake, that's not what happened*. But I couldn't. And when I went back to Hunter to say it had all gone too far and I needed to tell the truth, he said it wasn't that simple. Because if I tried to go back on everything I'd said, I'd get charged for lying and then I'd go to prison. That's when he showed me the photos again and reminded me what he could do with them.'

Now she was crying so hard I felt something melting inside me. And despite what she'd said and despite what she'd done, I searched in my bag for a handkerchief and handed it to her.

The moment she took it, I realised my error. The handkerchief was not mine after all. It belonged, instead, to my husband and was embroidered with his initials. I began to quake. *That's it*, I admonished myself. *This will be my undoing.*

But it wasn't.

Using the handkerchief to wipe up her tears, the girl didn't seem to notice a thing.

'So what did you do,' said DSC Johnston, 'after Hunter said all those things to you?'

'Nothing,' she sniffled, 'I didn't do anything.'

But DSC Johnston was shaking her head. 'That's not quite right now is it, Laetitia? You gave evidence at the trial.'

Once again dabbing her eyes, the girl gave a quick nod. 'Hunter told me to get it over and done with and just repeat what I'd said in my statement.'

When DSC Johnston asked her two final questions, her voice, very clear, rose again. 'And that's what you did, are you saying? That while under oath, you lied about Gordon O'Hanlon?'

And when the girl lowered her head and agreed that she had, DSC Johnston concluded the interview.

49

THE FOLLOWING DAY, WHEN I arrived home from school, Gillian Cooper rang me.

'You'll never guess what's happened,' she said. 'It's good news. Very good news.'

'What is it?' I asked, trying to keep my voice calm.

'I've just been on the phone to Vicky Johnston: you know, the detective. Or, more precisely, she's been on the phone to me. She's spoken to Laetitia Hartford. More than that, she's recorded an interview with her. Laetitia admitted she lied to the court; that what she said about Gordon was untrue. It seems some boy put her up to it.'

Hunter Carmichael, I wanted to snarl. *That's who.*

'A boy from Grandborough College,' she continued. 'One of Gordon's senior students. He'll be charged this week.'

'Oh,' I said, feigning surprise, 'that's extraordinary. And, Ti—' I began, before catching myself. 'The girl,' I said carefully instead, 'what will happen to her?'

'Good question,' she mused. 'They'll probably offer her some sort of deal—an immunity, even—to give evidence against the boy.'

'And Gordon?' finally I ventured. 'What about Gordon?'

'Well, he should apply for bail. At least I should, on his behalf.'

So she did. The very next day, she went to court and I went with her. Bernadette and Bridget came, too.

I said I was ill when I rang the school to tell them I wouldn't be in. It wasn't a lie; not really. All night my stomach was churning, and if I'd slept at all, it would have been minutes not hours. And when I got out of bed, my legs were shaky, my mouth was dry and I found it hard to swallow. So it was hardly a lie to say that I'd taken ill overnight.

In the bag I took to court were clothes for Gordon.

'Clothes?' I'd asked, when Gillian Cooper made the suggestion. Surely they wouldn't be bringing him in without clothes?

That made her laugh. 'The thing is, they could well send him to court in his prison greens,' she said, 'and he won't want to go home in that.'

So I packed his grey trousers and a white collared shirt, his black leather shoes and a pair of black socks.

And in the courtroom that morning—with Bernadette and Bridget beside me—I kept hold of that bag while we waited for things to begin.

But when the judge came onto the bench—an old man this time, with crackly white hair poking out of his wig—Gordon was still nowhere to be seen.

'Is the prisoner being brought in?' the judge enquired.

Gillian Cooper, who was appearing by herself this time, stood up to answer the question. 'Yes,' she said, 'he is.'

As she spoke, a side door opened and in walked a guard followed by Gordon who, as Gillian had predicted, was wearing a green prison tracksuit.

Turning to me and Bernadette and Bridget, he waved and, lifting my hand, I waved back. Then I took a deep breath and tried to stay patient.

As it happened, no patience was needed. Less than ten minutes later, that judge was reading out his decision. 'Well, Mr O'Hanlon,' he said at the end of it, 'now you're free to go home.'

⌐

I was ecstatic, of course, and relieved and delighted. For the weeks that followed, I was all of these things. During the daytime, I'd beam at my husband and he'd beam back and together we'd laugh for no reason. And at night time—in the dead of each night—I'd reach out my arm, half awake, half asleep, soothed to find him still there.

Yet in the mornings, still I'd wake startled—trembling and nervous—just as I had each day he'd been absent.

'It's okay,' he'd console me, holding me tight, his voice soft and tender. 'Ellen, my love, it's okay.'

'You're back,' I'd say, over and over and over again, still not quite believing it.

⌐

Two months later, my husband and I returned to the court-room together.

And when that awful rapping, tapping filled the room, I flinched as always I did.

'All rise,' came a voice that bounced off the walls, as three judges—not one—walked in.

As I watched on, my nervousness grew and my hands began to shake. *Don't hope, don't hope, don't hope,* I chided myself for fear this might bring it undone.

It did not. Instead it all unfolded so quickly, I wondered if I'd misunderstood what had happened.

I hadn't.

No, I hadn't.

Appeal conceded by the prosecution.

Leave to appeal granted.

Appeal allowed.

Conviction quashed.

That's what had happened.

It took me some time to truly believe that my Gordon was home for good, that no-one was coming to take him away; and that when I returned from school each day, the house would no longer be empty.

And oh the relief, the wonder, the joy of it.

Soon enough, he'd need to find work. Until then, there was that package from Grandborough College, the one he liked to call the 'Get Rid of Gordon Allowance'.

Gordon was, of course, most welcome to return to Grand-borough College, Dr Malcolm assured us. That, at least, was how he'd begun his reply to Gillian Cooper's demands.

Given the earlier media attention, however, this might not be so easy, he'd added. With this in mind, Grandborough College would happily—*yes, happily*—put Gordon back on the payroll until he'd secured employment elsewhere. In the meantime, he wouldn't be expected to teach or even set foot in the college.

And that's how Grandborough College managed to both keep and get rid of my husband.

It was an excellent result, Gillian Cooper declared, but I wasn't sure I agreed. For how on earth would my husband find work when his name had been destroyed?

Unlike his conviction and subsequent sentence, the appeal had gained no media interest. So how, I chafed, would anyone know his conviction was wrong, especially when, according to Google, he was still a sex offender.

Knowing this, reading this—but having no power to stop it—both enraged and distressed me. And whenever I thought of those children—the girl, yes, but mostly that boy—I'd become even more livid. When, I would curse, when would that boy be held to account?

Soon, as it happened, quite soon.

50

'I GOT A CALL FROM the prosecutor's office,' Gordon told me, his tone offhand as though this was nothing important.

It had been six weeks since we'd been to court and we were at home having dinner.

'Oh?' I said, a catch in my voice as my heart began to race. For whenever I heard the word prosecutor—no matter that Gordon was free and the case was over—my body would seize up and fear would overtake me.

'What for?' I asked.

'To give me the sentencing date for Hunter.'

'Oh,' I said, praying my voice would stay steady. 'And so when will that be?'

'The week after next. I think it's the sixth. They asked if I wanted to be there.'

'And?'

'I told them I didn't. I mean, why on earth would I choose to watch a kid being packed off to prison?'

I tried to agree or say something evasive, but I just couldn't do it. 'Because he tried to ruin your life,' I burst out. 'Doesn't that make you want to kill him?'

My husband considered the question. 'No,' he said, 'it doesn't. To be honest, I try not to think about Hunter at all. Or any of it, really. It's done. It's finished. Why keep mulling it over and over?'

I felt myself nod and heard myself murmur agreement. But later that night, I went to the calendar, marked the date with a capital H and began to count down the days.

And when that day finally arrived, I let Gordon believe I was headed for school, as usual. Instead, I parked in the city and returned to the courthouse where he'd been tried and sentenced. This time, however, I took a lift up two floors, not the stairs down and, once I'd found the courtroom I needed, sat in the back of the public gallery and hid myself in the corner.

A barrister stood at the front of the courtroom, his horsehair wig framing his florid face. Across from him was a younger woman with a serious face and light-coloured hair mostly tucked under her own barrister's wig. Closer to me were three people, their faces in profile: Hunter Carmichael flanked by his parents.

Lisa Carmichael stood with her shoulders slumped forward, unlike her son, who stood tall in his well-cut suit. Yet, despite his height and business attire, he looked surprisingly young: more like a child of fifteen than a man of eighteen. He was fidgety, too, with hands that wouldn't stay still.

As I took it all in, I inadvertently caught his eye then flinched, nervous he would recognise me. To my relief, his gaze slid away and he turned straight back to his father. Unlike his wife,

Richard Carmichael had not changed at all, or so it seemed. His frame was still squat and his skin, now shiny with sweat, was still pinkish. Missing was only his self-satisfied look, replaced by one of despair and confusion.

The judge who would be hearing Hunter's proceedings was a small, thin man with large rheumy eyes and skin a soft shade of yellow.

'Right,' he said when he came on the bench, 'let's get started.'

The young, robed woman stood up. 'Ms Dmitrovic,' she said, 'I appear for the Crown.' And in a voice that was slightly too quick, she read out the facts of the case.

The judge listened quietly. 'Is there anything else?' he asked once she'd finished.

'One thing,' she replied, 'there's a victim impact statement I'd like to tender.'

The judge gave a nod. 'Is the victim in court?'

Ms Dmitrovic shook her head. 'No,' she said, 'he didn't want to be present. But if I might read it onto the record?'

And with that, she read the statement I hadn't known Gordon had written. My fingers interlacing and my knuckles turning white, I sat bolt upright to listen.

In 2017, I was appointed to Grandborough College as deputy head of the English department. I was looking forward to the challenge of this new position. Less than six months into my appointment, I found myself suspended due to allegations of criminal behaviour towards one of my students. I was shocked by the allegations but, more than that, I was confused by them, both because they were untrue and because I couldn't understand why someone would make such an awful accusation. I kept thinking it would all sort itself out and everything would be resolved.

Instead, I found myself convicted and sentenced to a term of imprisonment for a crime I simply hadn't committed. I would not wish imprisonment on anyone.

The criminal proceedings that were brought against me have caused enormous distress. It is not pleasant to open your door to two police officers who look at you with such contempt you want to weep in despair and frustration. But I was not alone in being made to feel so humiliated. My wife—my beautiful wife—was forced to change her name and her work so people wouldn't find out we were married. It is not pleasant to be the wife of a man the world believes to be a sexual offender. So, too, my mother and sister have had to endure enormous distress and pain. The toll has been great. Even now it continues. I wish to return to teaching, for it has been my vocation, but I wonder if I'll ever have the courage to do it. With time, perhaps. I do hope so.

I understand that Hunter Carmichael is to be sentenced for perverting the course of justice and threatening to distribute intimate images. I wish to ask that, despite the gravity of the offences, he be treated with leniency. He is now eighteen years old and an adult; and it is as an adult that he will be sentenced. But at eighteen, a person is still very young and often immature, especially if that person happens to be a young man. Young men can be impulsive and thoughtless. They can act in ways that put themselves and others in danger, particularly if behind the wheel of a car or a motorcycle. They can behave badly, even criminally, and this behaviour may bring them before the police and the courts.

This is where Hunter now finds himself. It is a difficult position and one that must be causing him enormous stress. It must also be causing great pain to his parents. I am quite sure that Hunter Carmichael has learned from what he has done. I am certain that he did not truly understand the effects of his actions. When he encouraged lies to be told about me—to the police and then again at my trial—he was, I believe, thinking more about saving himself than about wishing me harm. He wanted to escape detection for cheating and he chanced upon a way of doing it. I don't think he ever considered that I might go to prison. I don't think that was his goal. He was impulsive and reckless and he behaved very badly. I believe he can learn from this experience and I would ask Your Honour to be mindful of this on sentencing. Being in prison was extremely unpleasant for me. I can only imagine how much worse it would be for a young man like Hunter Carmichael with such little life experience.

I do not seek retribution, I do not seek revenge against Hunter Carmichael for what he has done. Instead, I have forgiven him. For without forgiveness, hatred burns and life shrivels. And this is not how I wish my future to be.

Gordon O'Hanlon

And with that, Ms Dmitrovic sat down. My hands still clasped tightly together, I sat there, stunned.

Take no heed of my husband's entreaties, I wanted to call to that watery-eyed judge. *For why should that boy now get off scot-free when, because of him, my husband continues to carry the name of a sexual offender and a teacher who cannot be trusted?*

Instead, staying quiet, I waited to see what would happen.

51

ONCE THE LAWYERS HAD MADE their submissions, the judge took a break. On his return, a prison guard entered the court-room. Taking a seat at the front of the room, he lifted his head to the judge, who gave him a nod before he read out his judgment.

'The prisoner, Hunter Richard Carmichael, is to be sentenced for perverting the course of justice,' he began. 'In sentencing the prisoner, I take into account a further matter to which he also pleaded guilty, namely threatening to distribute intimate images of a fellow school student, who I'll simply call Miss L.

'I accept that the prisoner took intimate images of Miss L and that this occurred with her consent. She did not, however, consent to their distribution either online or to her parents. This had been something the prisoner had threatened to do if Miss L had refused to give false evidence in the trial of their teacher, Mr Gordon O'Hanlon. Miss L agreed to give this evidence in return for an undertaking that the prisoner would not distribute these intimate images. As a result of Miss L's evidence, Mr O'Hanlon was convicted and sentenced to a four-year term of imprisonment. He was dismissed from his teaching position, the case was widely reported and Mr O'Hanlon's reputation suffered accordingly.'

I was nodding now; vehemently nodding. *Yes, Your Honour,* I wanted to call out, *that is what happened. That is exactly how it was.*

'The High Court has confirmed that the course of justice is perverted by impairing the capacity of a court to do justice,' the judge advised. 'This would include being denied the truth of a case before it. Mr O'Hanlon was charged with indecently assaulting his student Miss L and was convicted on her false evidence. Miss L had, however, felt forced to give this evidence due to threats made by the prisoner. But for the immunity from prosecution she has been given, Miss L would have been charged with perjury. This, of course, was because of the false evidence she'd given.'

He stopped for a moment to reach under his wig and give his head a good scratch. Then he kept going. 'The offence to which the prisoner has pleaded guilty, namely perverting the course of justice, is a serious matter, carrying with it a maximum penalty of fourteen years imprisonment.'

From somewhere towards the front of the courtroom came an intake of breath that was close to a sob and, for a moment, the judge hesitated.

'Hunter Carmichael is a young man who excelled as a student of Grandborough College,' he continued. 'He represented his school in sport and public speaking and was actively involved in other activities, including the annual dramatic production. He has secured a place at university, and is enrolled in business studies. And although this is all very impressive, it cannot outweigh his offending behaviour and the criminality it entailed.

'I have before me a psychological report by Ms Jane Bedford. She describes the prisoner as a young man with a strong drive to succeed, who deeply regrets his behaviour. It is, however, difficult to say if this regret is more for himself and his current position, or whether he is truly sorry for the anguish caused to both Miss L and Mr O'Hanlon. As I have not heard from the prisoner himself, I can give only limited weight to the opinions expressed by Ms Bedford.

'Because of the seriousness of his offending behaviour, the sentence I impose on the prisoner must reflect many things: retribution and community condemnation, as well as general deterrence. Having regard to his early plea of guilty and some limited contrition, an overall discount of twenty-five per cent is appropriate. The prisoner has no prior criminal record. Indeed, this is the first time he has appeared in the courts and, I would hope, the last. Given the seriousness of the offence, however, a term of imprisonment is the only appropriate punishment to impose in this case.'

Looking up, the judge fixed his gaze on Hunter. 'Stand up,' he ordered, and the boy stood up.

'Hunter Richard Carmichael, for the offence of perverting the course of justice, I impose a non-parole period of imprison-ment of two years with a head sentence of four years. To make matters clear to you, this means that you will be eligible for parole two years from today.' The judge turned to address the uniformed man who'd arrived late to the court proceedings. 'Remove the prisoner,' he told him.

'No.' It was just one word, and uttered just once. It wasn't a cry, it wasn't a scream, it was more like a guttural groan. And it came from Lisa Carmichael.

I knew about that sort of sound. I knew how it splintered the mind and exhausted the body. I knew all about that.

I know, I almost called to that woman. *I know how this is. I know how you're feeling.*

But her sound could not stop what the judge had ordered and within seconds Hunter Carmichael was gone: whisked away by that guard through another well-hidden door.

And with that I left. I stood up, I made my way to the end of the row and I headed outside.

Back on the street, I felt myself blink and gulp in the daylight, breathing and breathing until I was gasping, until there was nothing left to breathe out; until I'd expelled everything still caught inside me—the relief and the anger, the grief and the sorrow, the panic, the vengeance, the horror.

52

LATER THAT NIGHT WHEN WE were in bed, my husband told me the news. 'The prosecutor rang,' he said. 'Hunter's been sent to prison.'

I feigned surprise. 'Did that come as a shock?'

He gave a small shrug and a sad little smile. 'Not really. I just don't like the thought of him being in jail. I mean, it won't solve anything. It won't make anything better.'

'But shouldn't he pay for his actions?' I countered.

He made a sound in his throat. 'I already did. I already paid the price for him.' He smiled as he spoke so I couldn't quite tell if he meant what he said or if it was more of a joke. With a gentle laugh at my puzzled face, he stroked the side of my neck. 'Why don't we talk about something more pleasant instead?'

'Like what?' I asked, as I snuggled into him.

Lifting an arm, he pulled me in closer. 'Like whether it's time for a change.'

'A change?' I repeated.

'A change,' he confirmed. 'I'm sick of being Gordon O'Hanlon. I want to be somebody new.'

Leaning against his shoulder, I craned my head up. 'What do you mean?'

'Just like I said. I want to be somebody new.'

I was completely confounded. 'Like who?'

'Like you,' he replied. 'I want to be a Wells, just like you.'

A Wells like me?

'Don't panic,' he said. 'It's just an idea I had in the shower. I was thinking how cleverly you managed that hideous time, and how you did it as Ellen Wells. That's when the thought came out of the blue: why couldn't I do the same thing? Why can't I just get rid of my name and become a Wells like you?'

I felt my face tighten in horror. My mother, my father and Reverend Burnett: what would they think about such a ludicrous suggestion?

Then I smiled. For after all that had happened, after everything Gordon and I had gone through, why on earth should I care about that? And anyway, how would they even find out?

'So instead of Gordon O'Hanlon, you'd be Gordon Wells,' I said slowly, surprising myself with a chuckle.

'Why not?' he replied. 'Just imagine it, El. It would give me the chance to start over.'

I thought about this a bit more. 'How would you do it?'

'By deed poll,' he said, cupping my face in his hands.

And although it was night and the room was dark, the air felt light as my husband leaned in to kiss me.

'Gordon,' I murmured. 'Gordon Patrick Wells.'

'Not so Irish,' he said, 'but I do like the sound of it.'

'Me too,' I said, as I started to giggle.

Acknowledgements

THIS NOVEL WAS MOSTLY WRITTEN on Gadigal land and I extend my thanks and respect to the Gadigal people.

To write *The Watchful Wife*, I received grants from the Copyright Agency's Cultural Fund and the Australia Council and I so appreciate their support. I'm also delighted to have been selected by Randwick City Council to be part of their Space to Create residency program which gave me a place to hide away so I could finish off the manuscript.

My thanks also to the Arthur Miller Estate for granting me the permission to quote from *The Crucible*.

On the eve of the release of my earlier novel, *The Deceptions*, I rang my agent, Margaret Connolly, in excitement. 'What could possibly go wrong?' I asked her. A week later, when the country went into lockdown, we had our answer.

Over the months that followed, Margaret was supportive, measured, calm and always available. I'm really not sure how I would have managed without her.

So it's a particular delight to be able to celebrate the release of *The Watchful Wife* together.

Heartfelt thanks to my publisher Jane Palfreyman, whose suggestions and insights have made *The Watchful Wife* a much better book.

It was wonderful to have Ali Lavau as my editor again. Her rigorous and meticulous structural edit gave me the blueprint I needed to rework the manuscript.

I've been so lucky to work with Christa Munns through the publication process and on the copyedit for *The Watchful Wife*. With the most careful eye, she scrupulously and meticulously combed through the manuscript.

Thank you to Alissa Dinallo for another beautiful cover.

Many thanks to the rest of the team at Allen & Unwin, with a special mention to Jennifer Thurgate, Genevieve Buzo, Samantha Ryan and Odette Droulers.

For their friendship and support while I was writing *The Watchful Wife*, I'd like to thank Denise Chapman, Ted and Dina Lawes, Karine Bastard, Kathy Crittenden, Pauline Jongma, Catherine du Peloux Menagé, Kathryn Heyman, Megan Tipping (née James), Allison Silink, Kelly Barlow, Jane Martin, Laurence Maisonhaute, Joanne Fedler, Ursula Dubosarsky, David Leal and Carol Mondeverde Leal.

The Reverend Anne Ryan was a great source of church-related knowledge and, once again, so generous with her time.

Patrick Bowe was a careful proofreader, as was my son, Alex, while Kate Nicol assisted me with important Biblical insights.

The Watchful Wife is the story of teachers and, in writing it, I gained an appreciation of my mother's vocation and her unwavering commitment to teaching her primary-school students.

Thank you to my children, Alex, Dominic, Xavier and Miranda, for being so supportive and encouraging and loving. I revel in your company and in watching you make your way in the world.

I met my husband, David Barrow, when we were both working at the Legal Aid Commission of New South Wales. David is my first reader and his legal expertise is of such enormous assistance in my writing. Clever and kind and funny and generous, he always puts the kids and me first, no matter what. Thank you, sweetheart: it's wonderful to be your wife.

In 2020, I began hosting Thursday Book Club, a relaxed, weekly online gathering which has become a warm and caring community of readers. To everyone who has joined us, thank you so much for your support, your company and your terrific book recommendations.

It's great to be a part of the writing community and I treasure the friendships I have with my fellow writers. To those of you who are librarians and booksellers, thank you for looking after us, your readers and writers. And to my readers, I love to imagine my books in your hands and so delight in your feedback.